W9-BUS-864

CARTOON HANGOVER

BRAVEST WARRIORS

CREATED by PENDLETON WARD

MAY 0 2 2017

The Blue Mountains Public Library
L.E. Shore Memorial Library
Thornbury, Ontario N0H 2P0

VOLUME SEVEN

www.kaboom-studios.com • www.youtube.com/cartoonhangover

ROSS RICHIE CEO & Founder • MATT GAGNON Editor-in-Chief • FILIP SABLIK President of Publishing & Marketing • STEPHEN CHRISTY President of Development • LANCE KREITER VP of Licensing & Merchandising
PHIL BARBARO VP of Finance • BRYCE CARLSON Managing Editor • MEL CAYLO Marketing Manager • SCOTT NEWMAN Production Design Manager • IRENE BRADISH Operations Manager
CHRISTINE DINH Brand Communications Manager • SIERRA HAHN Senior Editor • DAFNA PLEBAN Editor • SHANNON WATTERS Editor • ERIC HARBURN Editor • WHITNEY LEOPARD Associate Editor • JASMINE AMIRI Associate Editor
CHRIS ROSA Associate Editor • ALEX GALER Assistant Editor • CAMERON CHITTOCK Assistant Editor • MARY GUMPORT Assistant Editor • MATTHEW LEVINE Assistant Editor • KELSEY DIETERICH Production Designer
JILLIAN CRAB Production Designer • MICHELLE ANKLEY Production Design Assistant • GRACE PARK Production Design Assistant • AARON FERRARA Operations Coordinator • ELIZABETH LOUGHRIDGE Accounting Coordinator
JOSÉ MEZA Sales Assistant • JAMES ARRIOLA Mailroom Assistant • HOLLY AITCHISON Operations Assistant • STEPHANIE HOCUTT Marketing Assistant • SAM KUSEK Direct Market Representative

BRAVEST WARRIORS Volume Seven, July 2016. Published by KaBOOM!, a division of Boom Entertainment, Inc. Based on "Bravest Warriors" © 2016 Frederator Networks,
Inc. Originally published in single magazine form as BRAVEST WARRIORS No. 25-28. ™ & © 2014, 2015 Frederator Networks, Inc. All rights reserved. KaBOOM!™ and the
KaBOOM! logo are trademarks of Boom Entertainment, Inc., registered in various countries and categories. All characters, events, and institutions depicted herein are
fictional. Any similarity between any of the names, characters, persons, events, and/or institutions in this publication to actual names, characters, and persons, whether
living or dead, events, and/or institutions is unintended and purely coincidental. KaBOOM! does not read or accept unsolicited submissions of ideas, stories, or artwork.

A catalog record of this book is available from OCLC and from the KaBOOM! website, www.kaboom-studios.com, on the Librarians Page.

BOOM! Studios, 5670 Wilshire Boulevard, Suite 450, Los Angeles, CA 90036-5679. Printed in China. First Printing.
ISBN: 978-1-60886-844-5, eISBN: 978-1-61398-515-1

CREATED BY
PENDLETON WARD

WRITTEN BY
KATE LETH

ILLUSTRATED BY
IAN McGINTY

COLORS BY
LISA MOORE

LETTERS BY
STEVE WANDS CH. 25
COREY BREEN CH. 26-28

"BUGCAT BITES"
WRITTEN BY
KATE LETH
ILLUSTRATED BY
JAKE MYLER WITH LETTERS BY STEVE WANDS
MATT CUMMINGS
PAULINA GANUCHEAU
WOOK JIN CLARK
JESS FINK
PRANAS NAUJOKAITIS

SHORT MISSIONS

WRITTEN BY **MAD RUPERT**
ILLUSTRATED BY **KAT LEYH**

COVER BY
IAN McGINTY

DESIGNERS
**KELSEY DIETERICH
& GRACE PARK**

ASSISTANT EDITOR
CAMERON CHITTOCK

ORIGINAL SERIES EDITOR
REBECCA TAYLOR

COLLECTION EDITOR
SHANNON WATTERS

WITH SPECIAL THANKS TO BREEHN BURNS, ERIC HOMAN,
FRED SEIBERT, RUTH MORRISON, NATE OLSON, AND ALL OF
THE CLASSY FOLKS AT FREDERATOR STUDIOS.

CHAPTER
25

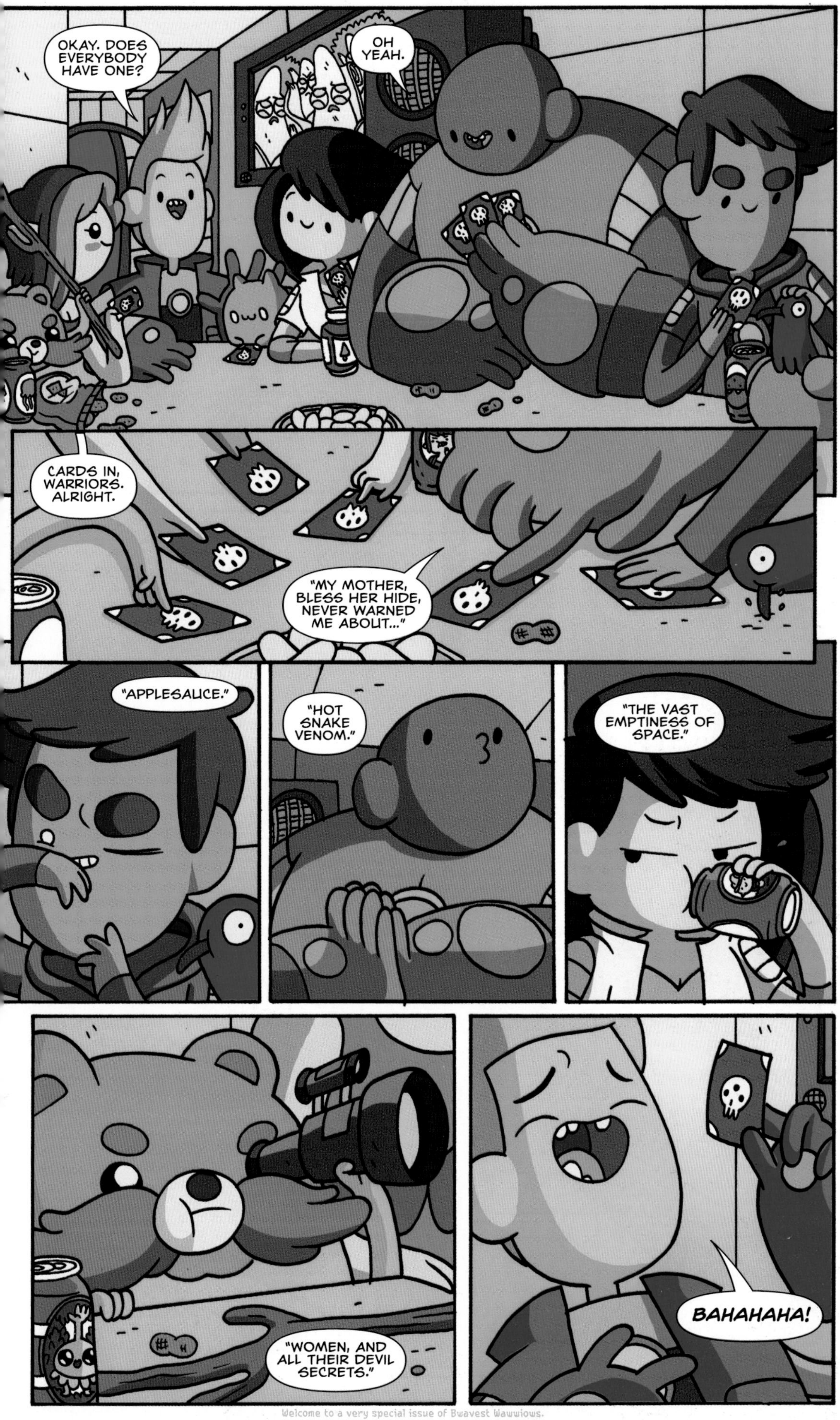
OKAY. DOES EVERYBODY HAVE ONE?
OH YEAH.
CARDS IN, WARRIORS. ALRIGHT.
"MY MOTHER, BLESS HER HIDE, NEVER WARNED ME ABOUT..."
"APPLESAUCE."
"HOT SNAKE VENOM."
"THE VAST EMPTINESS OF SPACE."
"WOMEN, AND ALL THEIR DEVIL SECRETS."
BAHAHAHA!

Welcome to a very special issue of Bwavest Wawwiows.

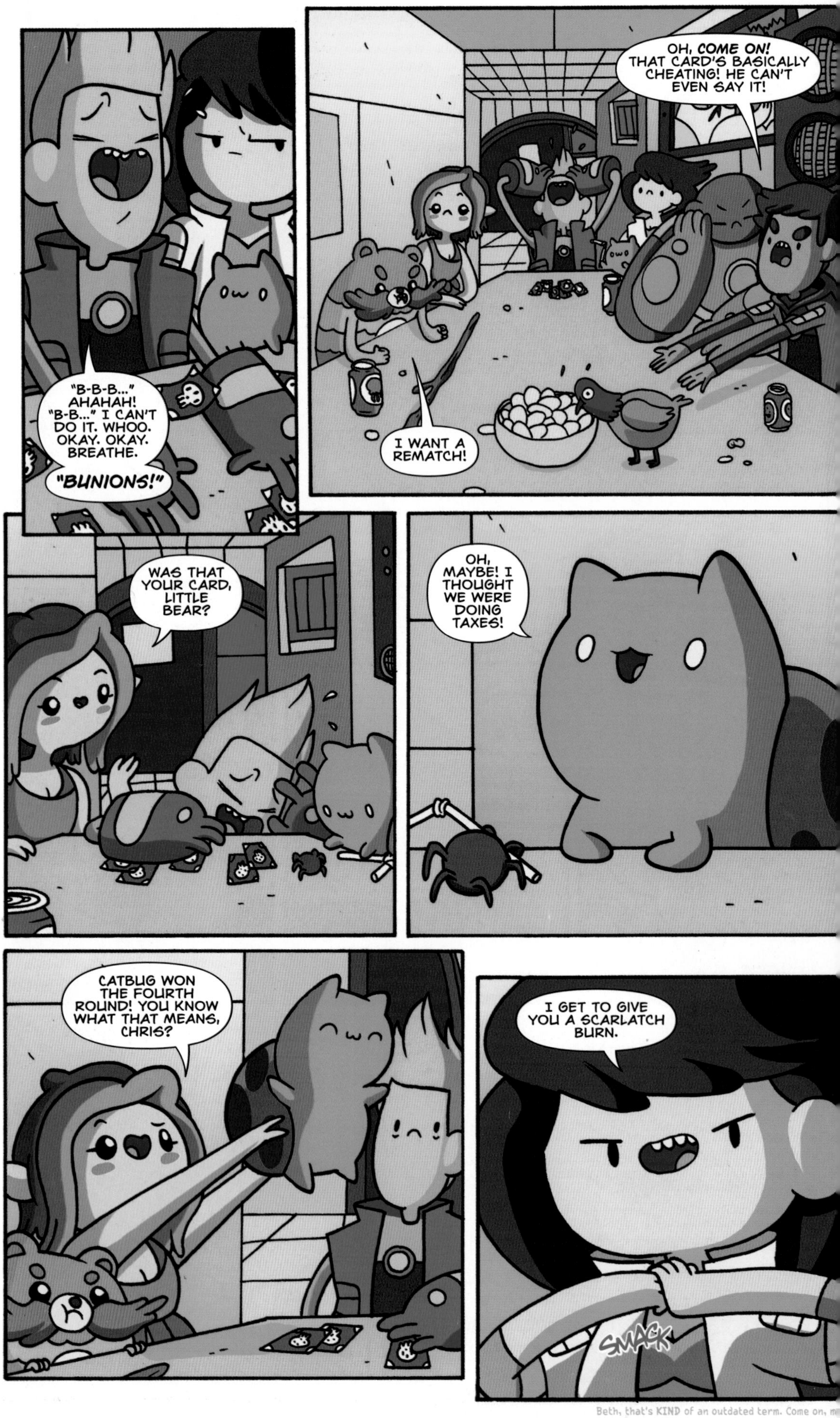

"B-B-B..." AHAHAH! "B-B..." I CAN'T DO IT. WHOO. OKAY. OKAY. BREATHE.
"BUNIONS!"
OH, COME ON! THAT CARD'S BASICALLY CHEATING! HE CAN'T EVEN SAY IT!
I WANT A REMATCH!
WAS THAT YOUR CARD, LITTLE BEAR?
OH, MAYBE! I THOUGHT WE WERE DOING TAXES!
CATBUG WON THE FOURTH ROUND! YOU KNOW WHAT THAT MEANS, CHRIS?
I GET TO GIVE YOU A SCARLATCH BURN.
SMACK

Beth, that's KIND of an outdated term. Come on, m

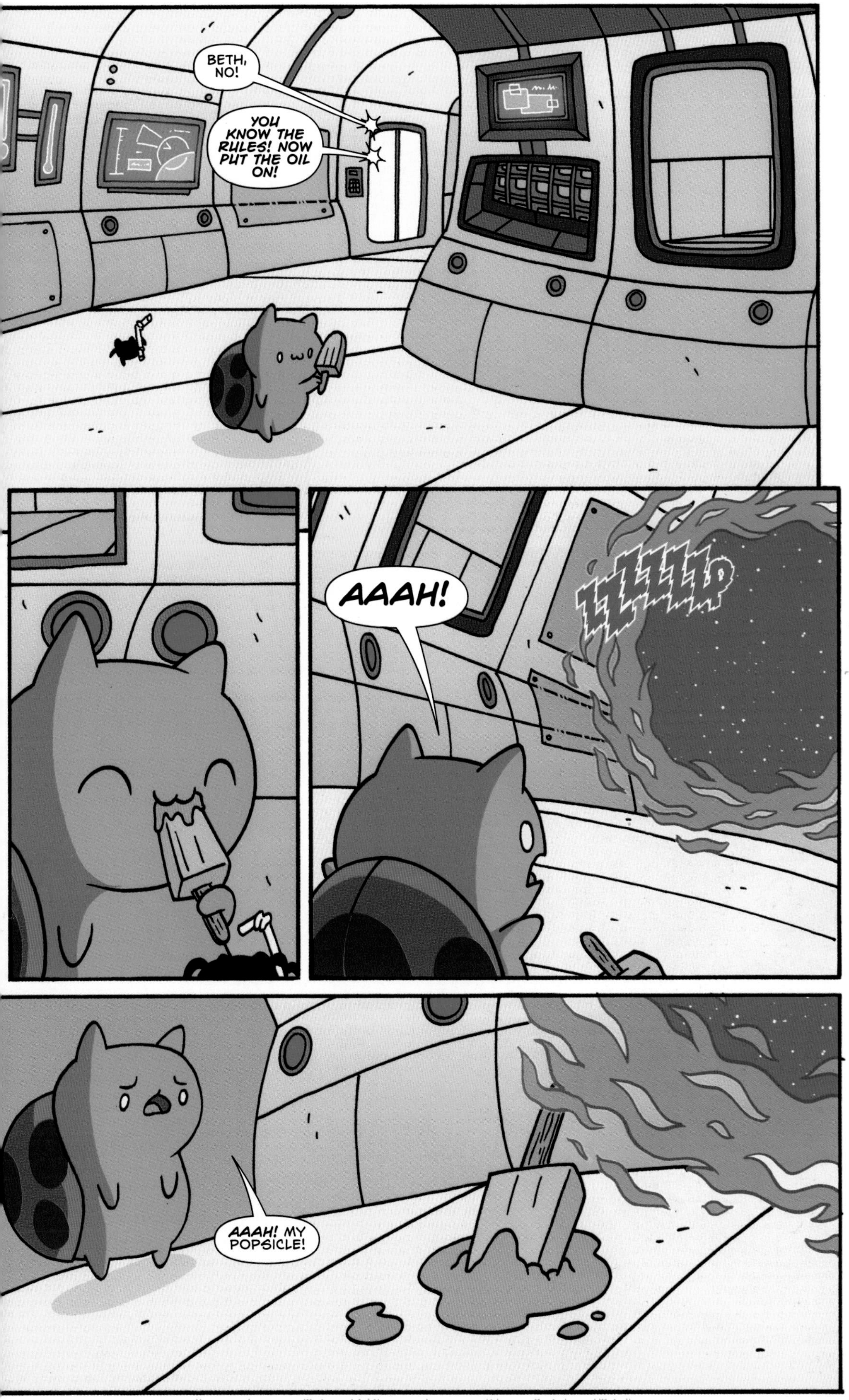
BETH, NO!
YOU KNOW THE RULES! NOW PUT THE OIL ON!
AAAH!
ZZZZZP
AAAH! MY POPSICLE!

No use crying over spilled popsicle! No use crying over anything, really, but we still do it.

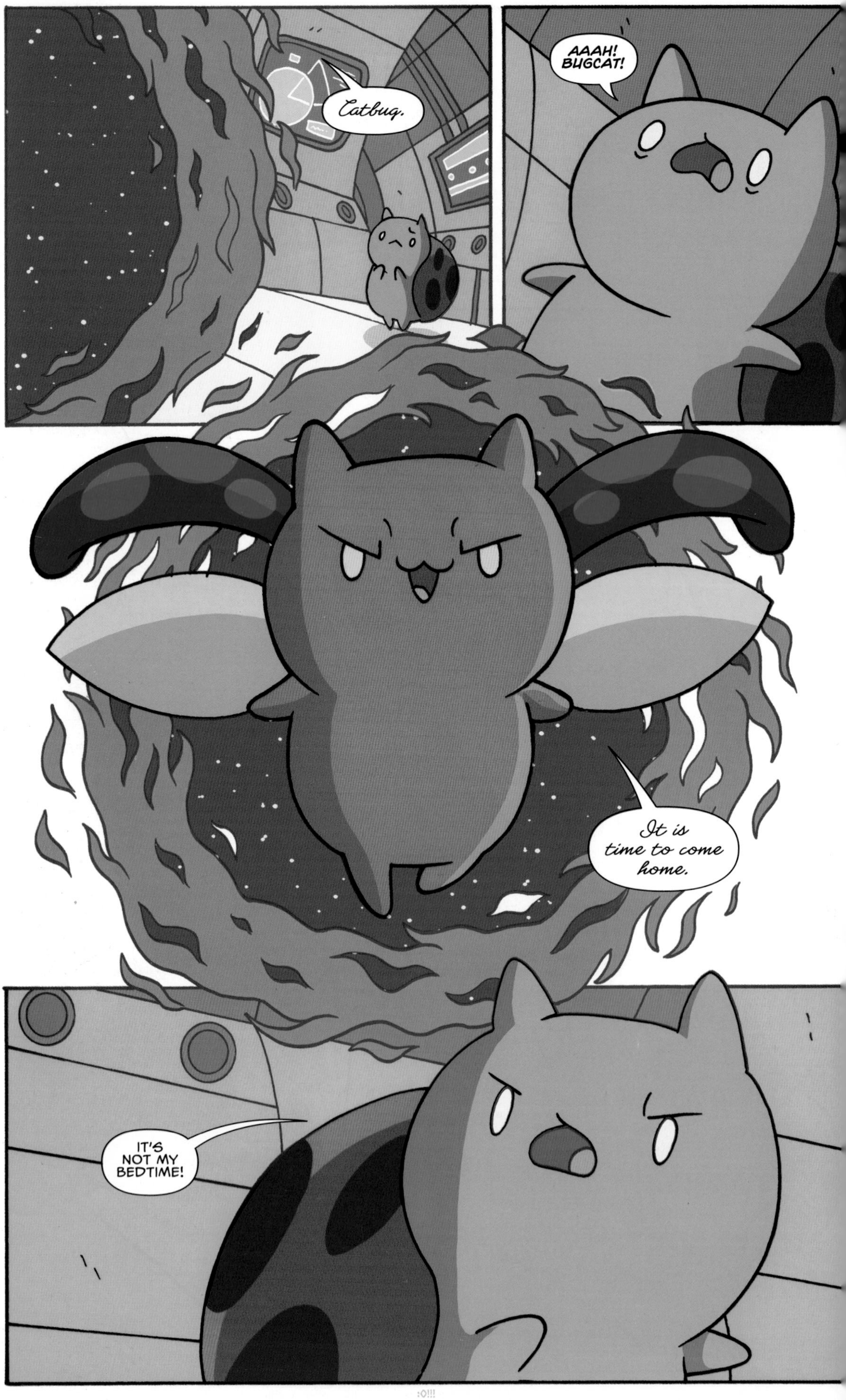
Catbug.
AAAH! BUGCAT!
It is time to come home.
IT'S NOT MY BEDTIME!

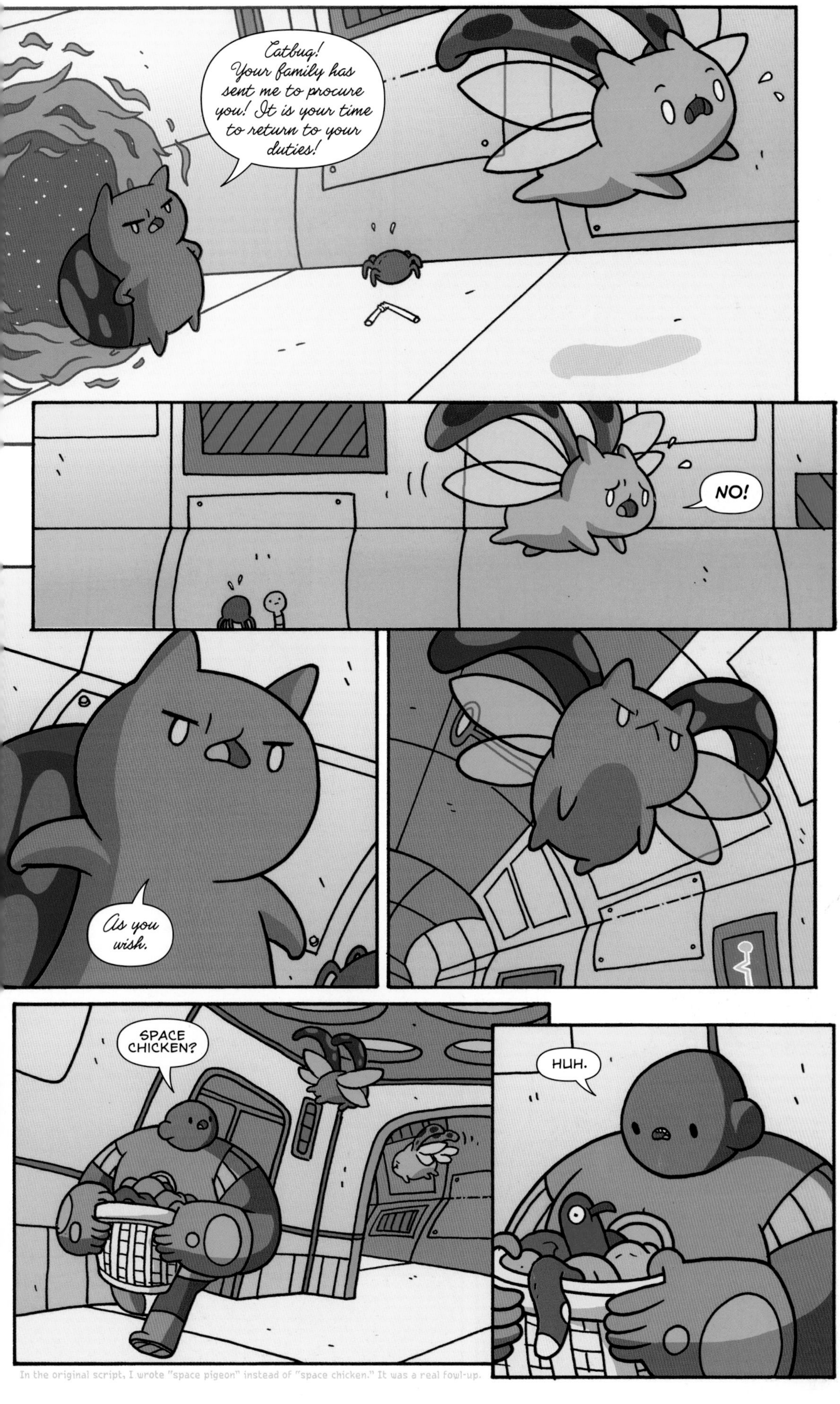
Catbug! Your family has sent me to procure you! It is your time to return to your duties!
NO!
As you wish.
SPACE CHICKEN?
HUH.
In the original script, I wrote "space pigeon" instead of "space chicken." It was a real fowl-up.

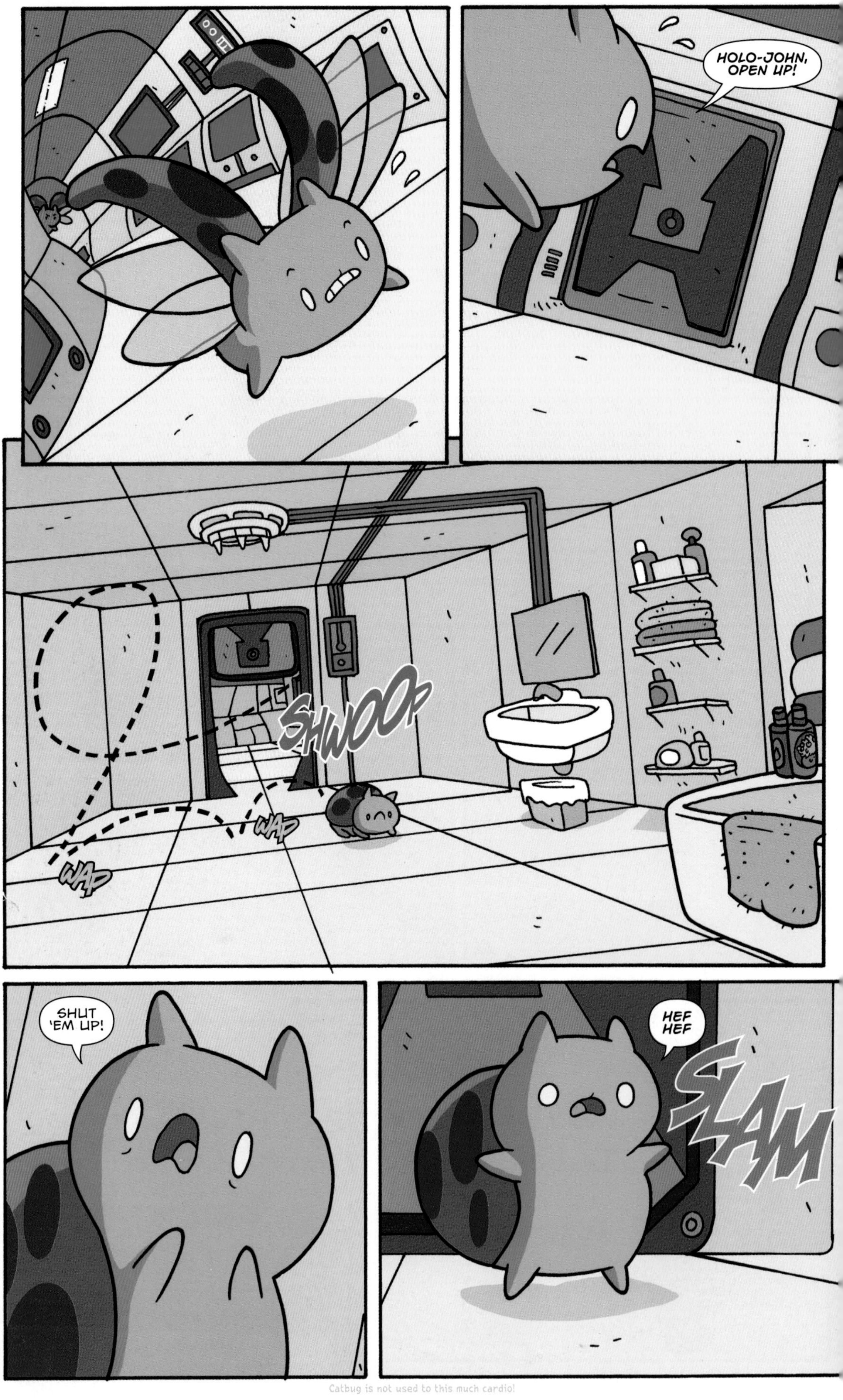
HOLO-JOHN, OPEN UP!
SHWOOP
WAP
WAP
SHUT 'EM UP!
HEF HEF
SLAM

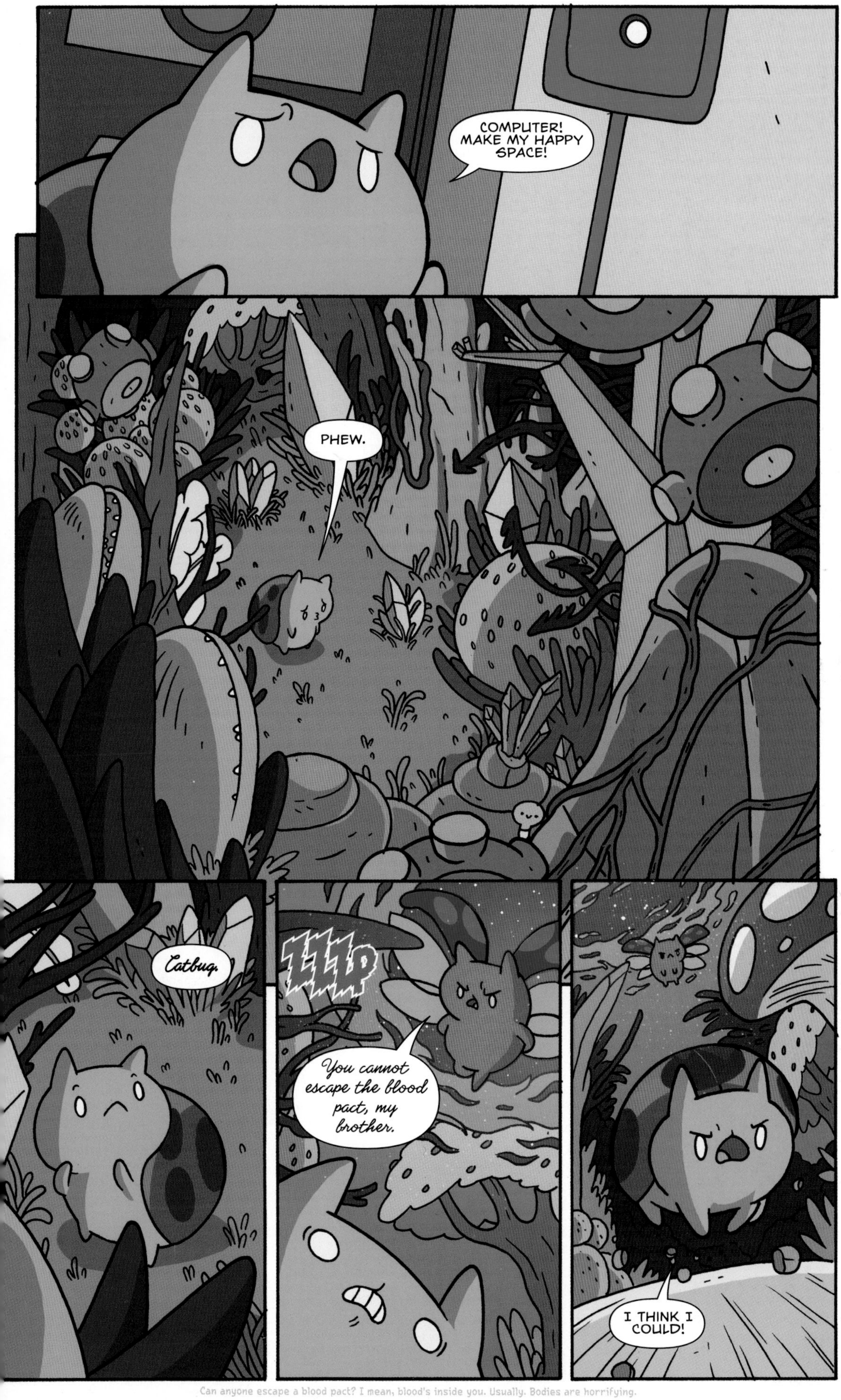
COMPUTER! MAKE MY HAPPY SPACE!
PHEW.
Catbug.
ZZZAP
You cannot escape the blood pact, my brother.
I THINK I COULD!

Can anyone escape a blood pact? I mean, blood's inside you. Usually. Bodies are horrifying.

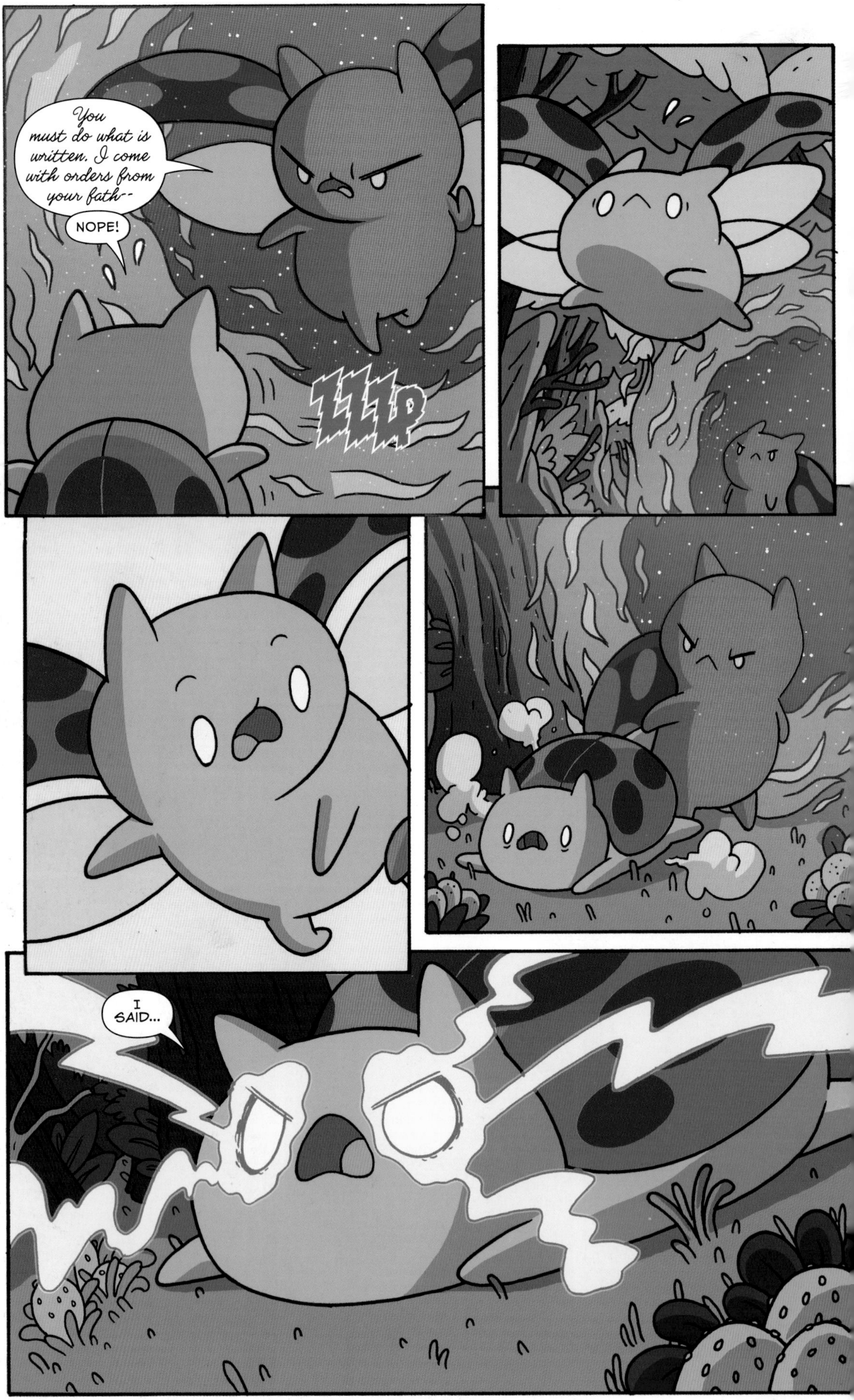
You must do what is written. I come with orders from your fath--
NOPE!
ZZZP
I SAID...

OH MY GOSH WHAT'S GONNA HAPPEN

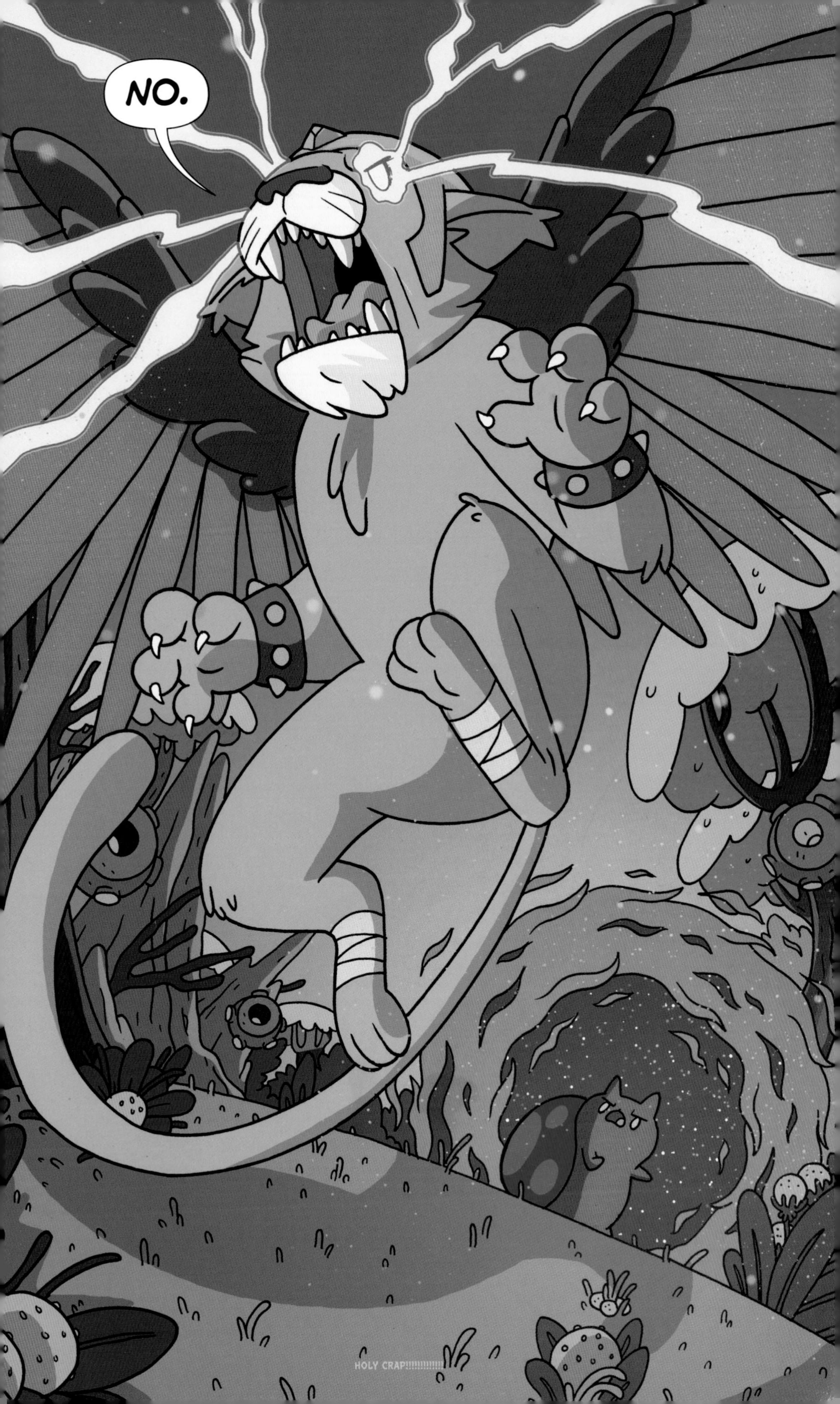
NO.
HOLY CRAP!!!!!!!!!!!!!!

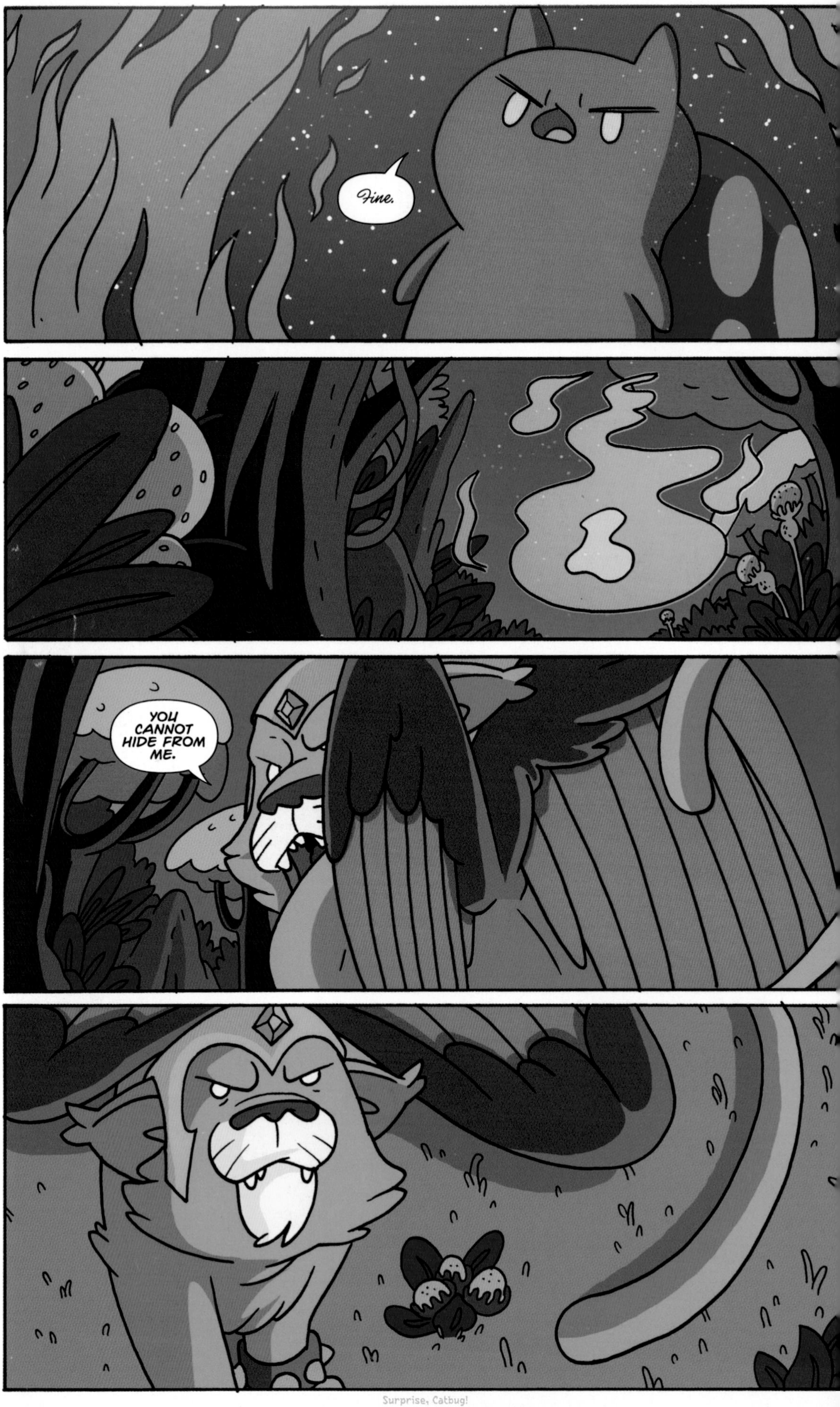
Fine.
YOU CANNOT HIDE FROM ME.

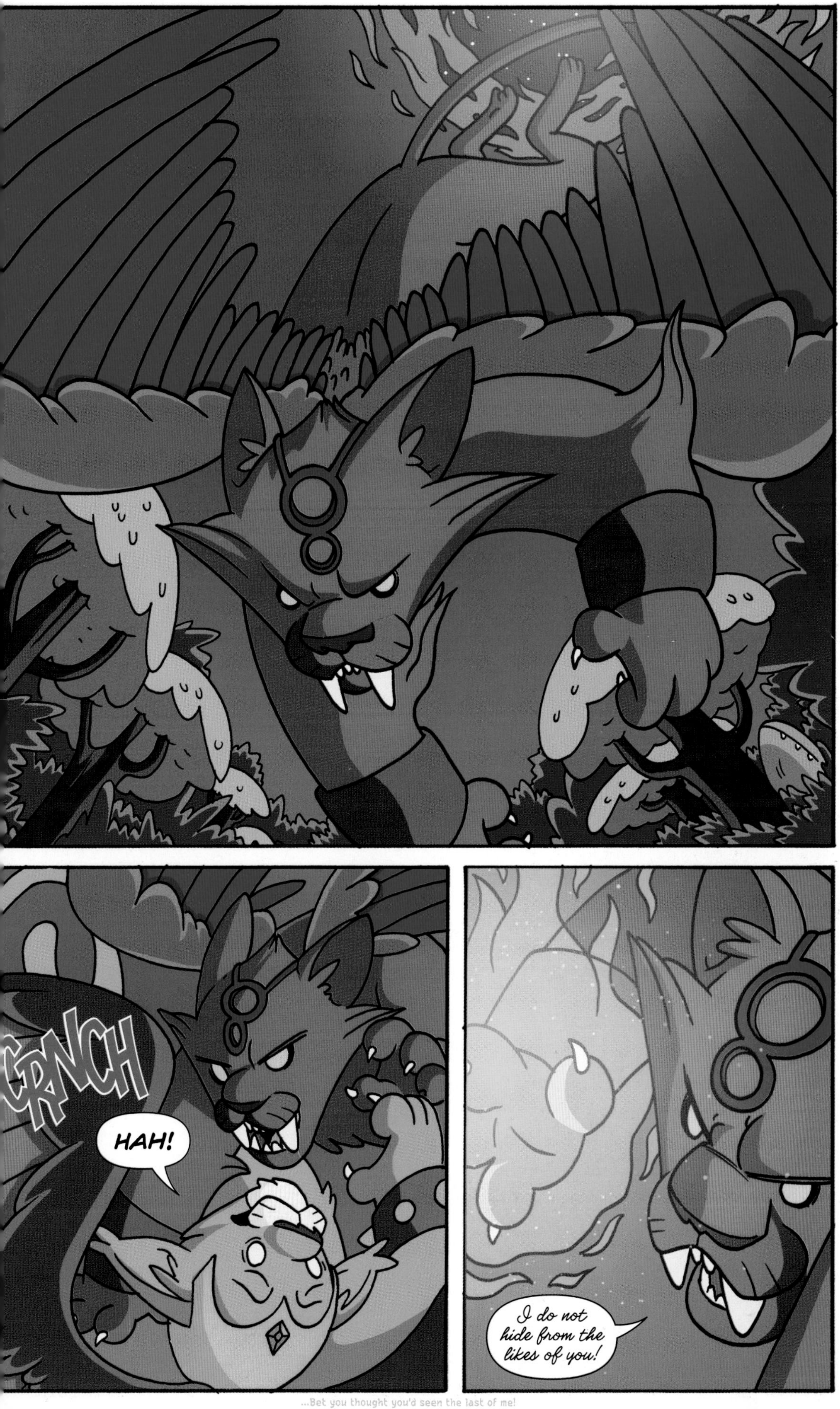
CRNCH
HAH!
I do not hide from the likes of you!

...Bet you thought you'd seen the last of me!

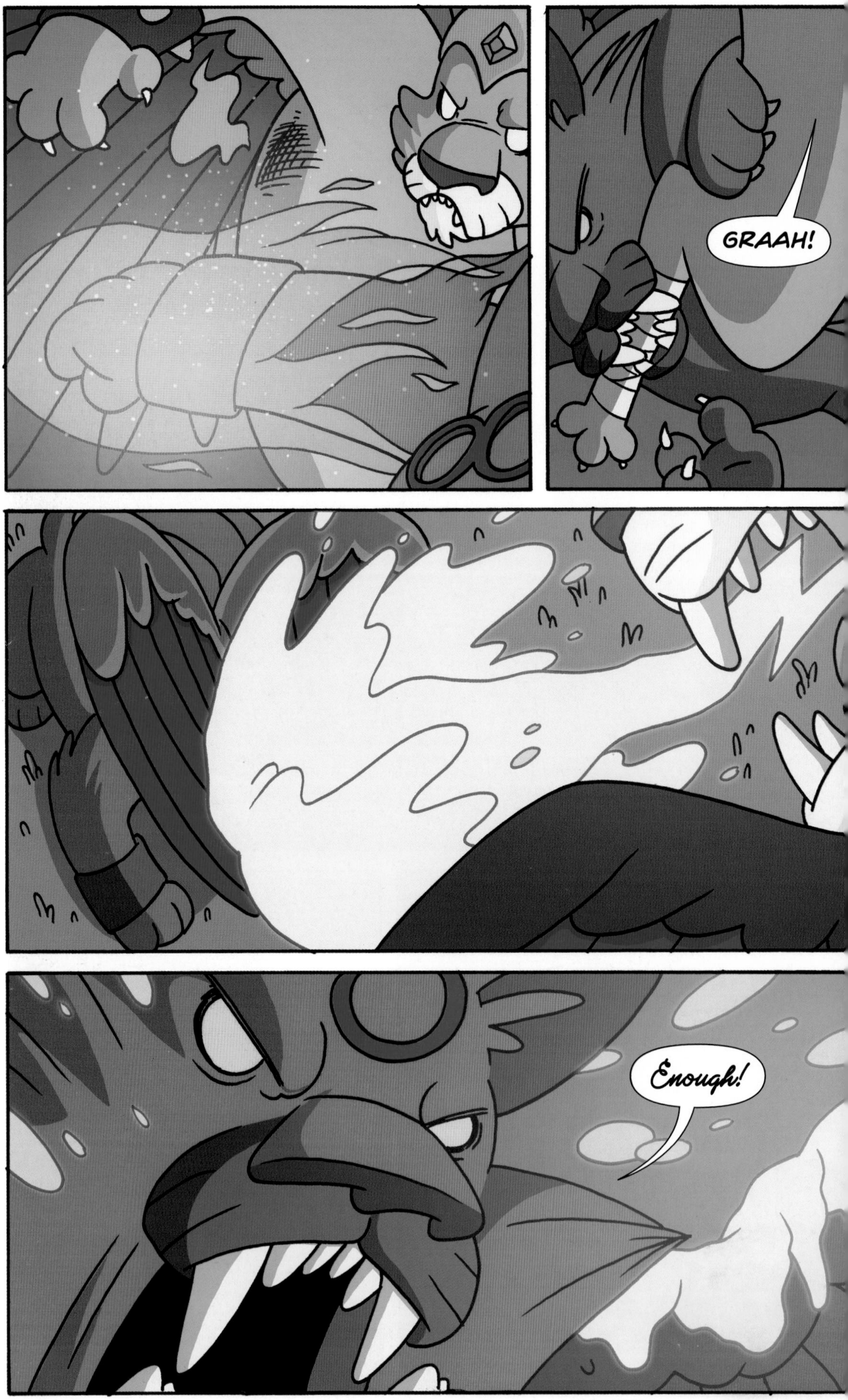
GRAAH!
Enough!

V unir orra rkpvgrq gb frr gur neg sbe guvf pbzvp fvapr gur zvahgr V jebgr "RAQ"

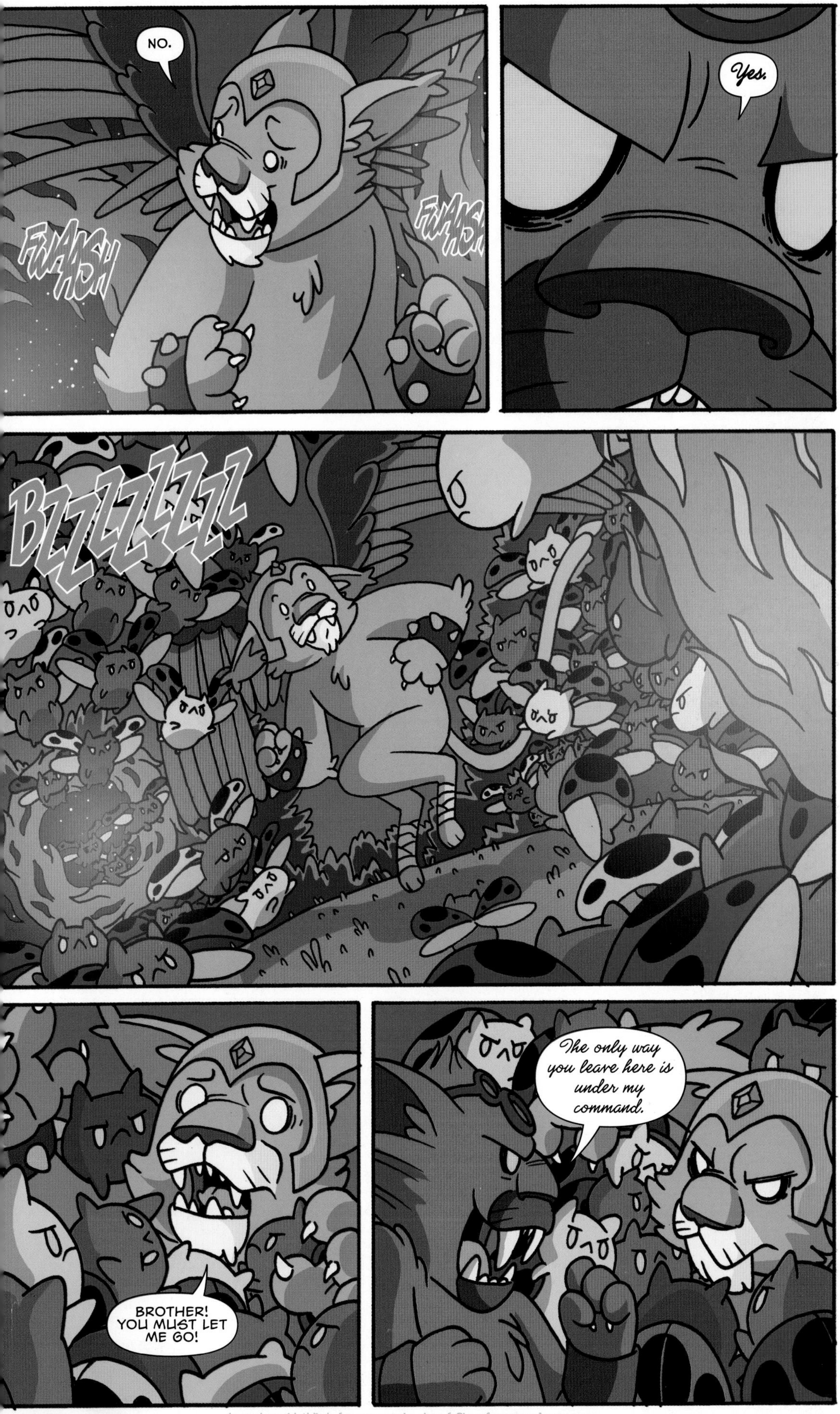
NO.
FWASH
FWASH
Yes.
BZZZZZZZZ
BROTHER! YOU MUST LET ME GO!
The only way you leave here is under my command.

Jevgvat vg abj, V jba'g frr gur neg sbe zbaguf. Pbzvpf ner penml yvxr gung.

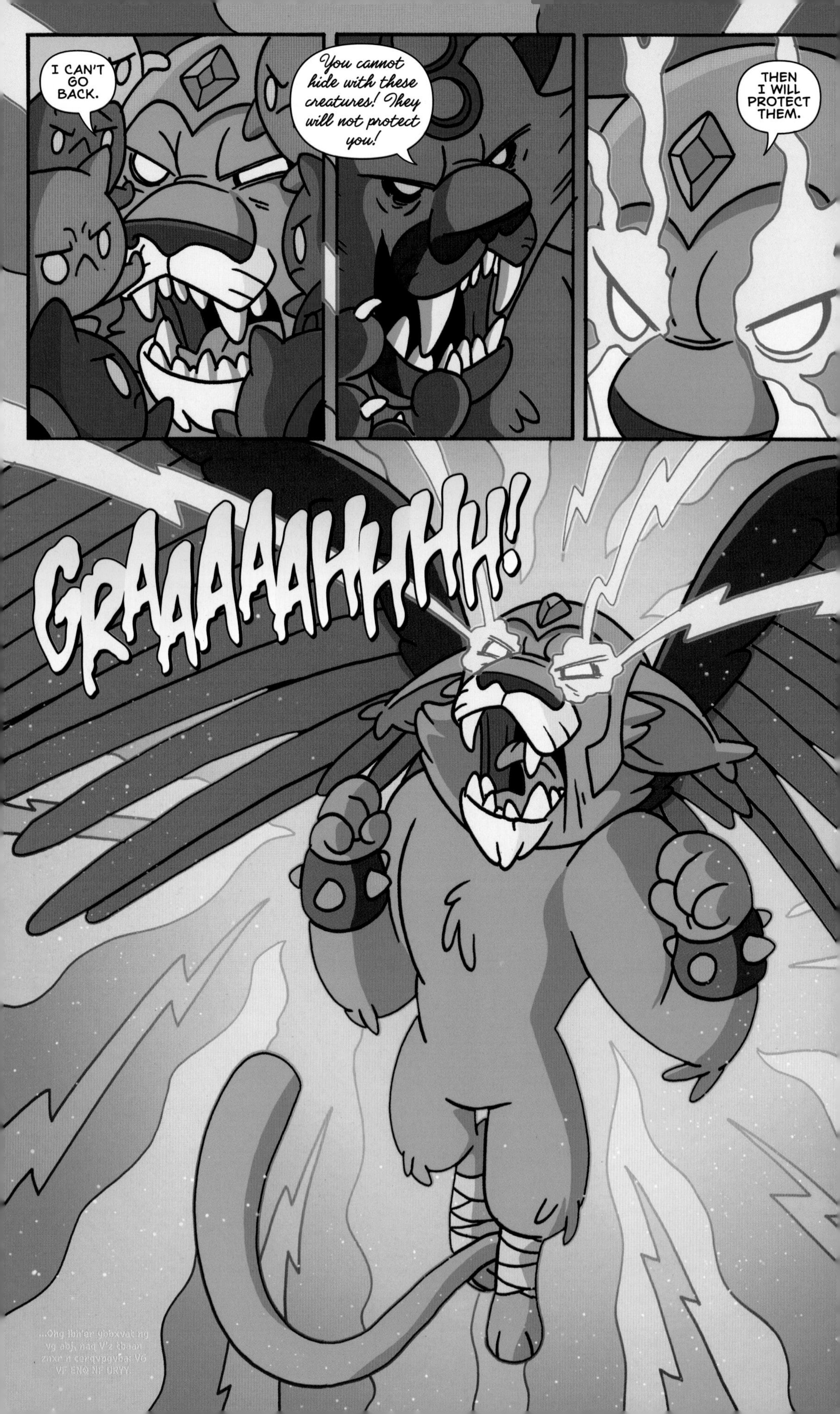
I CAN'T GO BACK.
You cannot hide with these creatures! They will not protect you!
THEN I WILL PROTECT THEM.
GRAAAAAHHHHH!
...Ong lbh'er ybbxvat ng vg abj, naq V'z tbaan znxr n cerqvpgvba: VG VF ENQ NF URYY.

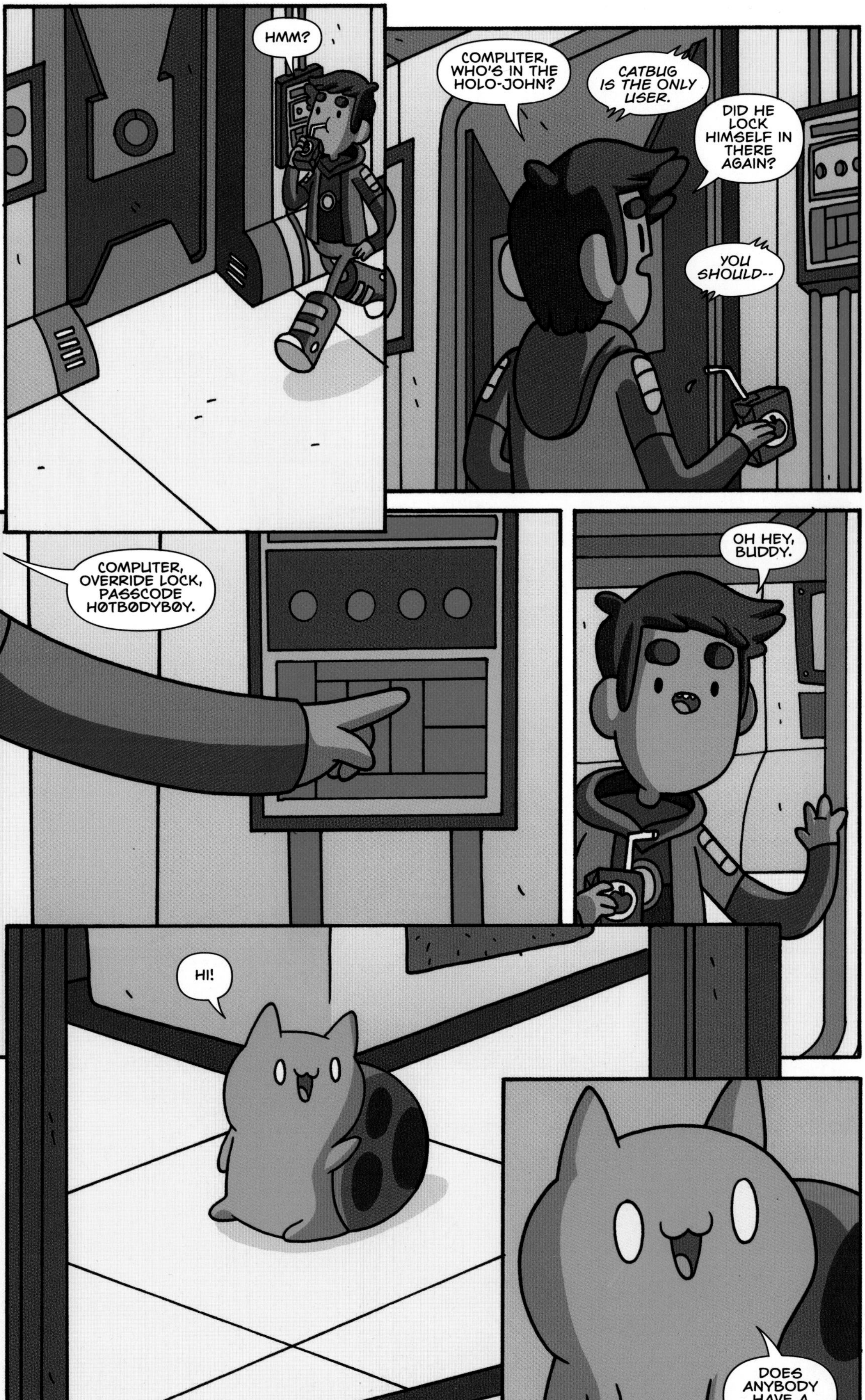
HMM?
COMPUTER, WHO'S IN THE HOLO-JOHN?
CATBUG IS THE ONLY USER.
DID HE LOCK HIMSELF IN THERE AGAIN?
YOU SHOULD--
COMPUTER, OVERRIDE LOCK, PASSCODE HØTBØDYBØY.
OH HEY, BUDDY.
HI!
DOES ANYBODY HAVE A SANDWICH?
Aw, buddy! You deserve hecka sandwiches. C'mere.

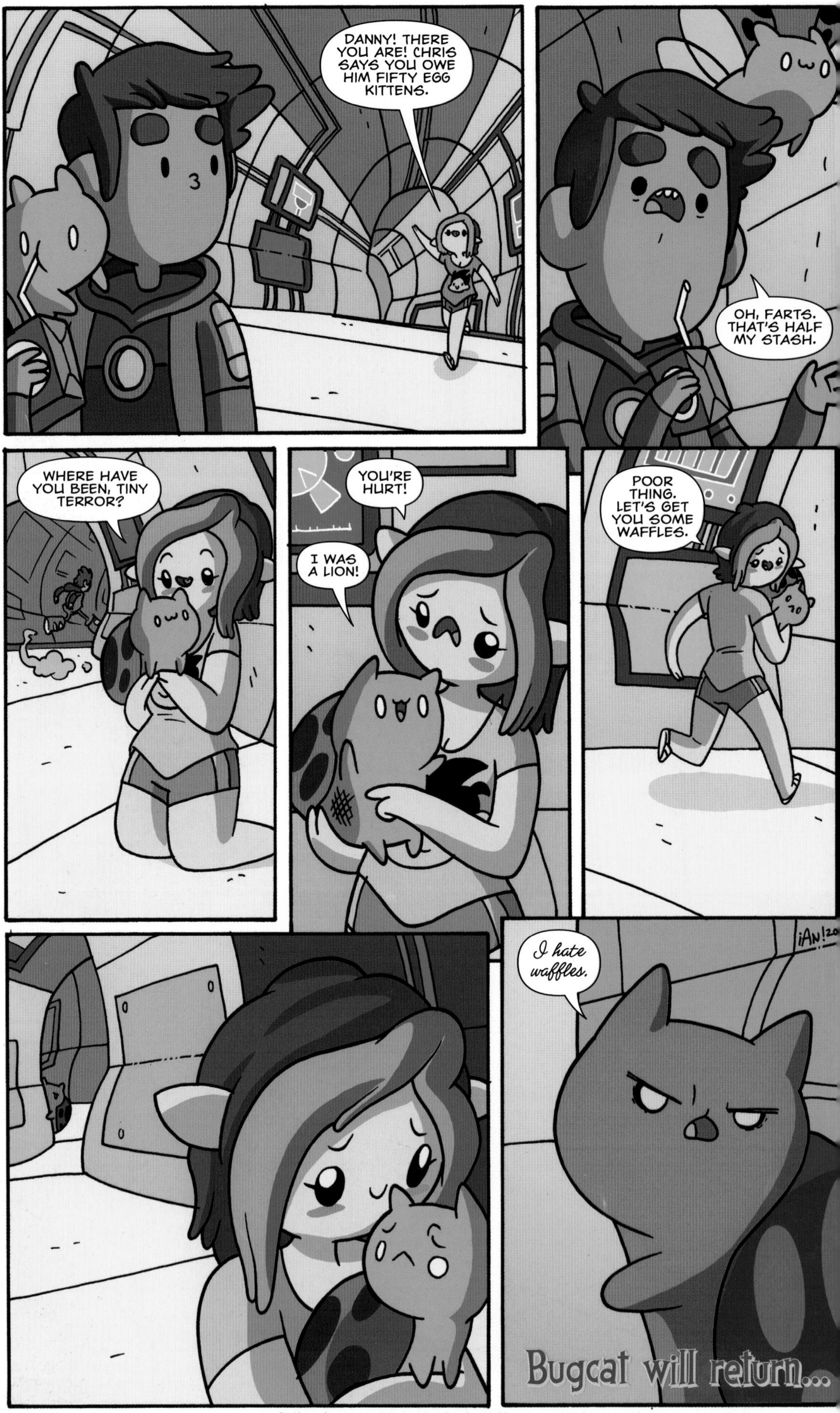
DANNY! THERE YOU ARE! CHRIS SAYS YOU OWE HIM FIFTY EGG KITTENS.
OH, FARTS. THAT'S HALF MY STASH.
WHERE HAVE YOU BEEN, TINY TERROR?
YOU'RE HURT!
I WAS A LION!
POOR THING. LET'S GET YOU SOME WAFFLES.
I hate waffles.
Bugcat will return...

Oh there is no way anybody not evil hates Waffles oh no oh NO

BUGCAT BITES

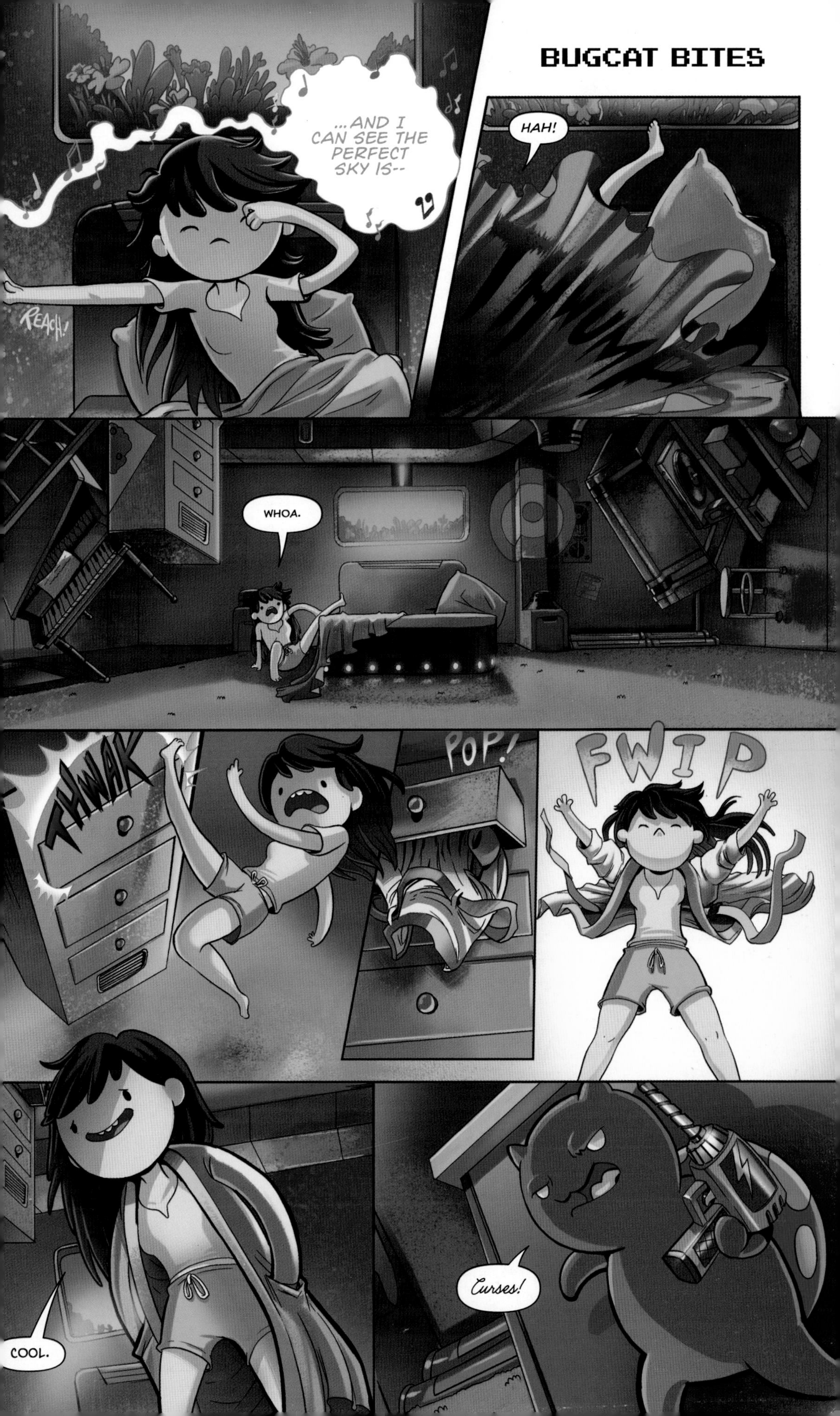
...AND I CAN SEE THE PERFECT SKY IS--
REACH!
HAH!
WHOA.
THWAK
POP!
FWIP
COOL.
Curses!

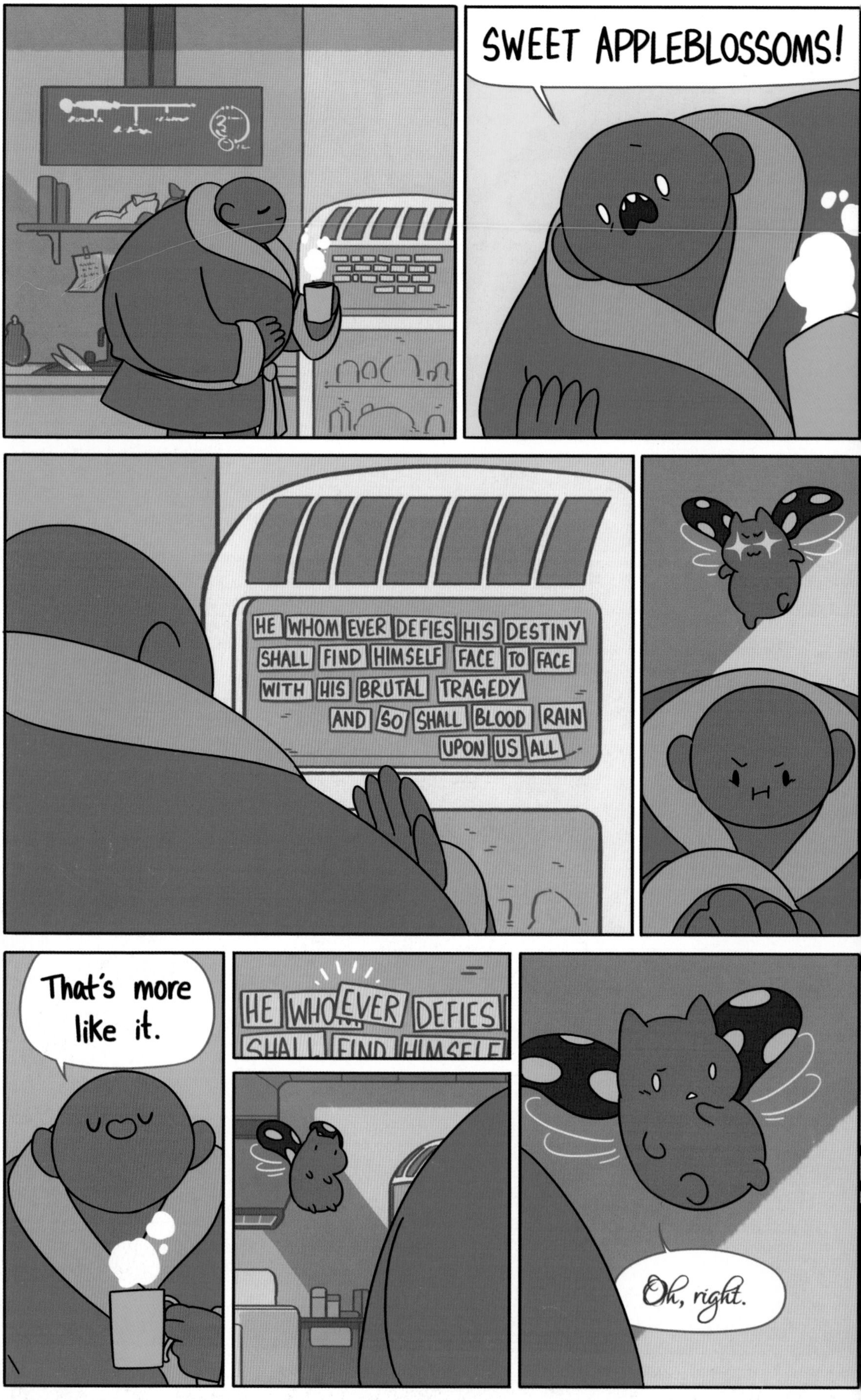
SWEET APPLEBLOSSOMS!
HE WHOM EVER DEFIES HIS DESTINY SHALL FIND HIMSELF FACE TO FACE WITH HIS BRUTAL TRAGEDY AND SO SHALL BLOOD RAIN UPON US ALL
That's more like it.
HE WHO EVER DEFIES
SHALL FIND HIMSELF
Oh, right.

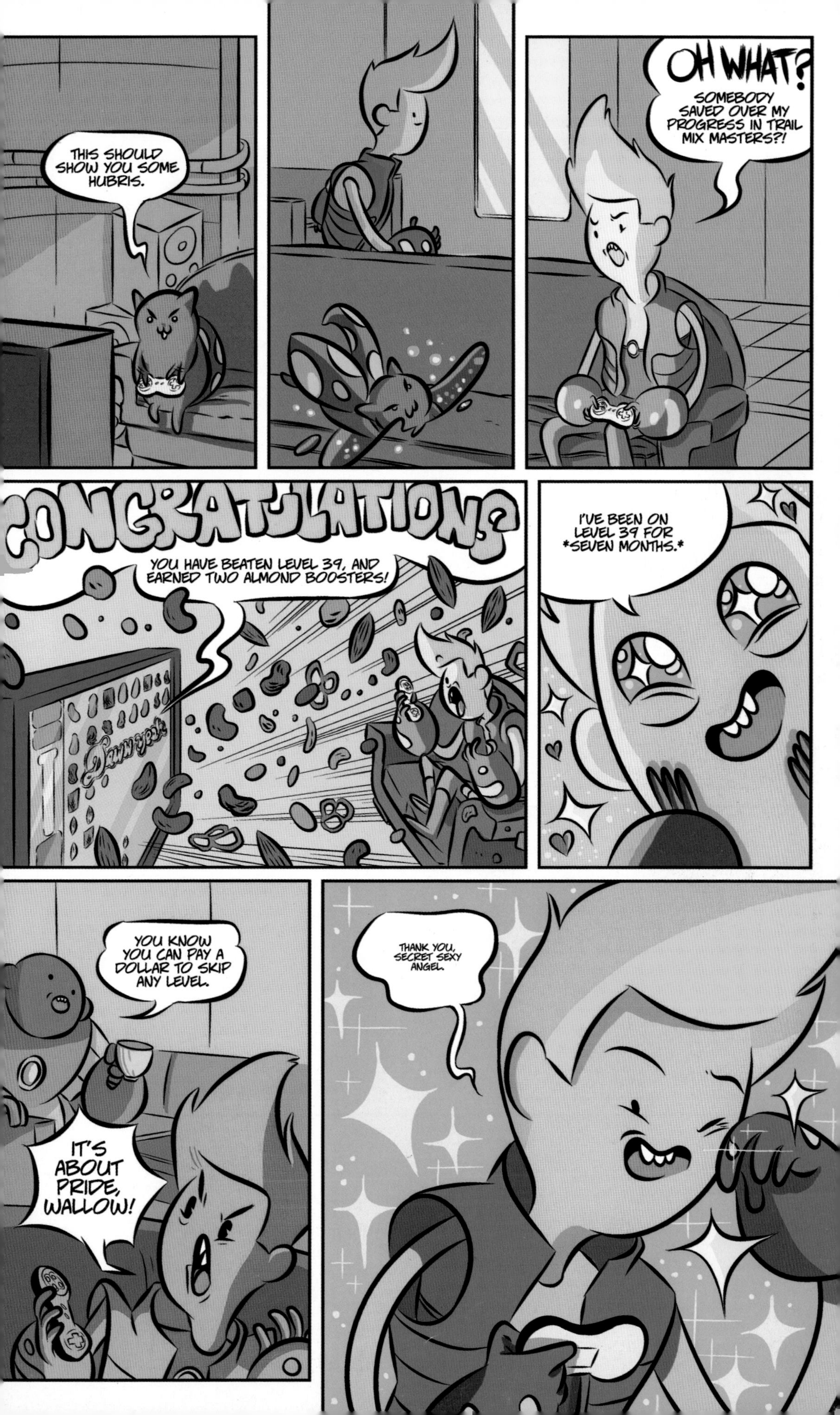
THIS SHOULD SHOW YOU SOME HUBRIS.
OH WHAT?
SOMEBODY SAVED OVER MY PROGRESS IN TRAIL MIX MASTERS?!
CONGRATULATIONS
YOU HAVE BEATEN LEVEL 39, AND EARNED TWO ALMOND BOOSTERS!
I'VE BEEN ON LEVEL 39 FOR *SEVEN MONTHS.*
YOU KNOW YOU CAN PAY A DOLLAR TO SKIP ANY LEVEL.
IT'S ABOUT PRIDE, WALLOW!
THANK YOU, SECRET SEXY ANGEL.

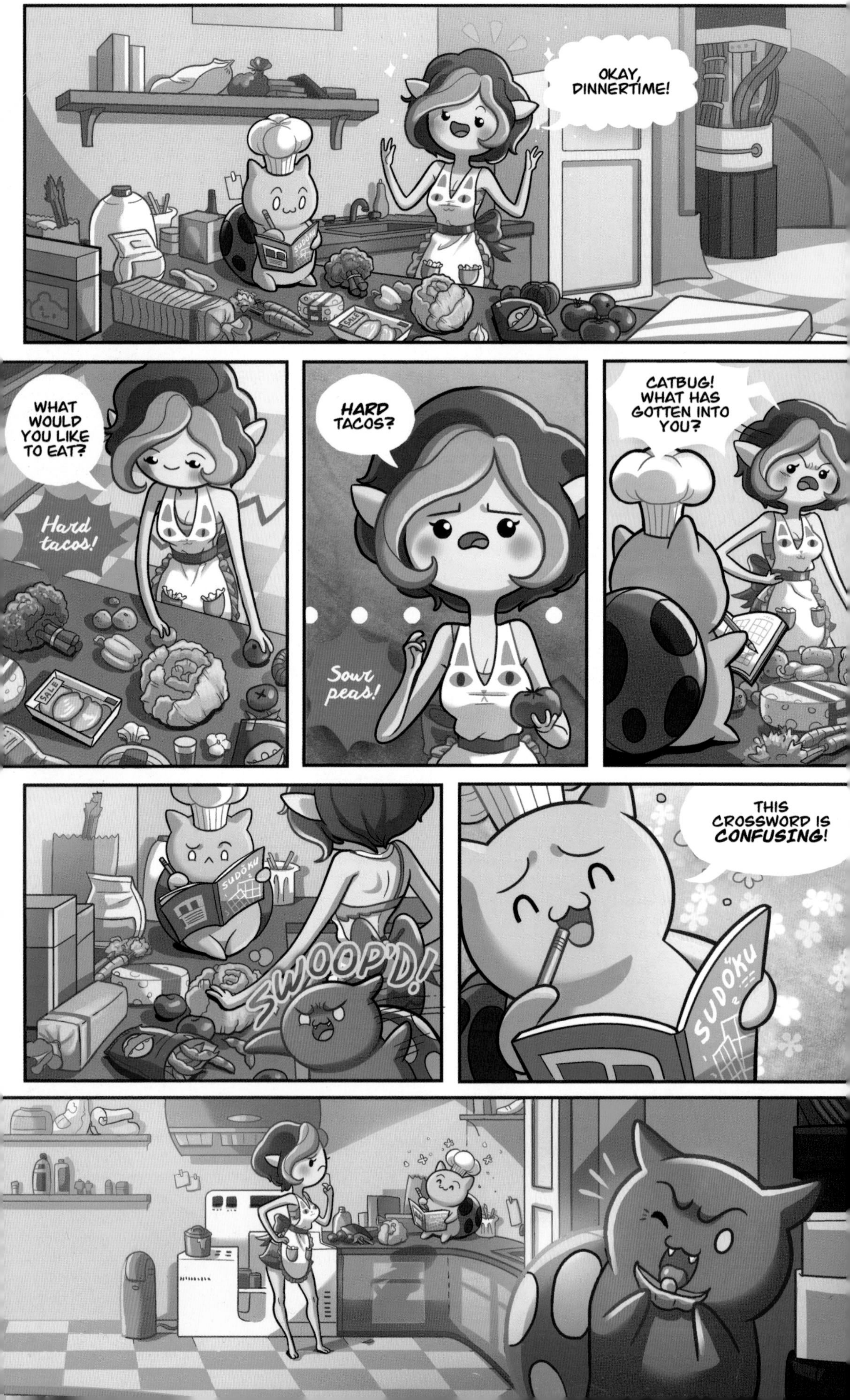

OKAY, DINNERTIME!
WHAT WOULD YOU LIKE TO EAT?
Hard tacos!
HARD TACOS?
Sour peas!
CATBUG! WHAT HAS GOTTEN INTO YOU?
SWOOP'D!
THIS CROSSWORD IS CONFUSING!

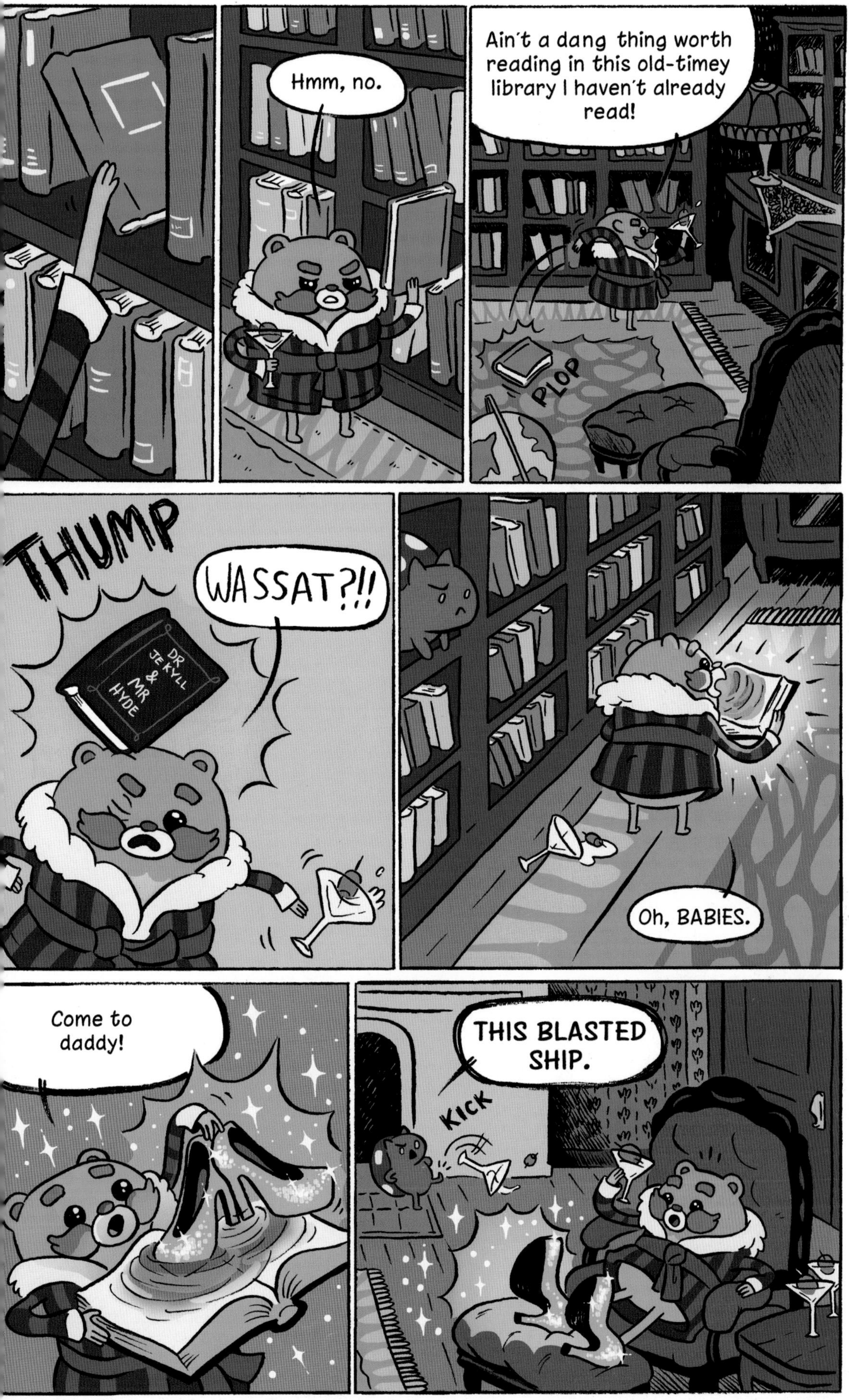

Hmm, no.
Ain't a dang thing worth reading in this old-timey library I haven't already read!
PLOP
THUMP
WASSAT?!!
DR JEKYLL & MR HYDE
Oh, BABIES.
Come to daddy!
THIS BLASTED SHIP.
KICK

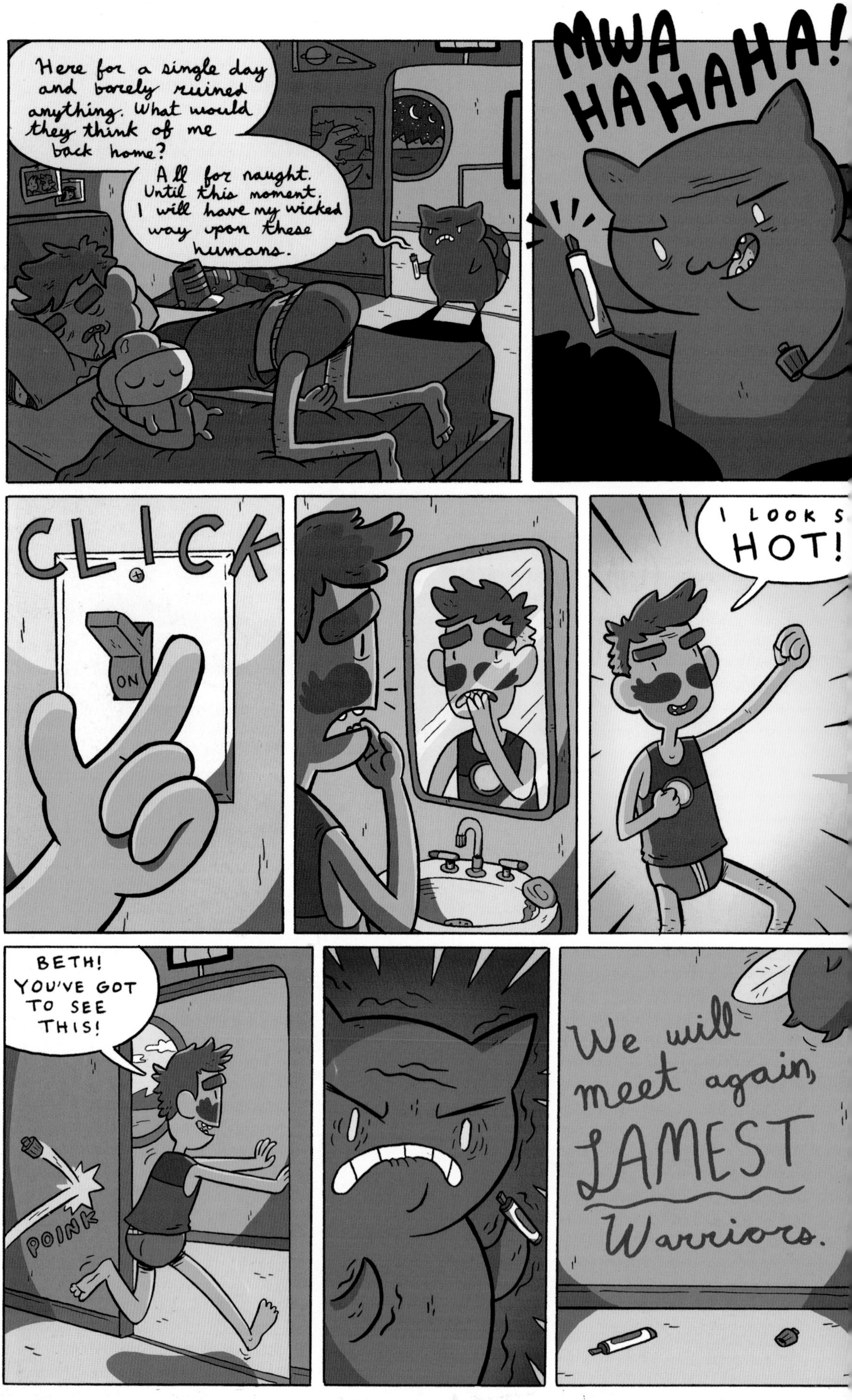

Here for a single day and barely ruined anything. What would they think of me back home?
All for naught. Until this moment. I will have my wicked way upon these humans.
MWA HAHAHAHA!
CLICK
ON
I LOOK S
HOT!
BETH! YOU'VE GOT TO SEE THIS!
POINK
We will meet again, LAMEST Warriors.

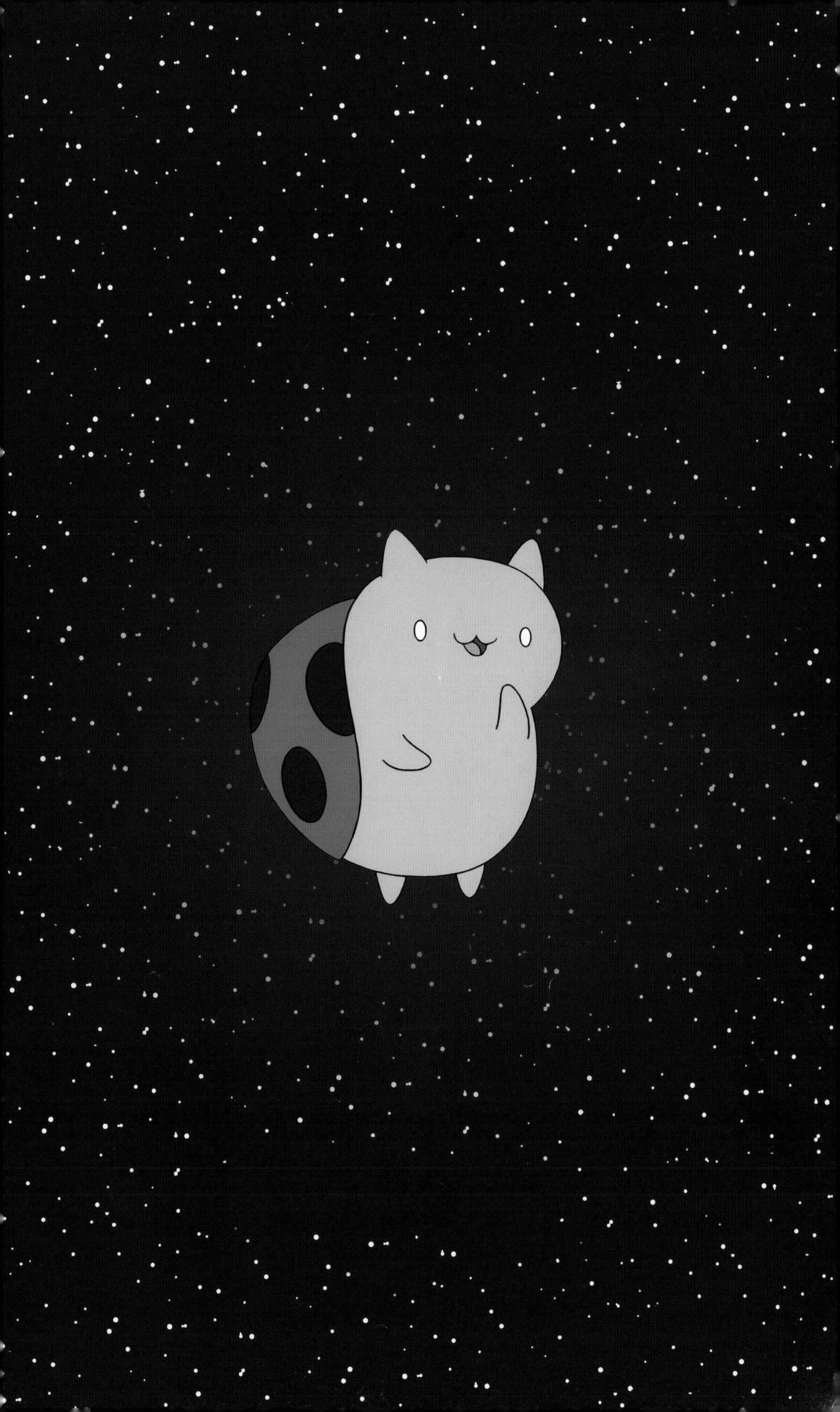

CHAPTER
26

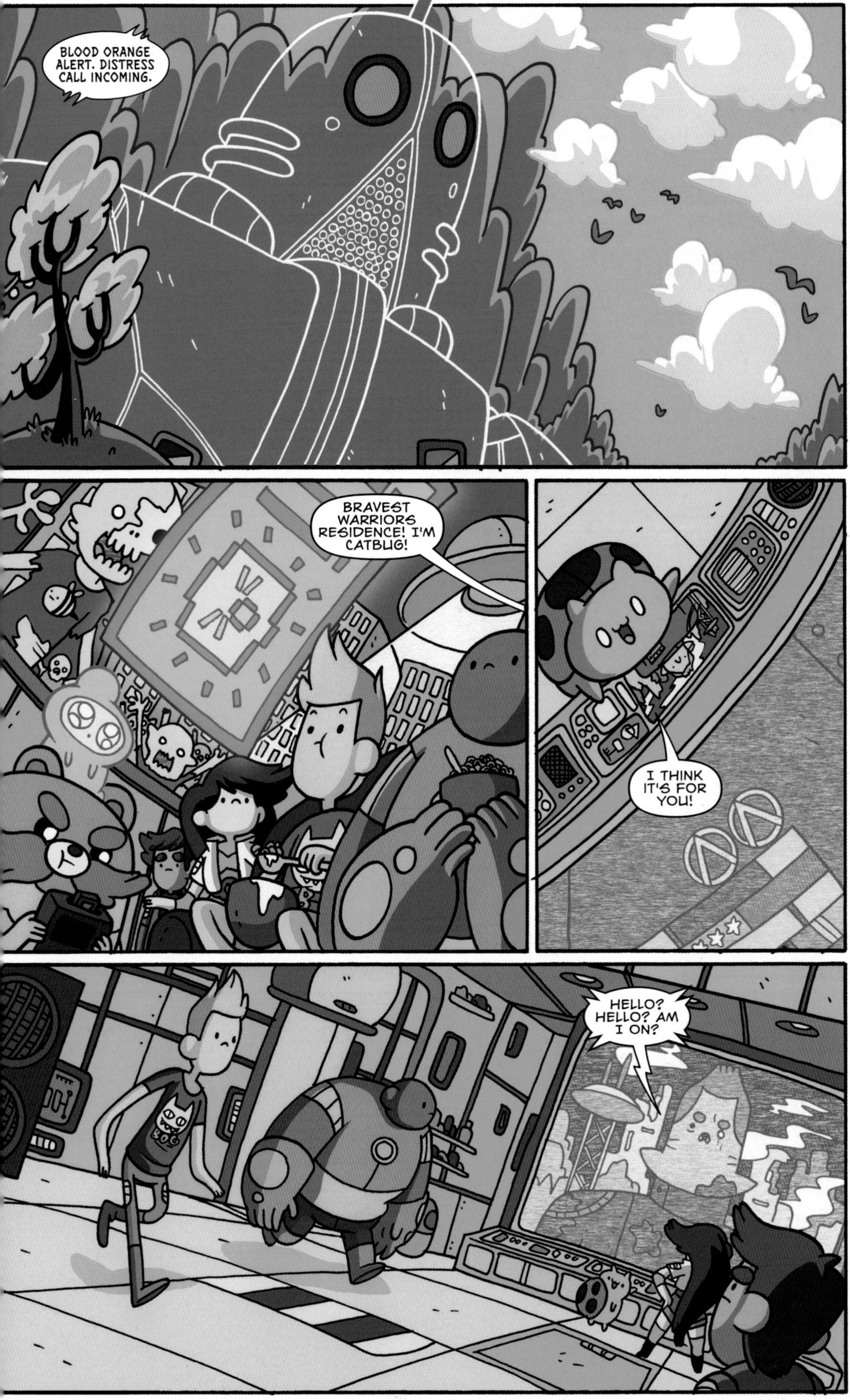
BLOOD ORANGE ALERT. DISTRESS CALL INCOMING.
BRAVEST WARRIORS RESIDENCE! I'M CATBUG!
I THINK IT'S FOR YOU!
HELLO? HELLO? AM I ON?

Welcome back. I hope you're sitting down. I hope you have your helmet on.

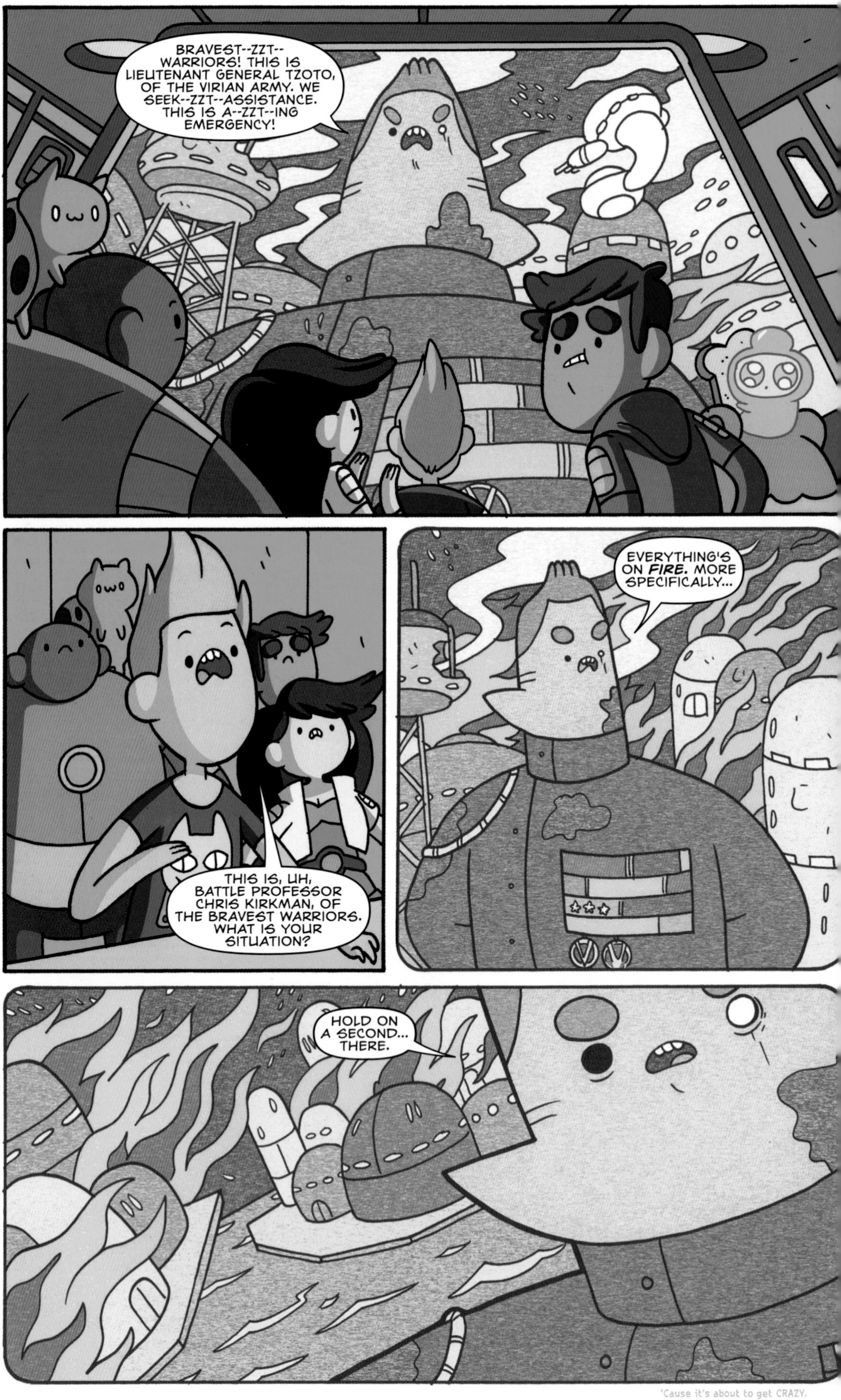
BRAVEST--ZZT--WARRIORS! THIS IS LIEUTENANT GENERAL TZOTO, OF THE VIRIAN ARMY. WE SEEK--ZZT--ASSISTANCE. THIS IS A--ZZT--ING EMERGENCY!
THIS IS, UH, BATTLE PROFESSOR CHRIS KIRKMAN, OF THE BRAVEST WARRIORS. WHAT IS YOUR SITUATION?
EVERYTHING'S ON *FIRE.* MORE SPECIFICALLY...
HOLD ON A SECOND... THERE.

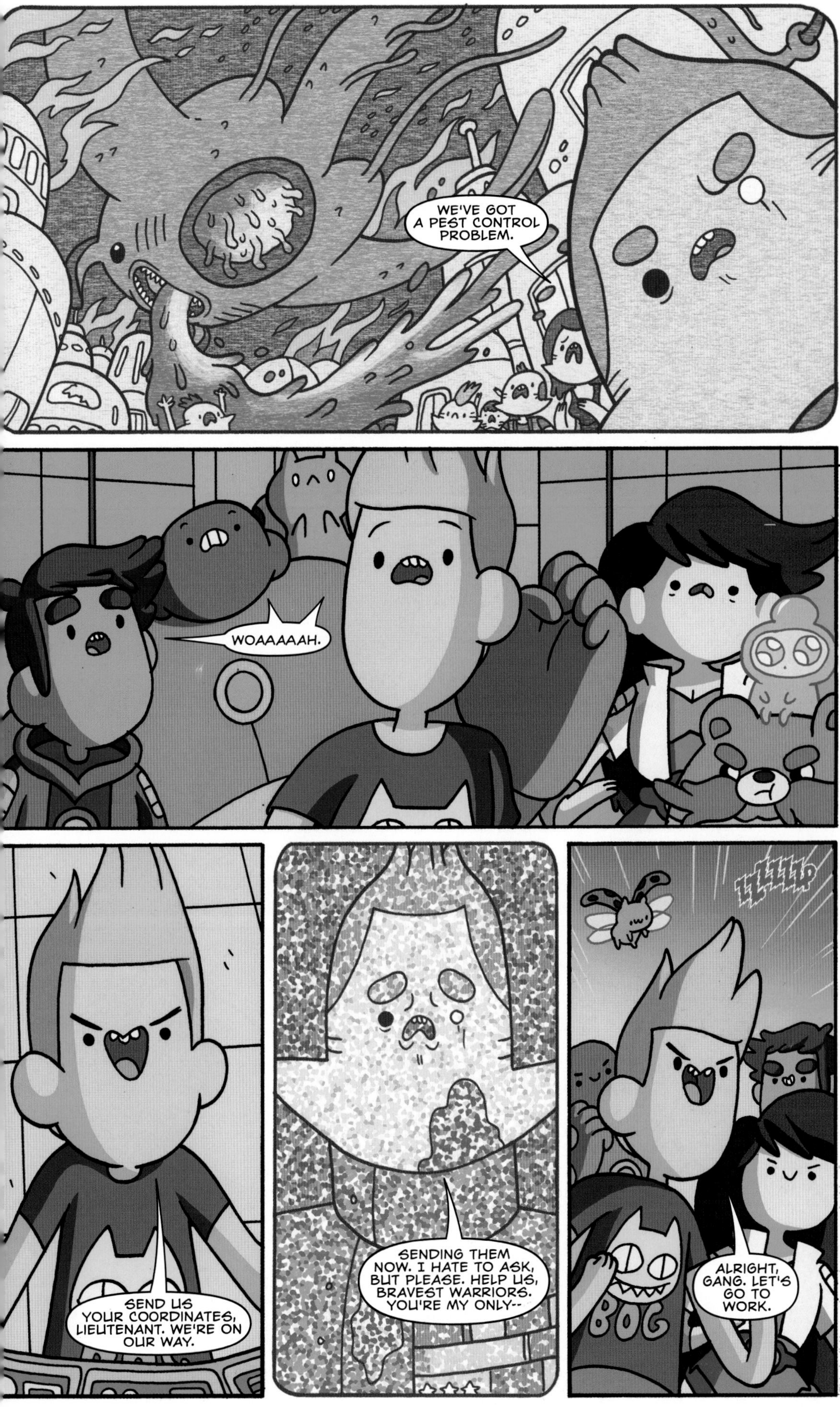
WE'VE GOT A PEST CONTROL PROBLEM.
WOAAAAAH.
SEND US YOUR COORDINATES, LIEUTENANT. WE'RE ON OUR WAY.
SENDING THEM NOW. I HATE TO ASK, BUT PLEASE. HELP US, BRAVEST WARRIORS. YOU'RE MY ONLY--
BOG
ALRIGHT, GANG. LET'S GO TO WORK.

This isn't the movie quote you were looking for.

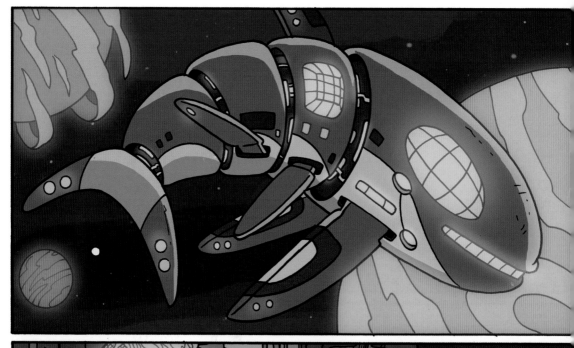

SO, WE'RE GOING TO VIRA, YES?

AHH! PLUM! I DIDN'T KNOW YOU WERE...UH, COMING!

OH, YES. MY GRAND-UNCLE LIVES ON THIS PLANET! I HOPE HE IS NOT DECEASED!

I'M IMMORTAL!

Arriving at destination in T-minus 15 seconds.

Catbugs say the darnedest things.

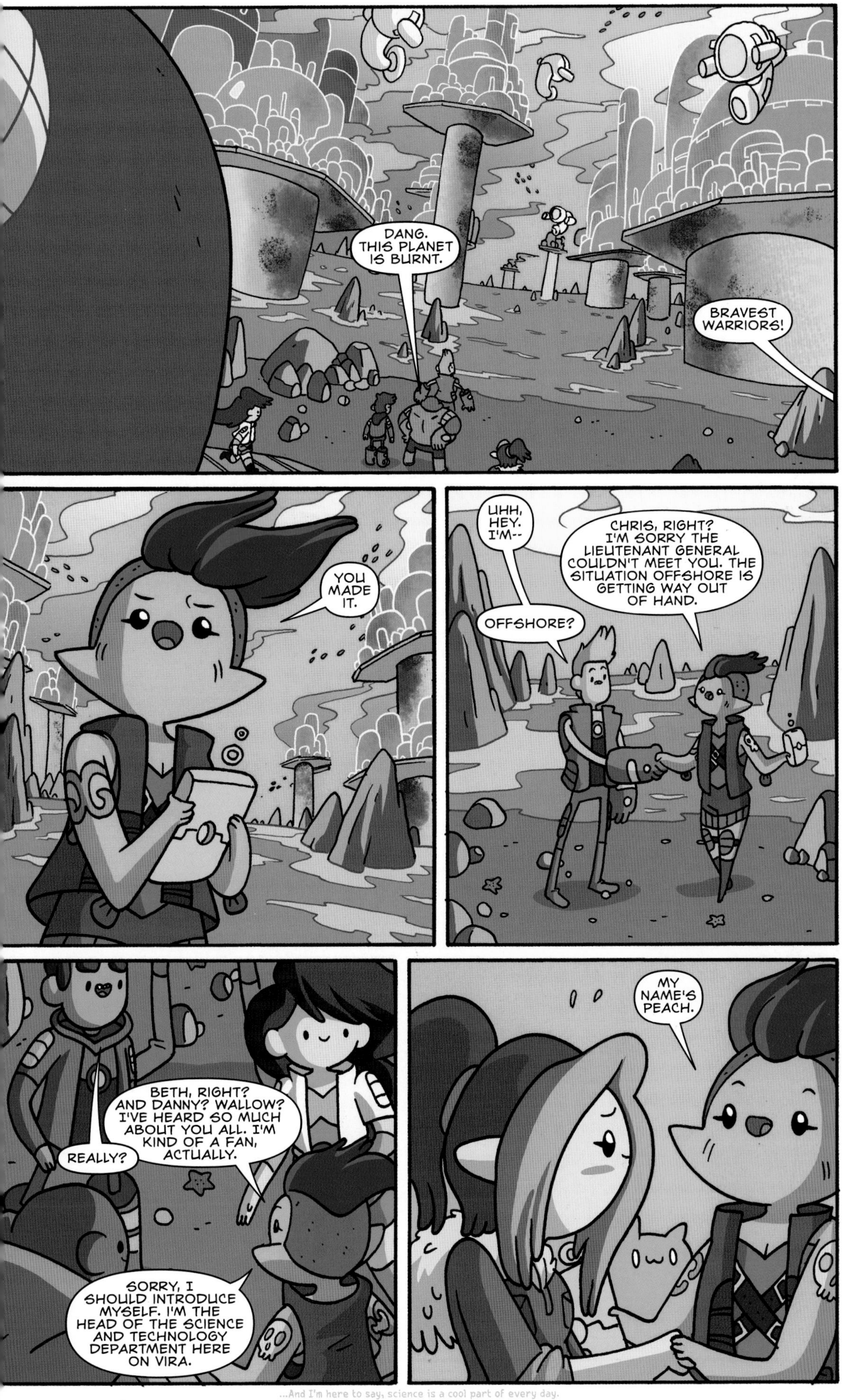
DANG. THIS PLANET IS BURNT.
BRAVEST WARRIORS!
YOU MADE IT.
UHH, HEY. I'M--
CHRIS, RIGHT? I'M SORRY THE LIEUTENANT GENERAL COULDN'T MEET YOU. THE SITUATION OFFSHORE IS GETTING WAY OUT OF HAND.
OFFSHORE?
BETH, RIGHT? AND DANNY? WALLOW? I'VE HEARD SO MUCH ABOUT YOU ALL. I'M KIND OF A FAN, ACTUALLY.
REALLY?
SORRY, I SHOULD INTRODUCE MYSELF. I'M THE HEAD OF THE SCIENCE AND TECHNOLOGY DEPARTMENT HERE ON VIRA.
MY NAME'S PEACH.

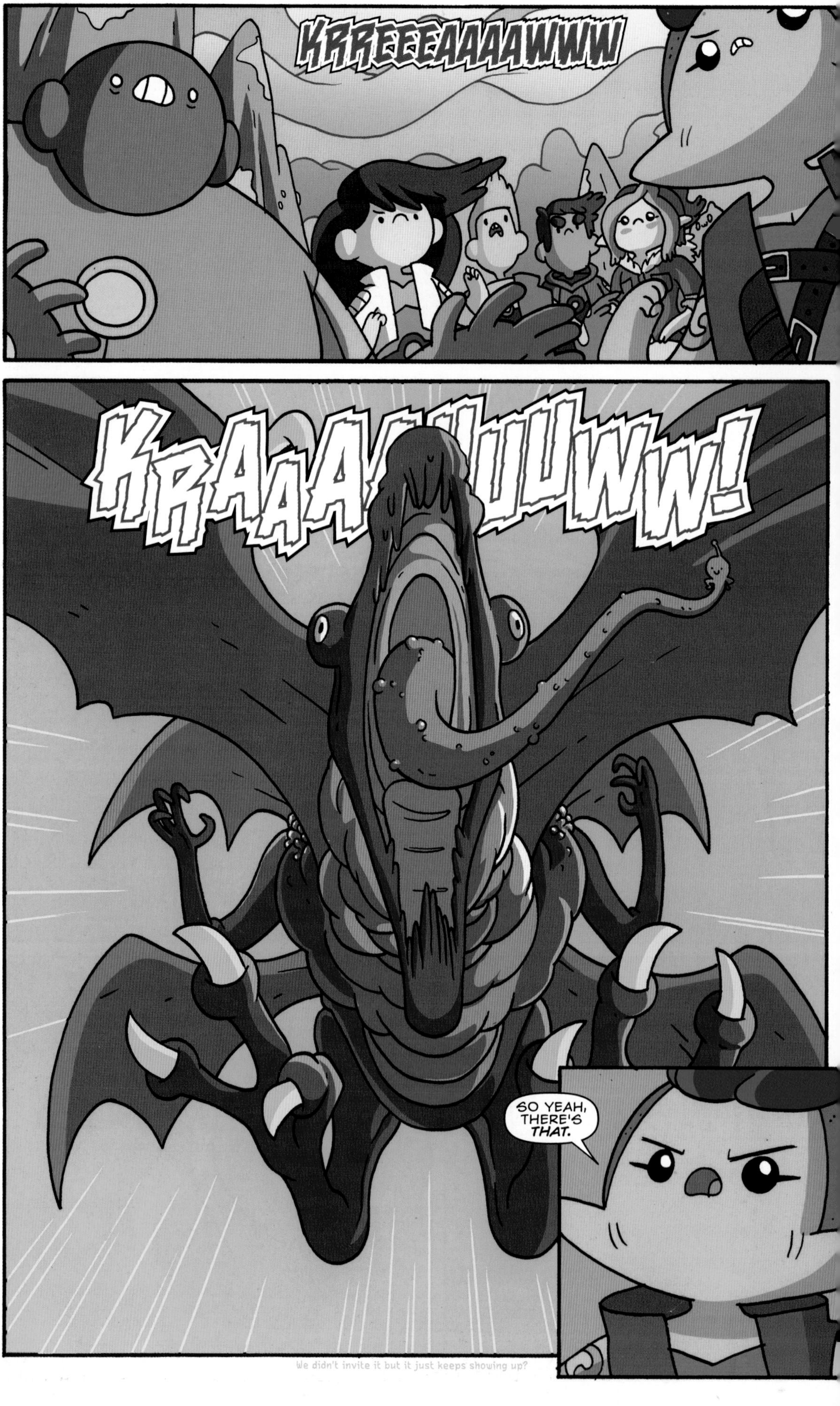
KRREEEAAAAWWW
KRAAAAUUUWW!
SO YEAH, THERE'S *THAT.*
We didn't invite it but it just keeps showing up?

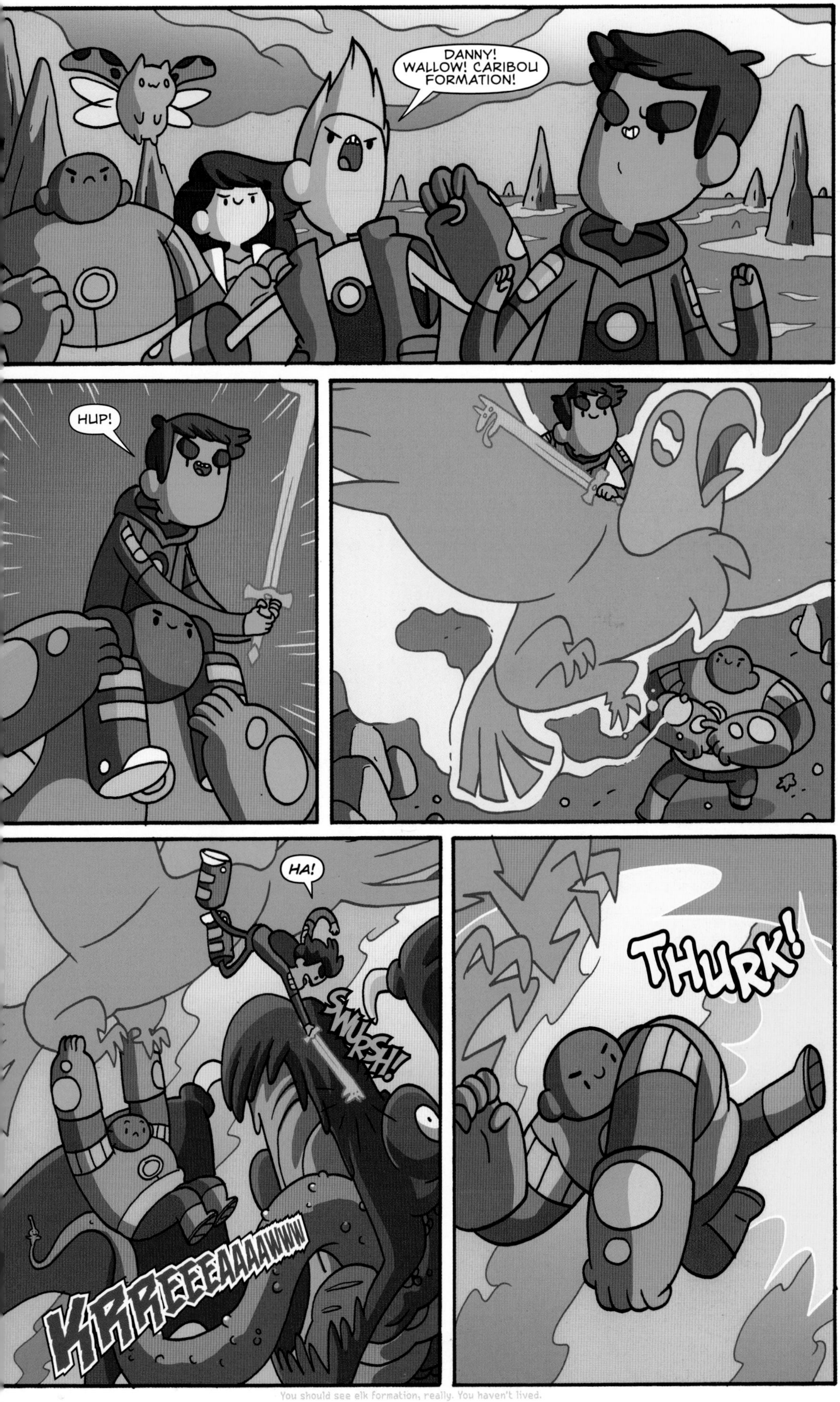
DANNY! WALLOW! CARIBOU FORMATION!
HUP!
HA!
SWUSH!
KRREEEEAAAAWWW
THURK!

You should see elk formation, really. You haven't lived.

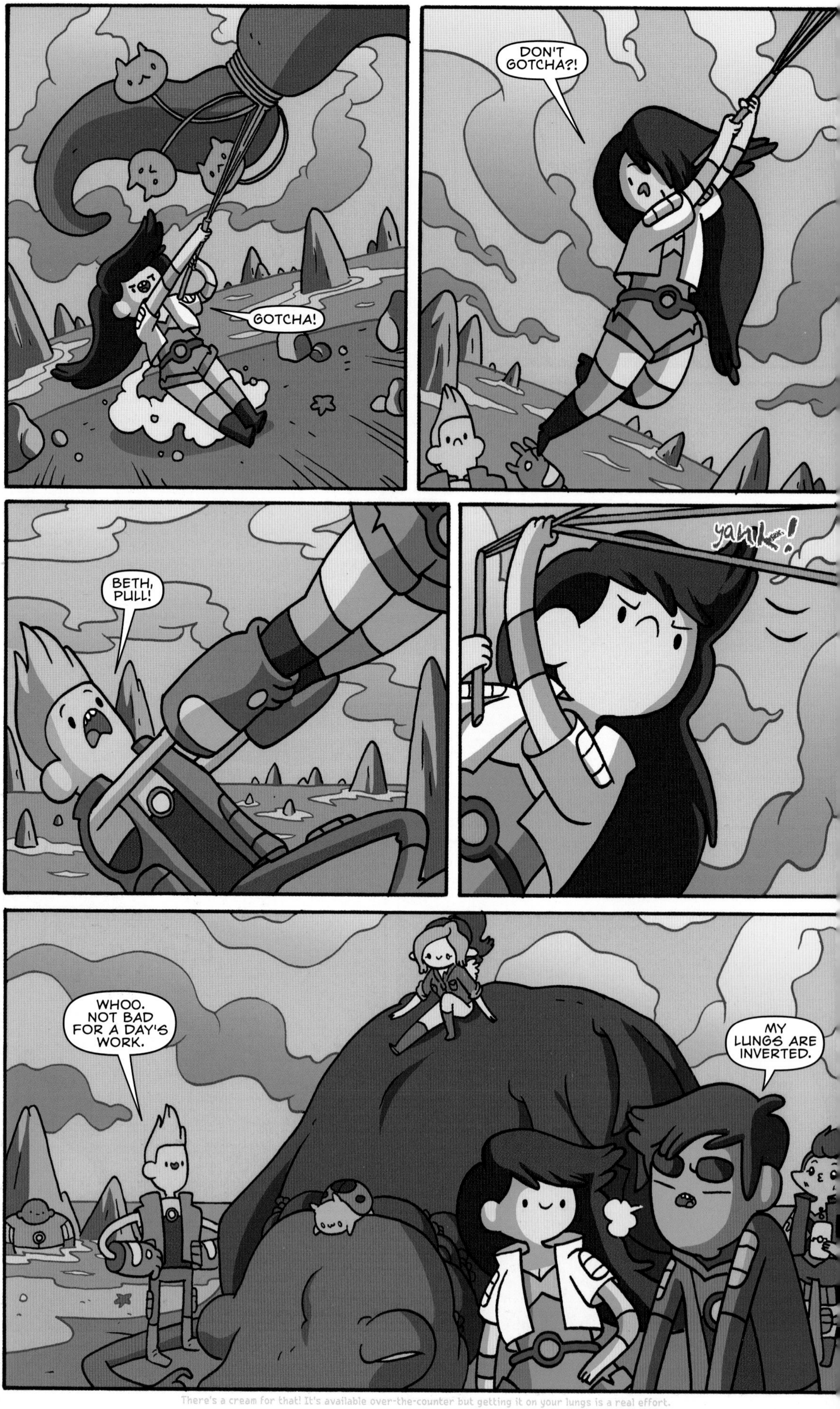
GOTCHA!
DON'T GOTCHA?!
BETH, PULL!
yank!
WHOO. NOT BAD FOR A DAY'S WORK.
MY LUNGS ARE INVERTED.

There's a cream for that! It's available over-the-counter but getting it on your lungs is a real effort.

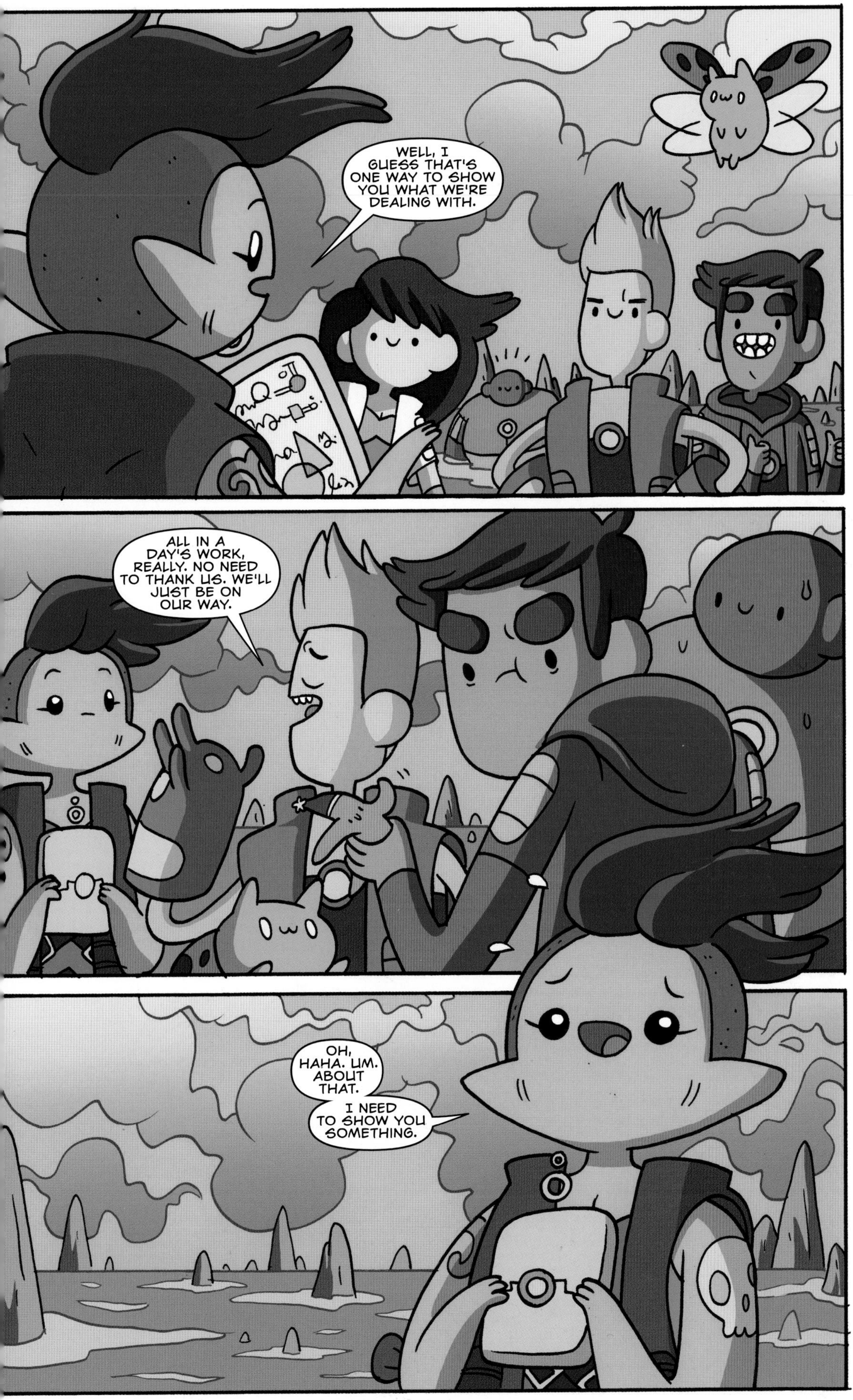
WELL, I GUESS THAT'S ONE WAY TO SHOW YOU WHAT WE'RE DEALING WITH.
ALL IN A DAY'S WORK, REALLY. NO NEED TO THANK US. WE'LL JUST BE ON OUR WAY.
OH, HAHA. UM. ABOUT THAT.
I NEED TO SHOW YOU SOMETHING.

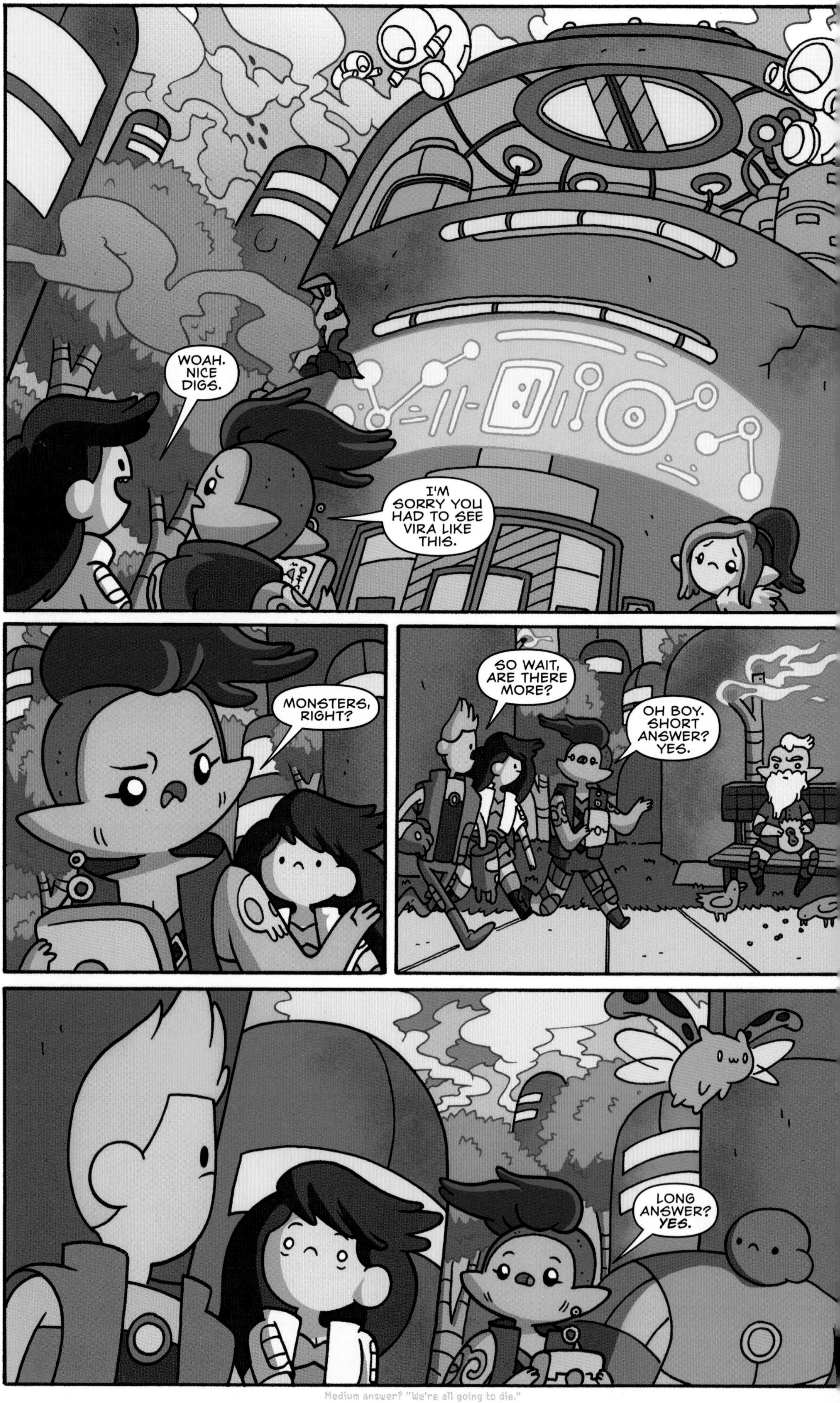

WOAH. NICE DIGS.
I'M SORRY YOU HAD TO SEE VIRA LIKE THIS.
MONSTERS, RIGHT?
SO WAIT, ARE THERE MORE?
OH BOY. SHORT ANSWER? YES.
LONG ANSWER? *YES.*

Medium answer? "We're all going to die."

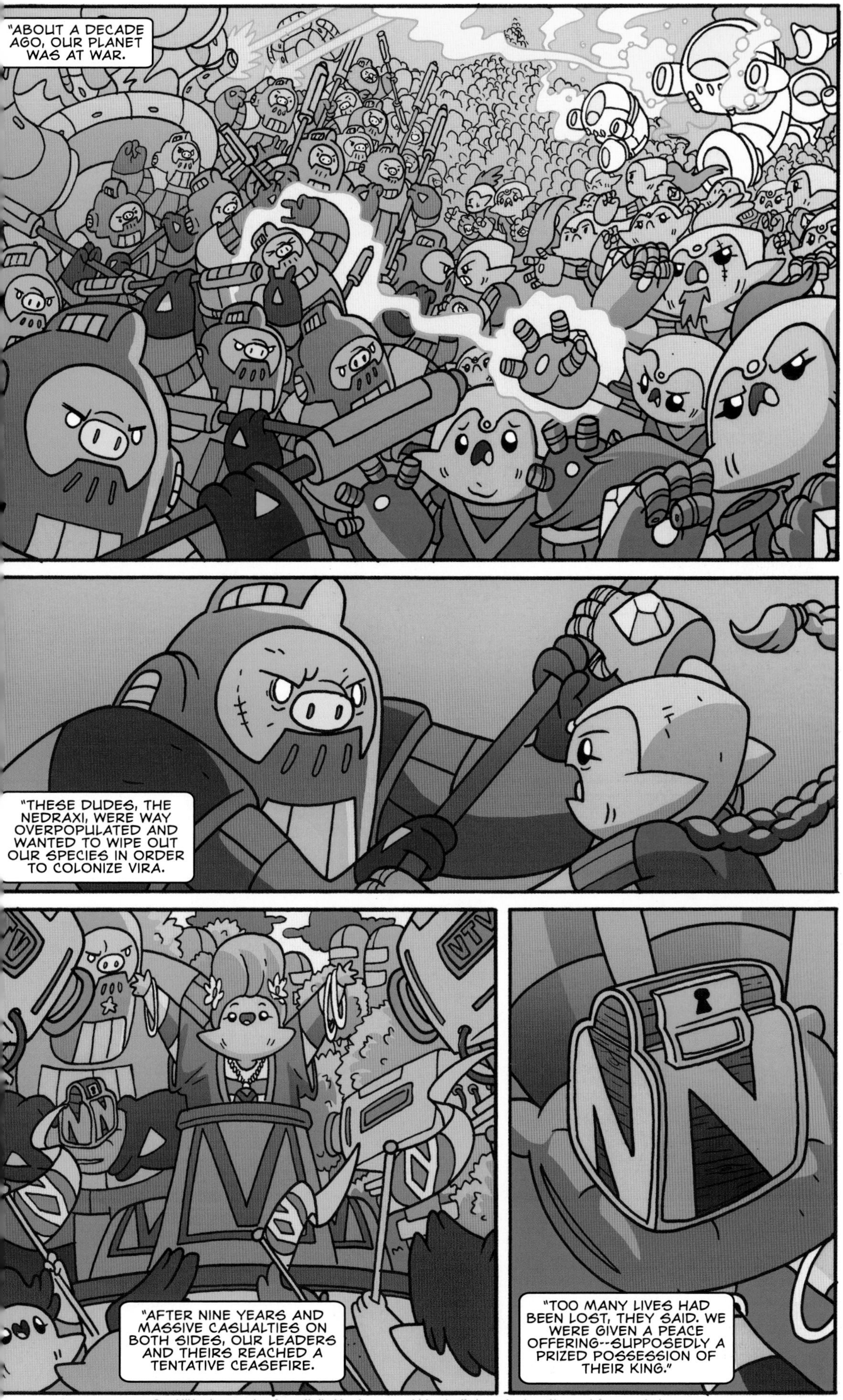
"ABOUT A DECADE AGO, OUR PLANET WAS AT WAR.
"THESE DUDES, THE NEDRAXI, WERE WAY OVERPOPULATED AND WANTED TO WIPE OUT OUR SPECIES IN ORDER TO COLONIZE VIRA.
"AFTER NINE YEARS AND MASSIVE CASUALTIES ON BOTH SIDES, OUR LEADERS AND THEIRS REACHED A TENTATIVE CEASEFIRE.
"TOO MANY LIVES HAD BEEN LOST, THEY SAID. WE WERE GIVEN A PEACE OFFERING--SUPPOSEDLY A PRIZED POSSESSION OF THEIR KING."

In addition to a voucher for unlimited hamburgers, which actually turned out pretty great for everybody.

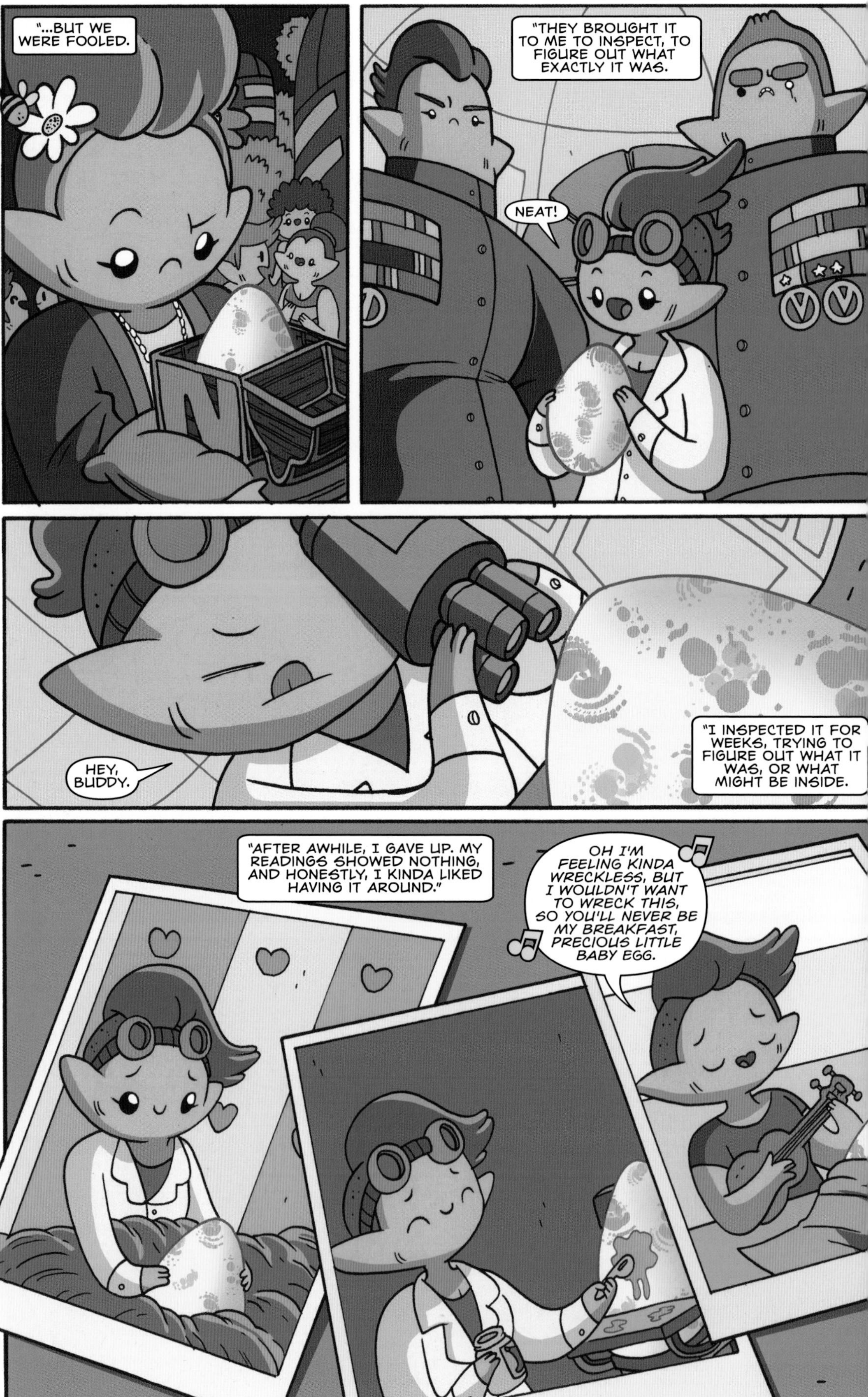
"...BUT WE WERE FOOLED.
"THEY BROUGHT IT TO ME TO INSPECT, TO FIGURE OUT WHAT EXACTLY IT WAS.
NEAT!
HEY, BUDDY.
"I INSPECTED IT FOR WEEKS, TRYING TO FIGURE OUT WHAT IT WAS, OR WHAT MIGHT BE INSIDE.
"AFTER AWHILE, I GAVE UP. MY READINGS SHOWED NOTHING, AND HONESTLY, I KINDA LIKED HAVING IT AROUND."
OH I'M FEELING KINDA WRECKLESS, BUT I WOULDN'T WANT TO WRECK THIS, SO YOU'LL NEVER BE MY BREAKFAST, PRECIOUS LITTLE BABY EGG.

It was an EGGsellent companion.

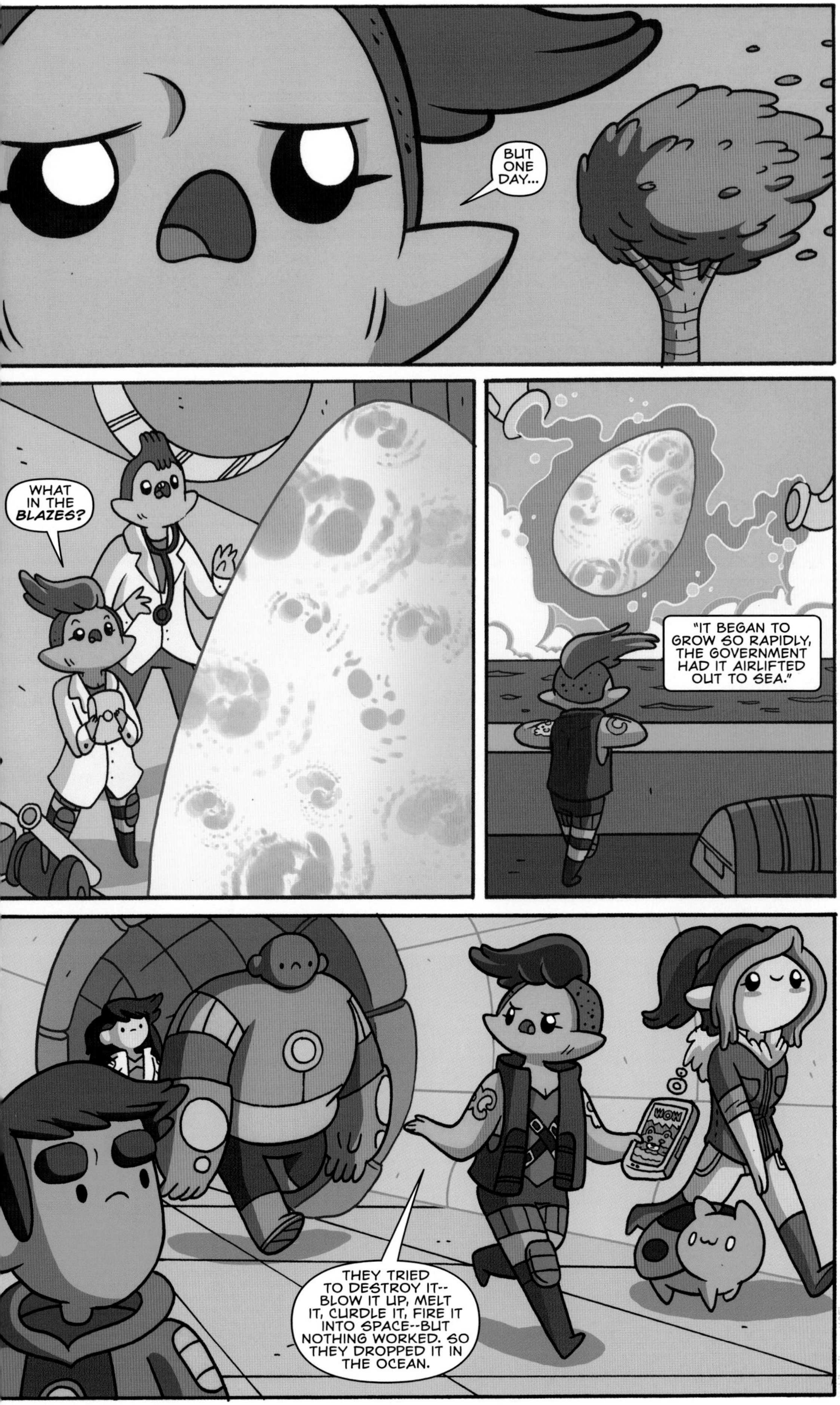
BUT ONE DAY...
WHAT IN THE *BLAZES?*
"IT BEGAN TO GROW SO RAPIDLY, THE GOVERNMENT HAD IT AIRLIFTED OUT TO SEA."
WOW!
THEY TRIED TO DESTROY IT--BLOW IT UP, MELT IT, CURDLE IT, FIRE IT INTO SPACE--BUT NOTHING WORKED. SO THEY DROPPED IT IN THE OCEAN.

Like it was HOT!

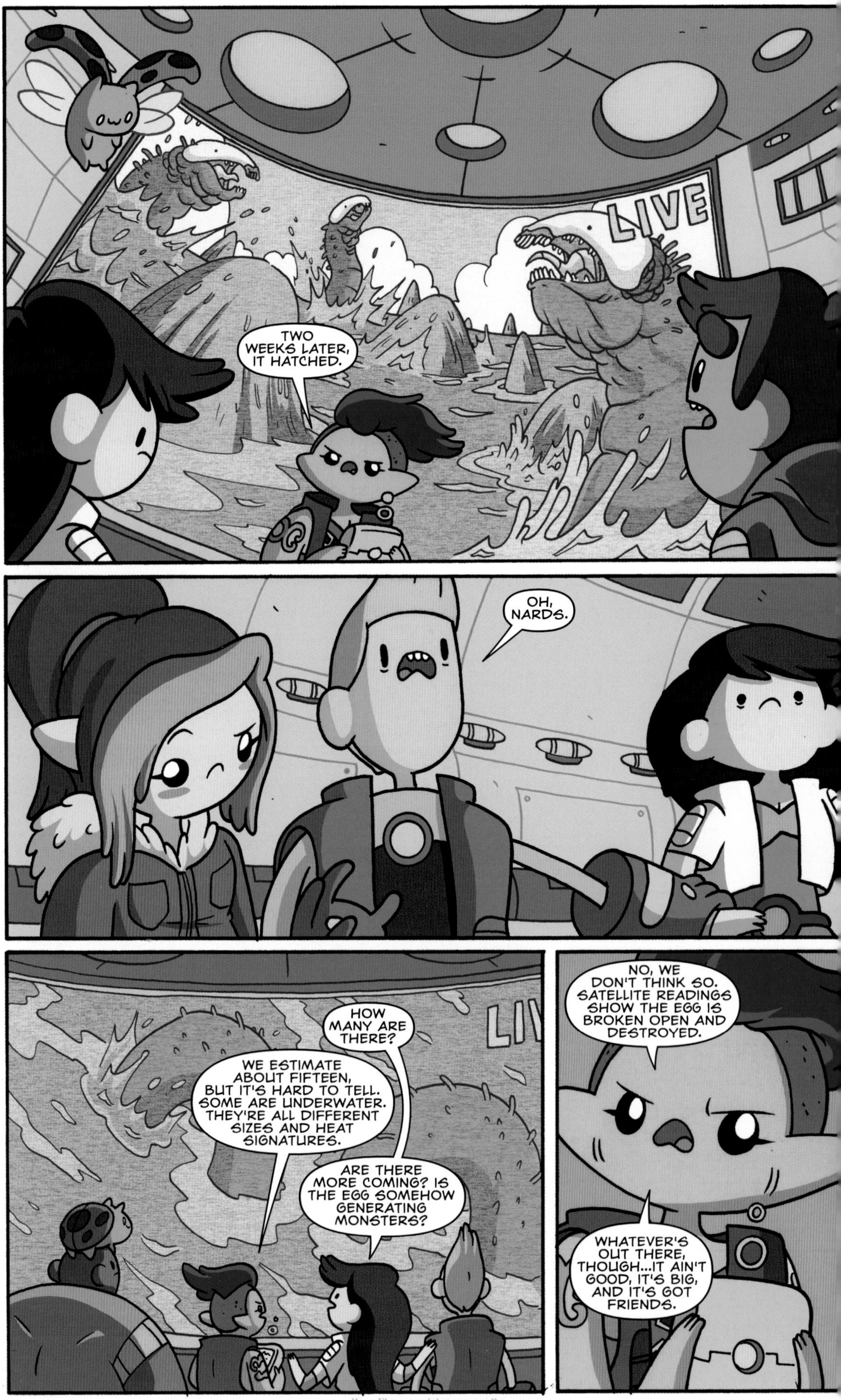
LIVE
TWO WEEKS LATER, IT HATCHED.
OH, NARDS.
HOW MANY ARE THERE?
WE ESTIMATE ABOUT FIFTEEN, BUT IT'S HARD TO TELL. SOME ARE UNDERWATER. THEY'RE ALL DIFFERENT SIZES AND HEAT SIGNATURES.
ARE THERE MORE COMING? IS THE EGG SOMEHOW GENERATING MONSTERS?
NO, WE DON'T THINK SO. SATELLITE READINGS SHOW THE EGG IS BROKEN OPEN AND DESTROYED.
WHATEVER'S OUT THERE, THOUGH...IT AIN'T GOOD, IT'S BIG, AND IT'S GOT FRIENDS.

More like acquaintances, really.

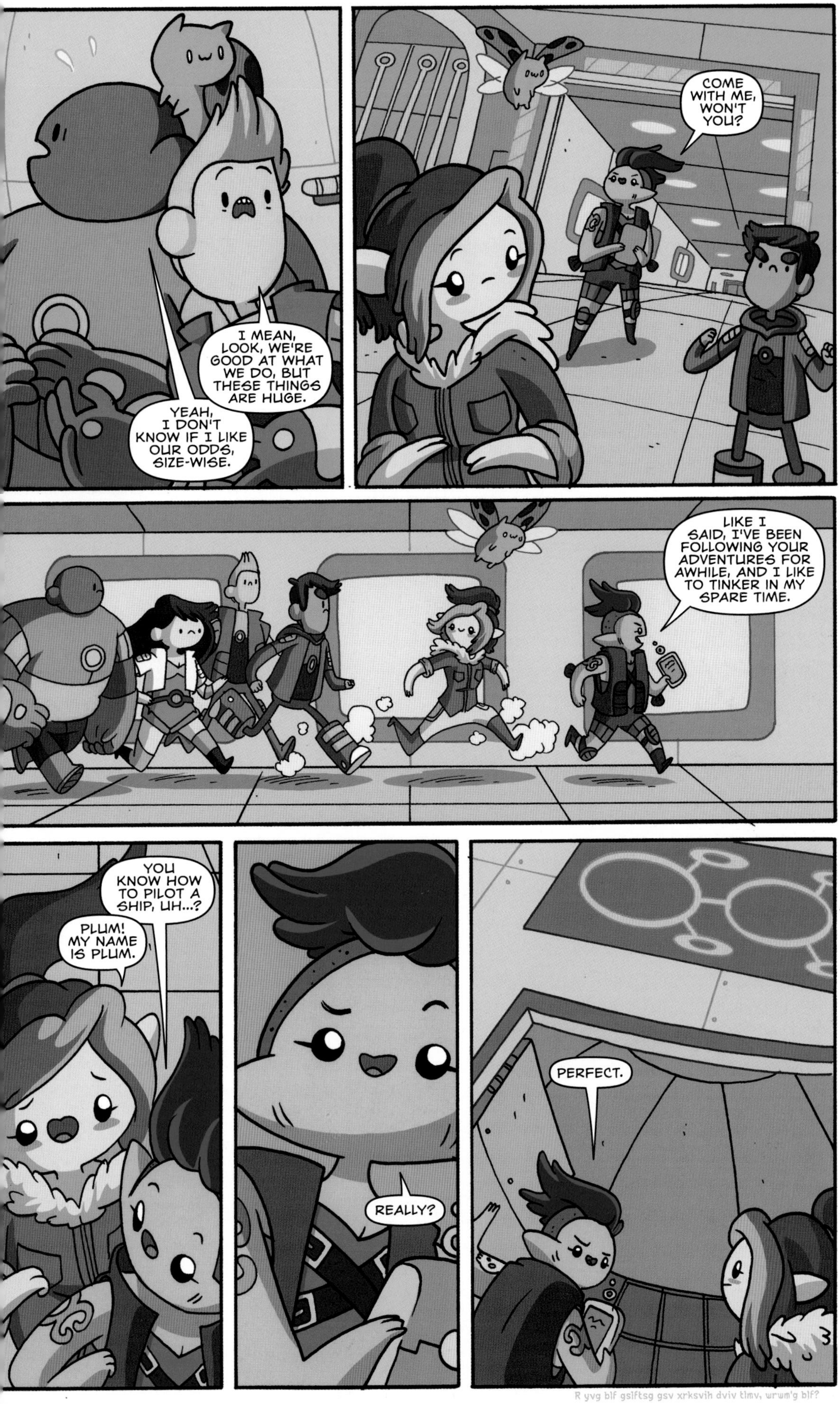

I MEAN, LOOK, WE'RE GOOD AT WHAT WE DO, BUT THESE THINGS ARE HUGE.
YEAH, I DON'T KNOW IF I LIKE OUR ODDS, SIZE-WISE.
COME WITH ME, WON'T YOU?
LIKE I SAID, I'VE BEEN FOLLOWING YOUR ADVENTURES FOR AWHILE, AND I LIKE TO TINKER IN MY SPARE TIME.
YOU KNOW HOW TO PILOT A SHIP, UH...?
PLUM! MY NAME IS PLUM.
REALLY?
PERFECT.

R yvg blf gslftsg gsv xrksvih dviv tlmv, wrwm'g blf?

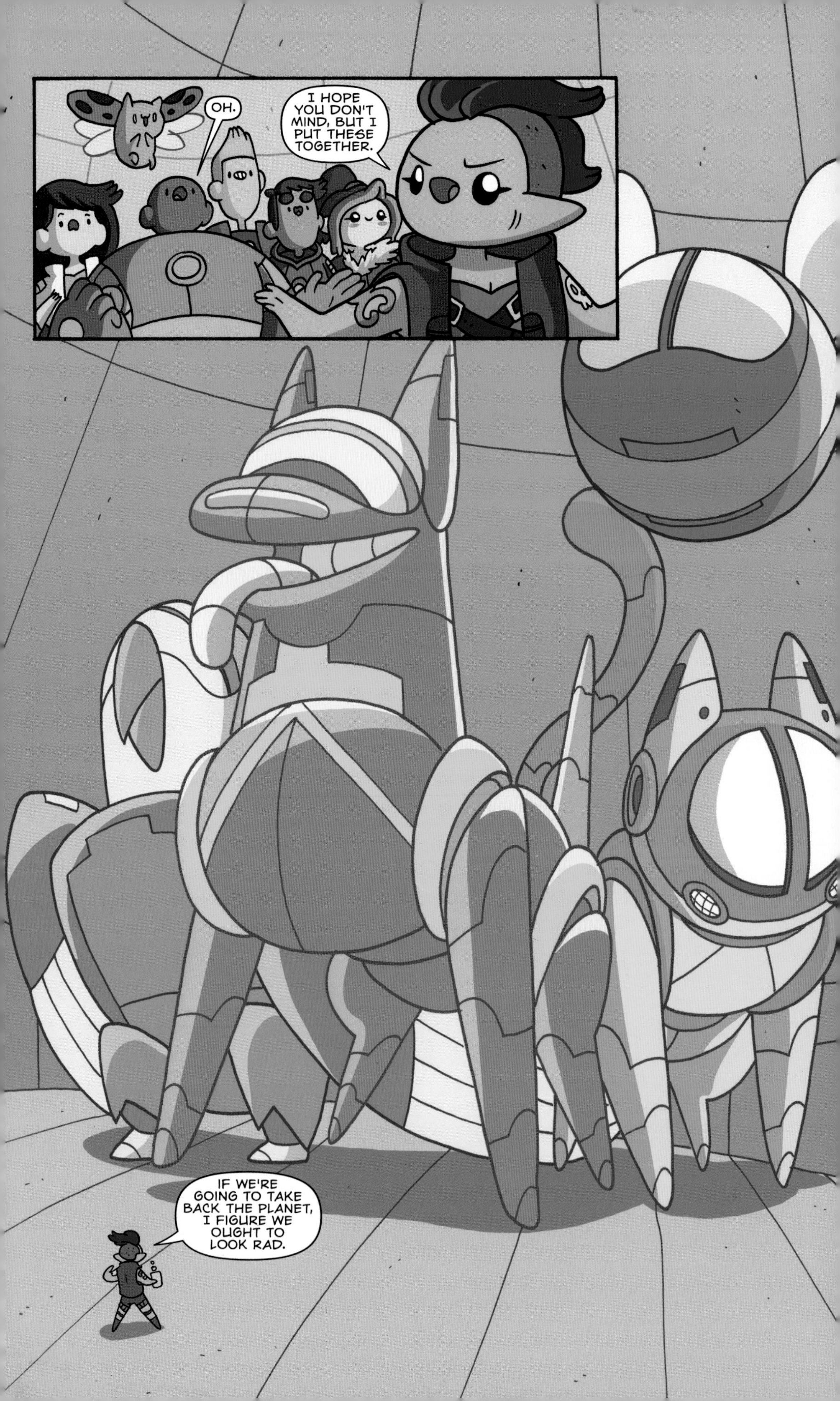
OH.
I HOPE YOU DON'T MIND, BUT I PUT THESE TOGETHER.
IF WE'RE GOING TO TAKE BACK THE PLANET, I FIGURE WE OUGHT TO LOOK RAD.

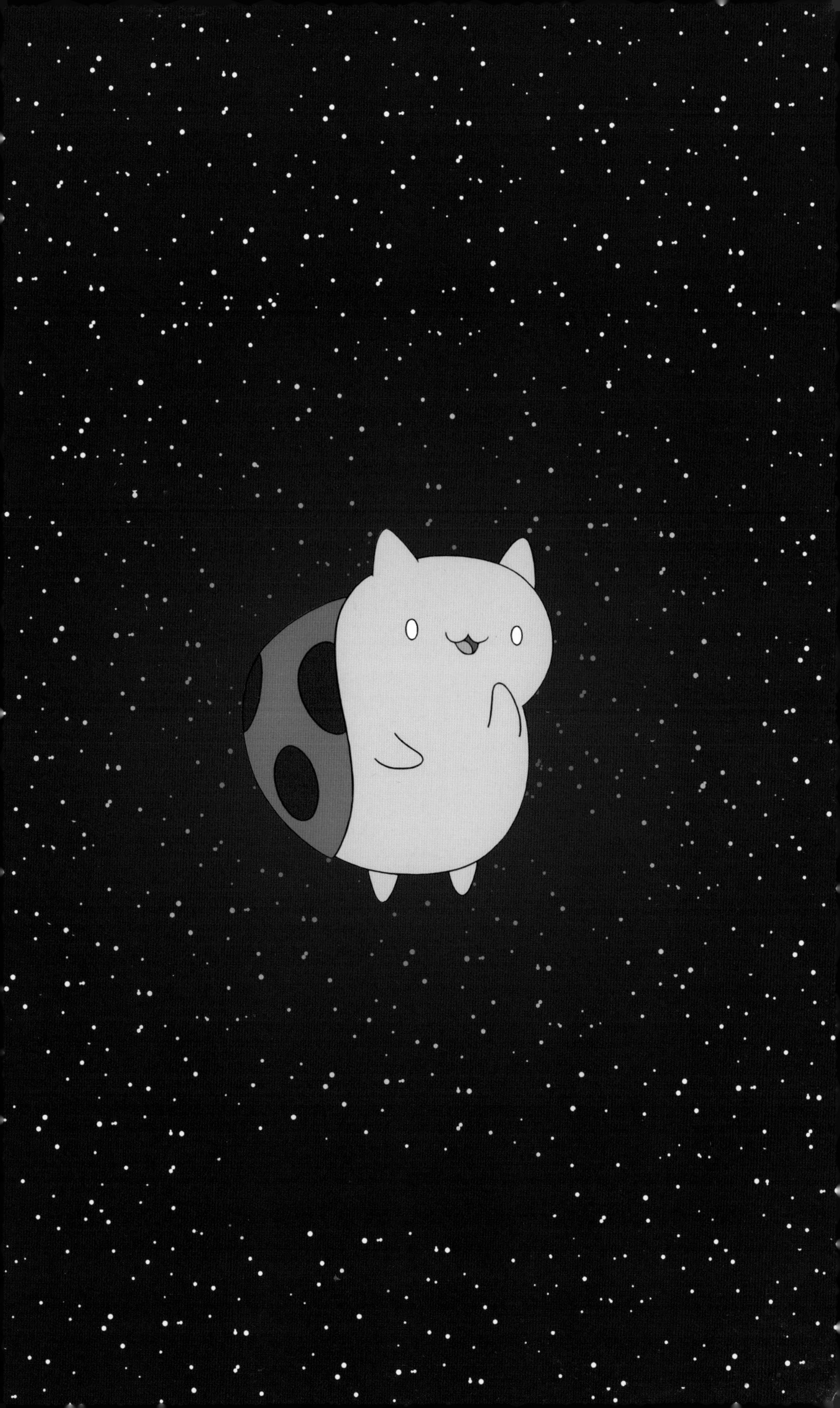

CHAPTER
27

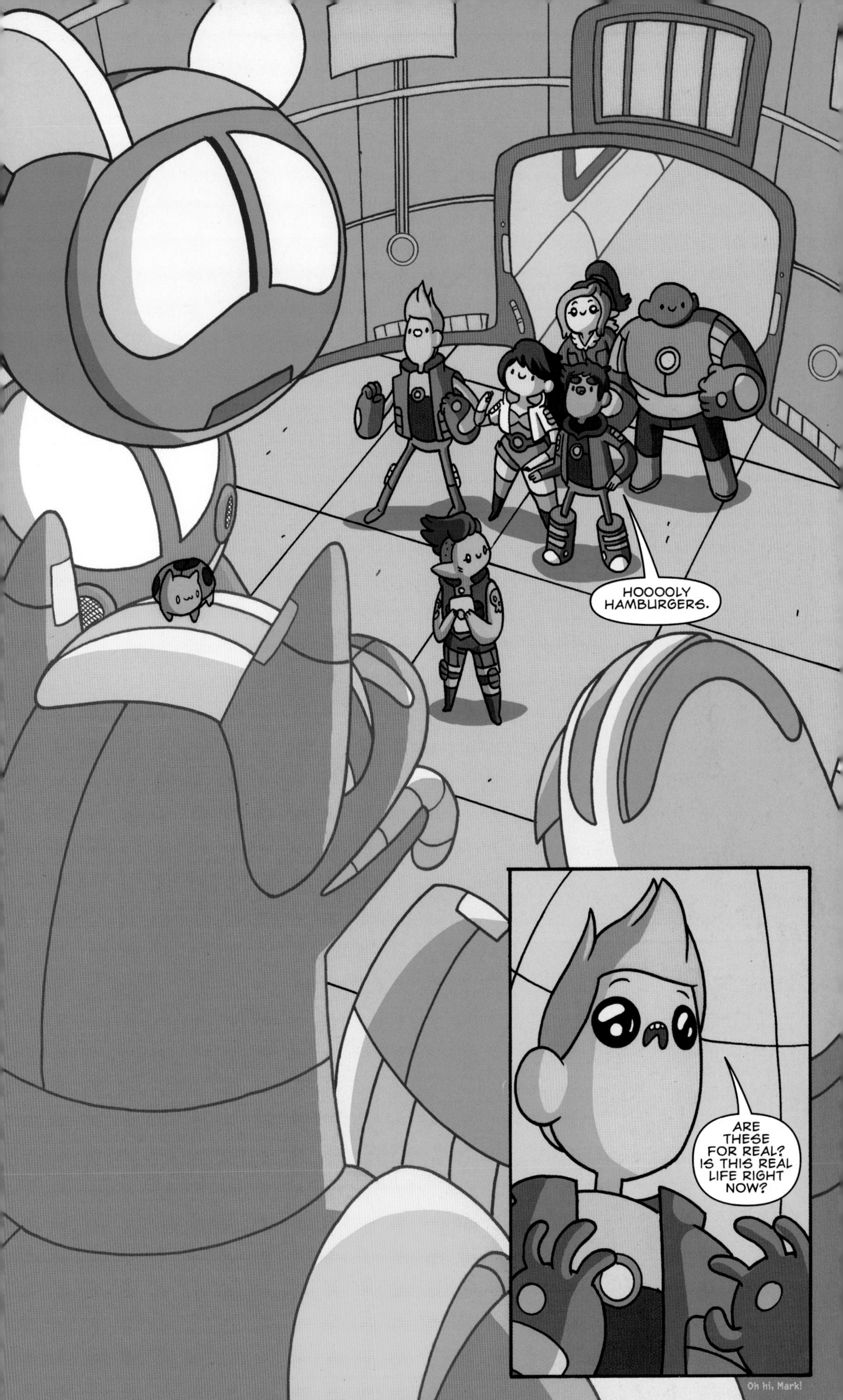
HOOOOLY HAMBURGERS.
ARE THESE FOR REAL? IS THIS REAL LIFE RIGHT NOW?

Oh hi, Mark!

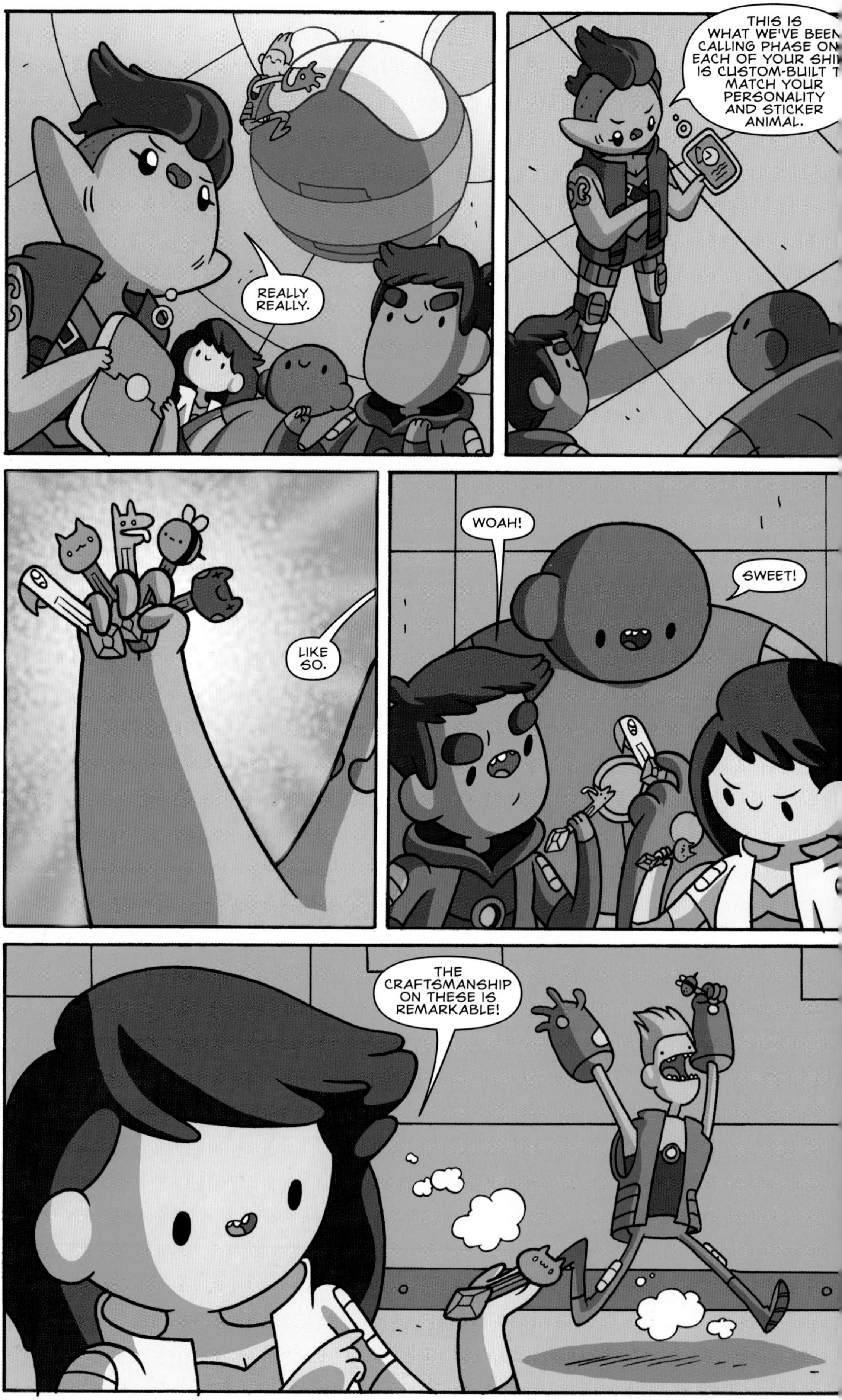
REALLY
REALLY.
THIS IS
WHAT WE'VE BEEN
CALLING PHASE ON
EACH OF YOUR SHI
IS CUSTOM-BUILT T
MATCH YOUR
PERSONALITY
AND STICKER
ANIMAL.
LIKE
SO.
WOAH!
SWEET!
THE
CRAFTSMANSHIP
ON THESE IS
REMARKABLE!

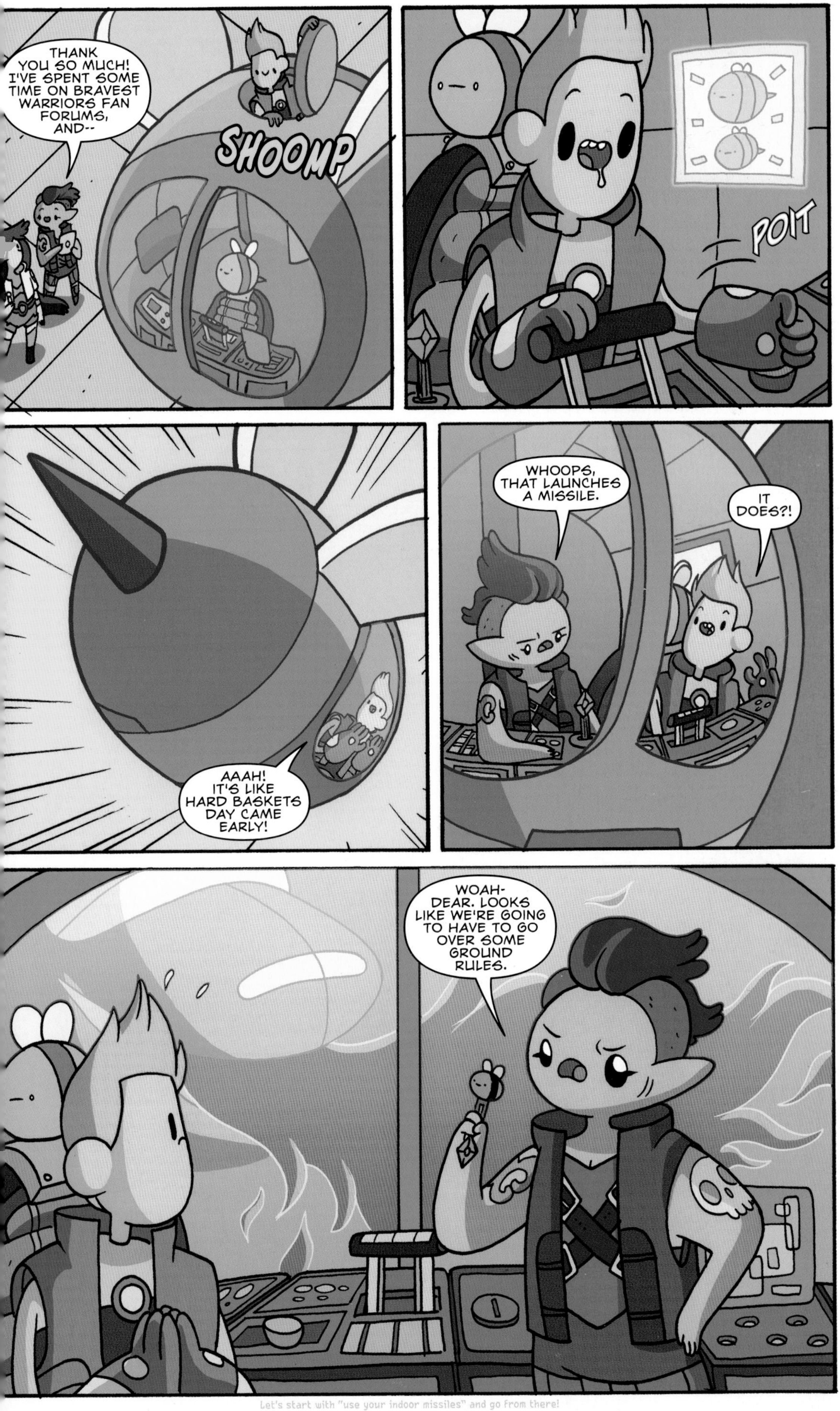
THANK YOU SO MUCH! I'VE SPENT SOME TIME ON BRAVEST WARRIORS FAN FORUMS, AND--
SHOOMP
POIT
AAAH! IT'S LIKE HARD BASKETS DAY CAME EARLY!
WHOOPS, THAT LAUNCHES A MISSILE.
IT DOES?!
WOAH-DEAR. LOOKS LIKE WE'RE GOING TO HAVE TO GO OVER SOME GROUND RULES.

Let's start with "use your indoor missiles" and go from there!

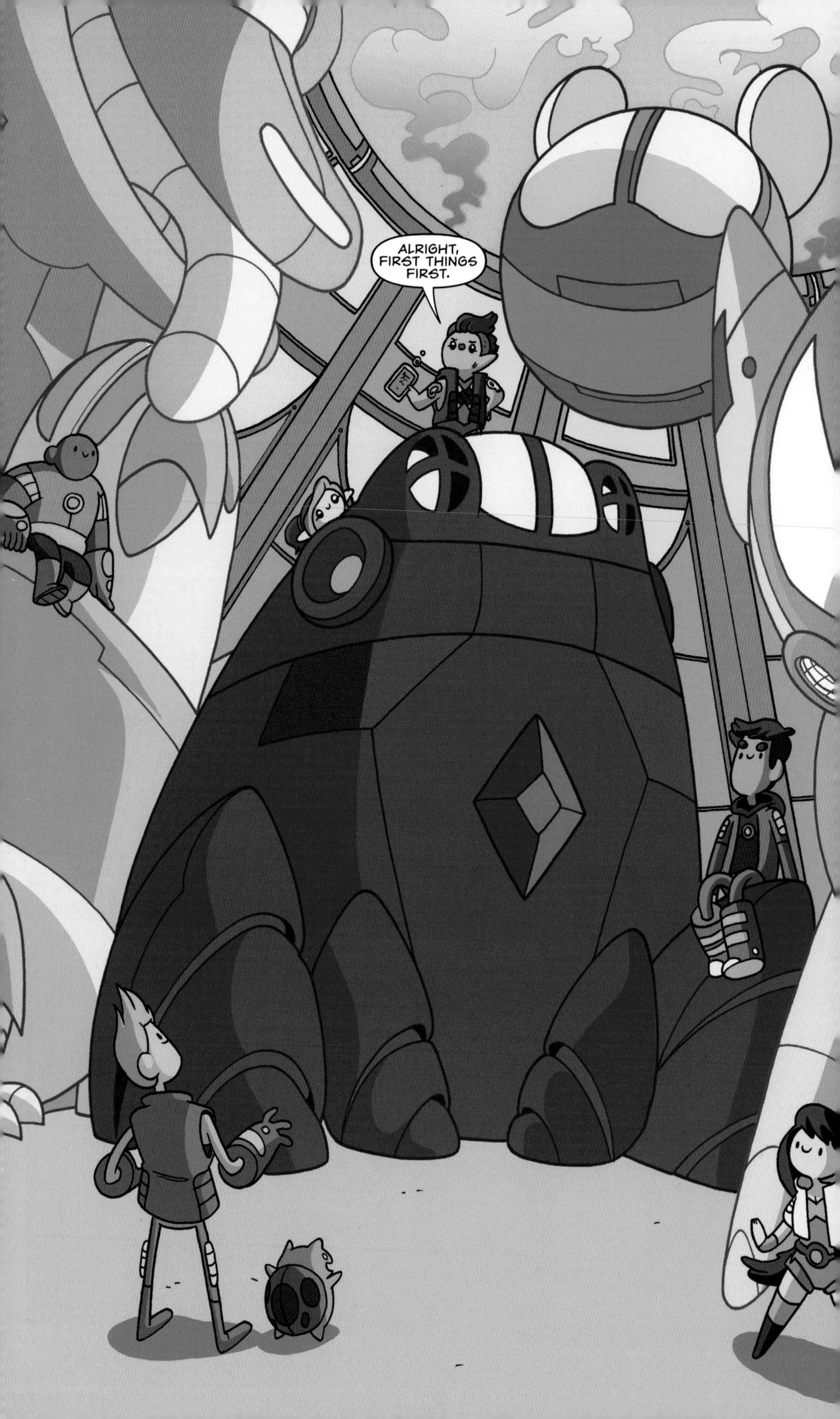
ALRIGHT, FIRST THINGS FIRST.

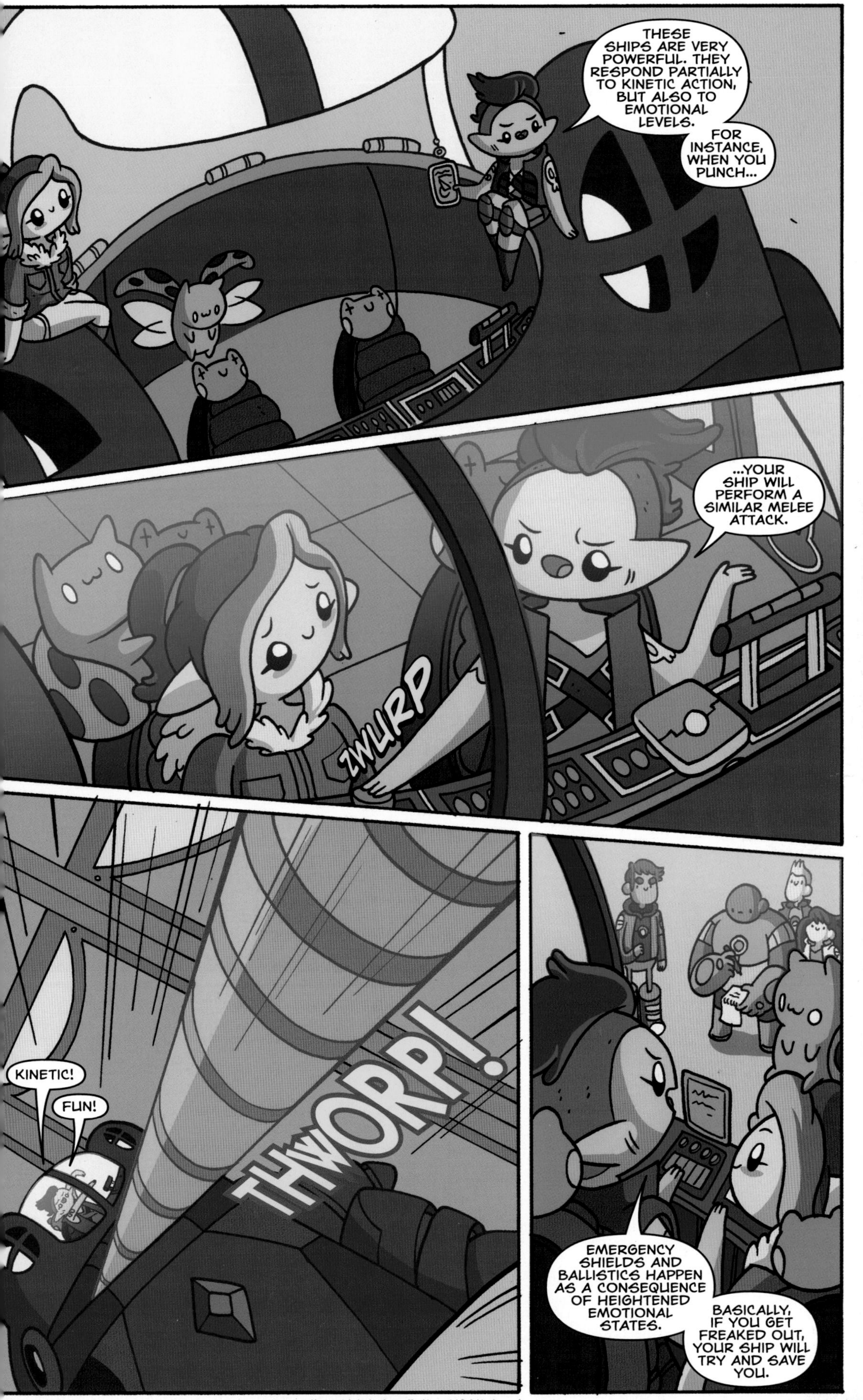
THESE SHIPS ARE VERY POWERFUL. THEY RESPOND PARTIALLY TO KINETIC ACTION, BUT ALSO TO EMOTIONAL LEVELS.
FOR INSTANCE, WHEN YOU PUNCH...
...YOUR SHIP WILL PERFORM A SIMILAR MELEE ATTACK.
ZWURP
KINETIC!
FUN!
THWORP!
EMERGENCY SHIELDS AND BALLISTICS HAPPEN AS A CONSEQUENCE OF HEIGHTENED EMOTIONAL STATES.
BASICALLY, IF YOU GET FREAKED OUT, YOUR SHIP WILL TRY AND SAVE YOU.

Your ship's just really thoughtful that way!

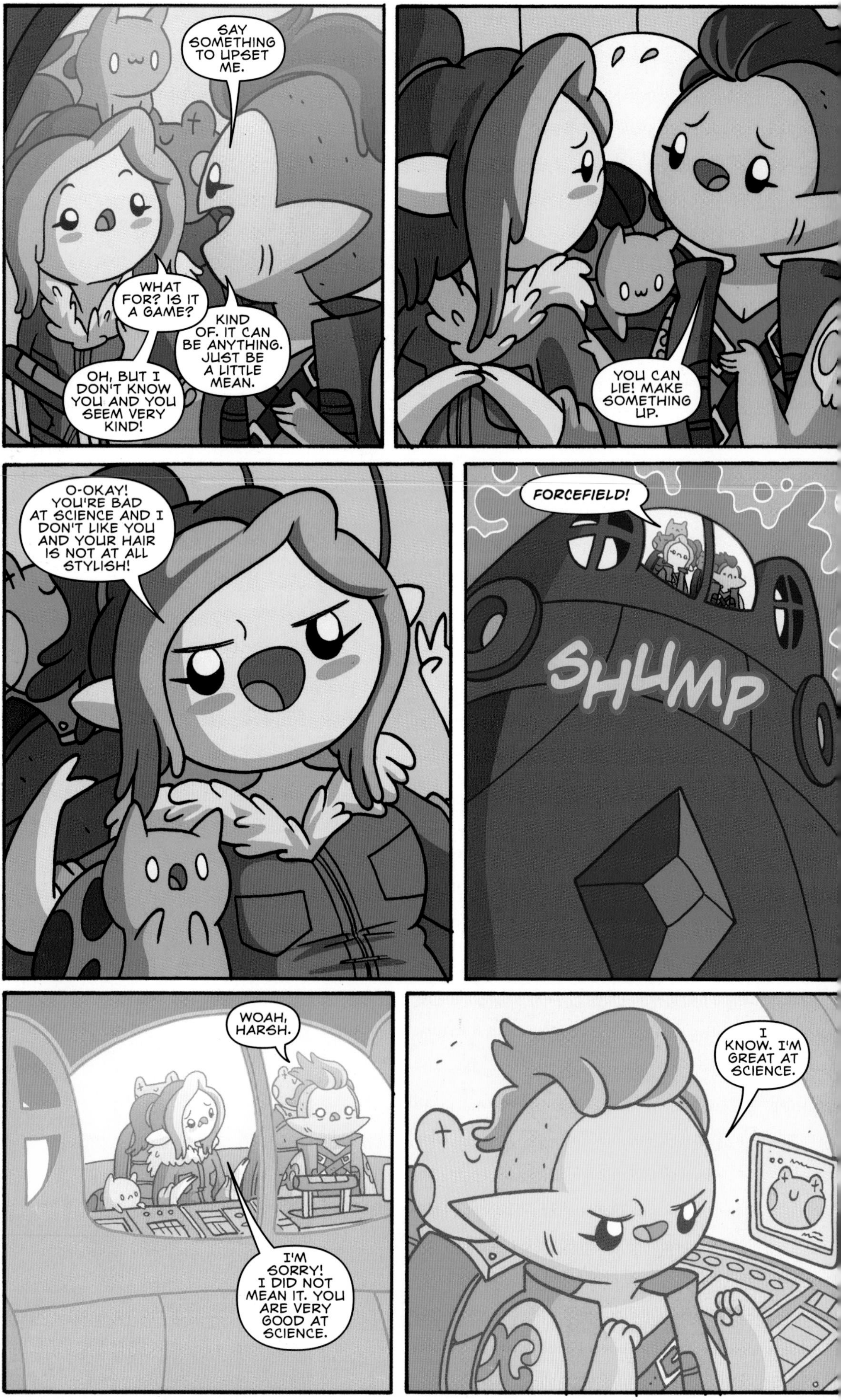
SAY SOMETHING TO UPSET ME.
WHAT FOR? IS IT A GAME?
KIND OF. IT CAN BE ANYTHING. JUST BE A LITTLE MEAN.
OH, BUT I DON'T KNOW YOU AND YOU SEEM VERY KIND!
YOU CAN LIE! MAKE SOMETHING UP.
O-OKAY! YOU'RE BAD AT SCIENCE AND I DON'T LIKE YOU AND YOUR HAIR IS NOT AT ALL STYLISH!
FORCEFIELD!
SHUMP
WOAH, HARSH.
I'M SORRY! I DID NOT MEAN IT. YOU ARE VERY GOOD AT SCIENCE.
I KNOW. I'M GREAT AT SCIENCE.

Someone call a medical professional to treat that sick burn.

I'm great at boa

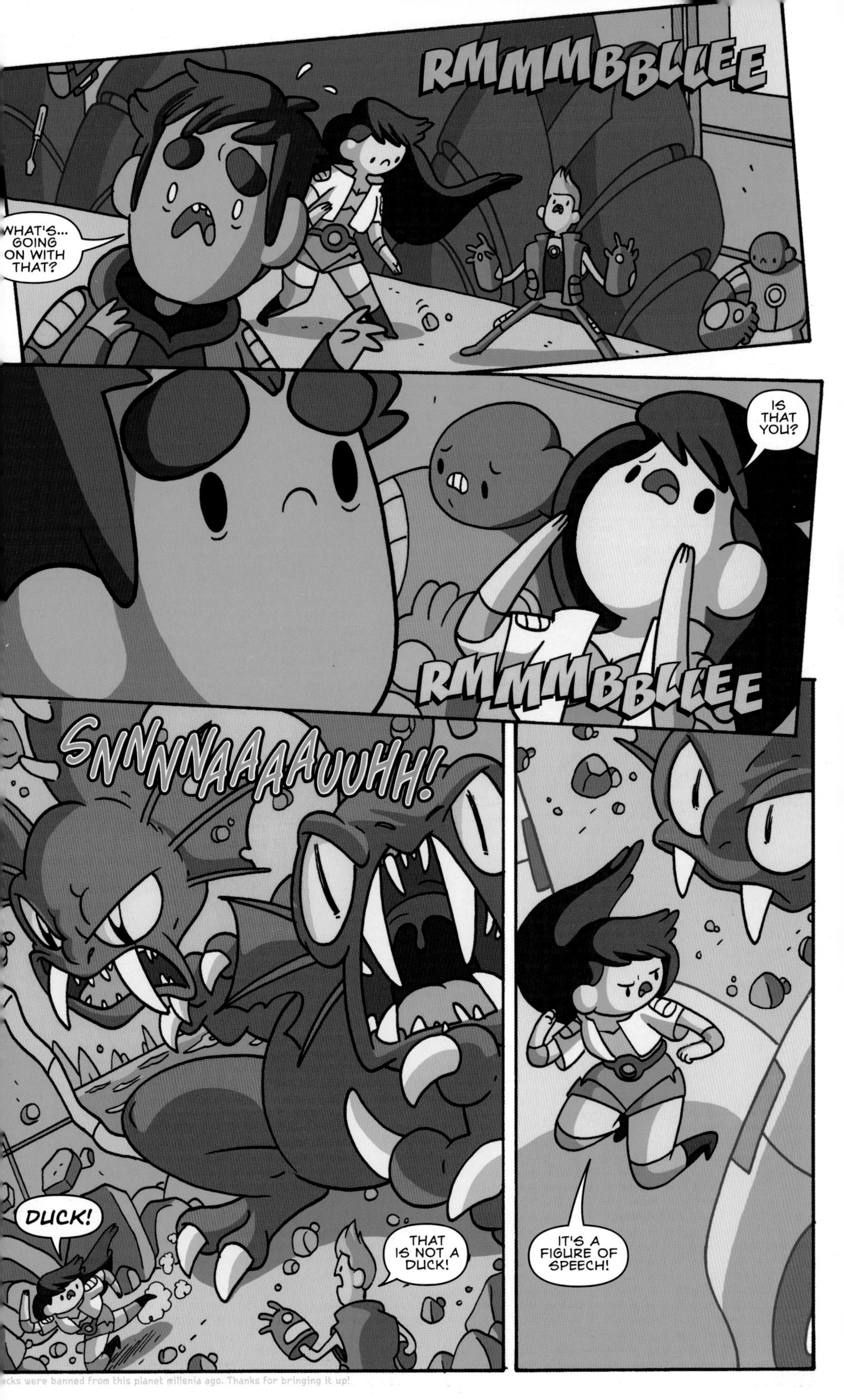
RMMMBBLLEE
WHAT'S... GOING ON WITH THAT?
IS THAT YOU?
RMMMBBLLEE
SNNNNAAAAUUHH!
DUCK!
THAT IS NOT A DUCK!
IT'S A FIGURE OF SPEECH!
...cks were banned from this planet millenia ago. Thanks for bringing it up!

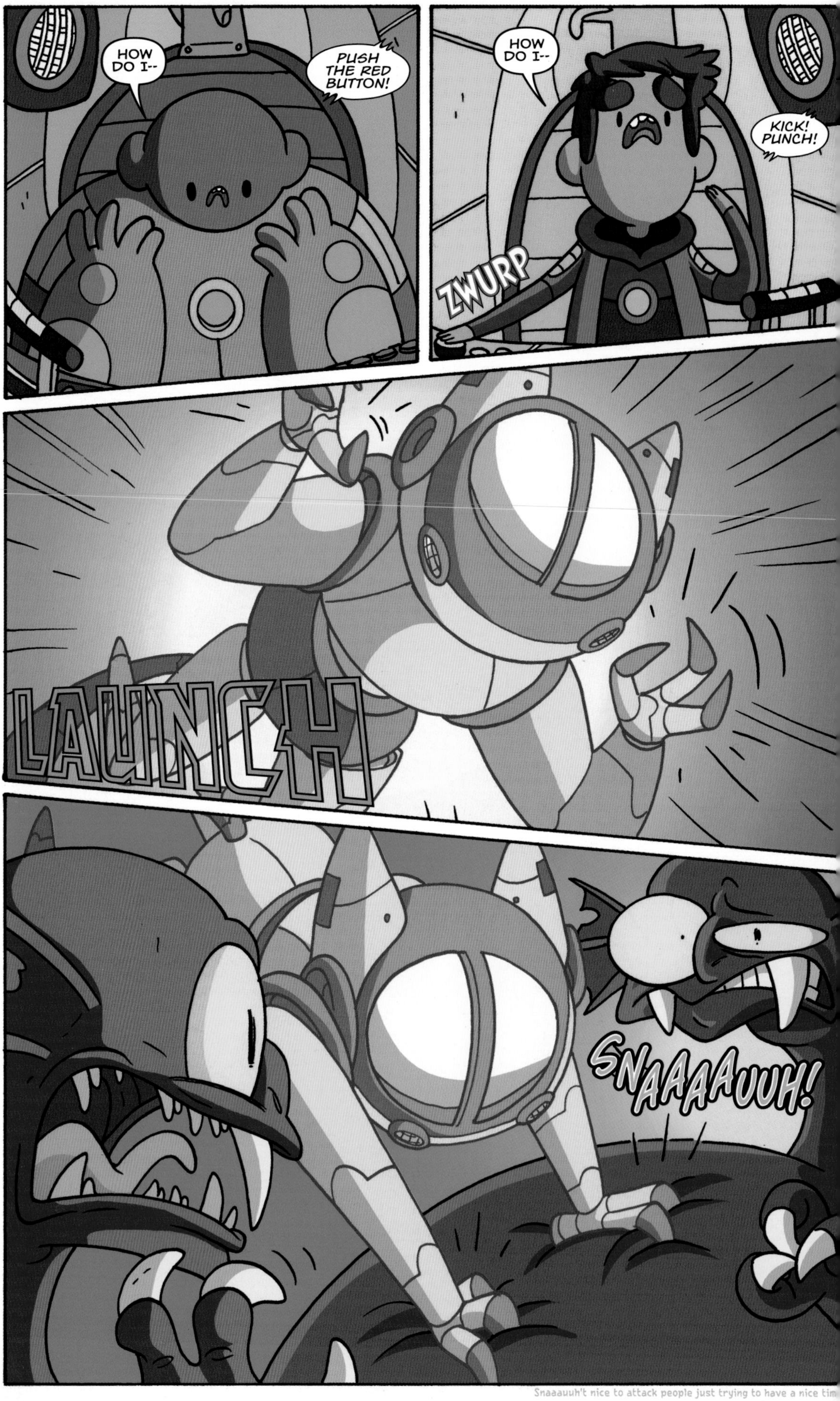
HOW DO I--
PUSH THE RED BUTTON!
HOW DO I--
KICK! PUNCH!
ZWURP
LAUNCH
SNAAAAUUH!

Snaaauuh't nice to attack people just trying to have a nice tim

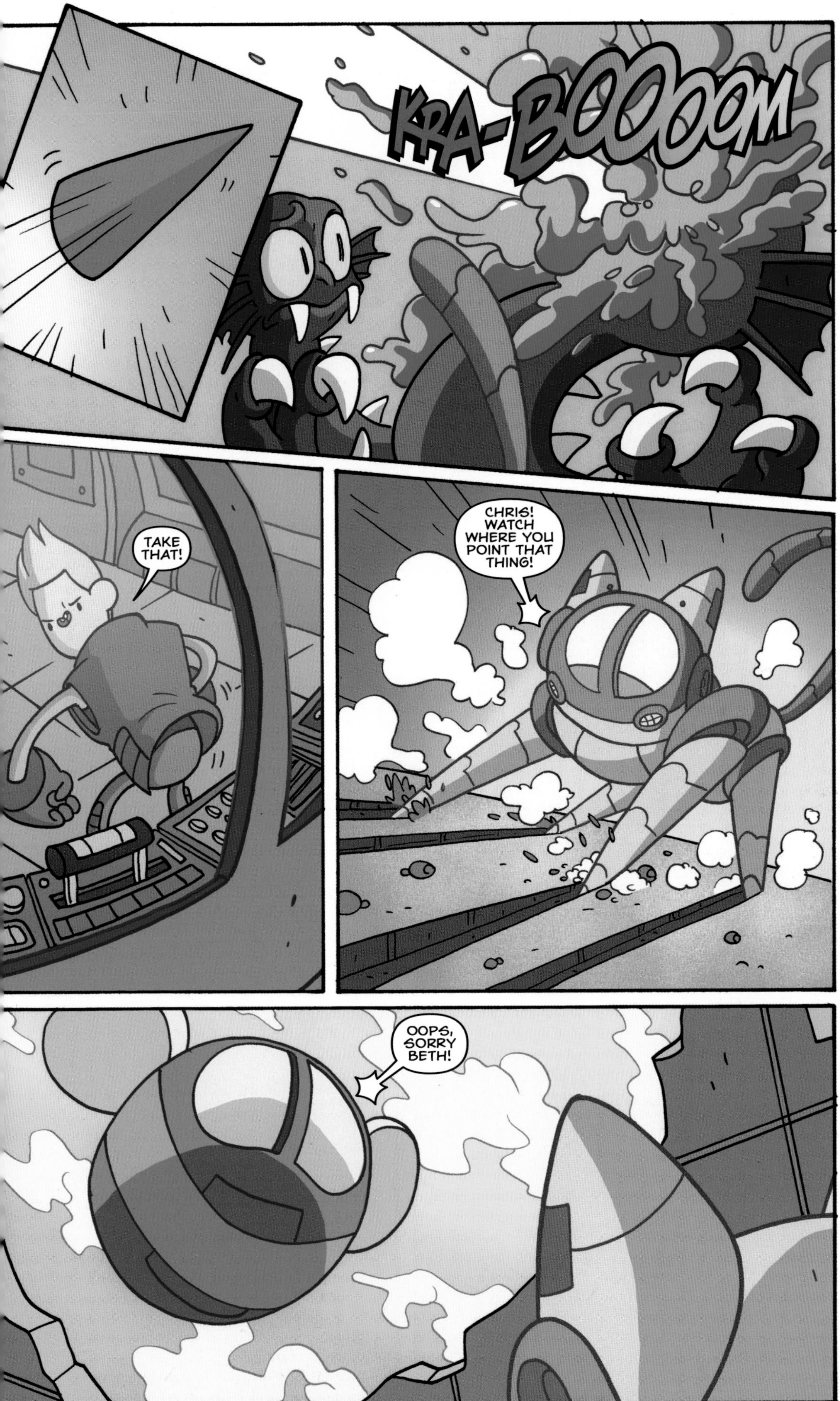
KRA-BOOOoOM
TAKE THAT!
CHRIS! WATCH WHERE YOU POINT THAT THING!
OOPS, SORRY BETH!

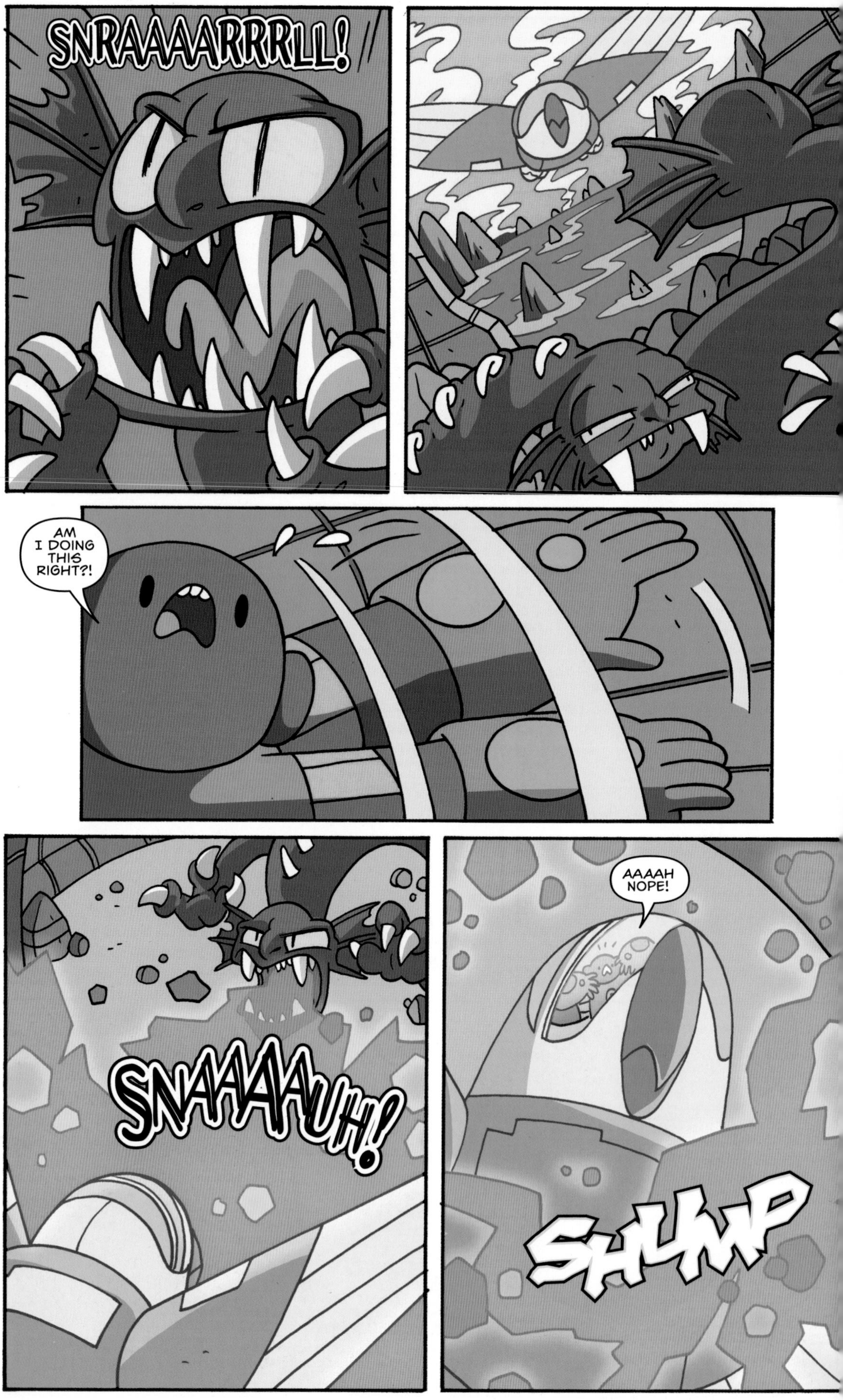
SNRAAAARRRLL!
AM I DOING THIS RIGHT?!
SNAAAAUH!
AAAAH NOPE!
SHUMP

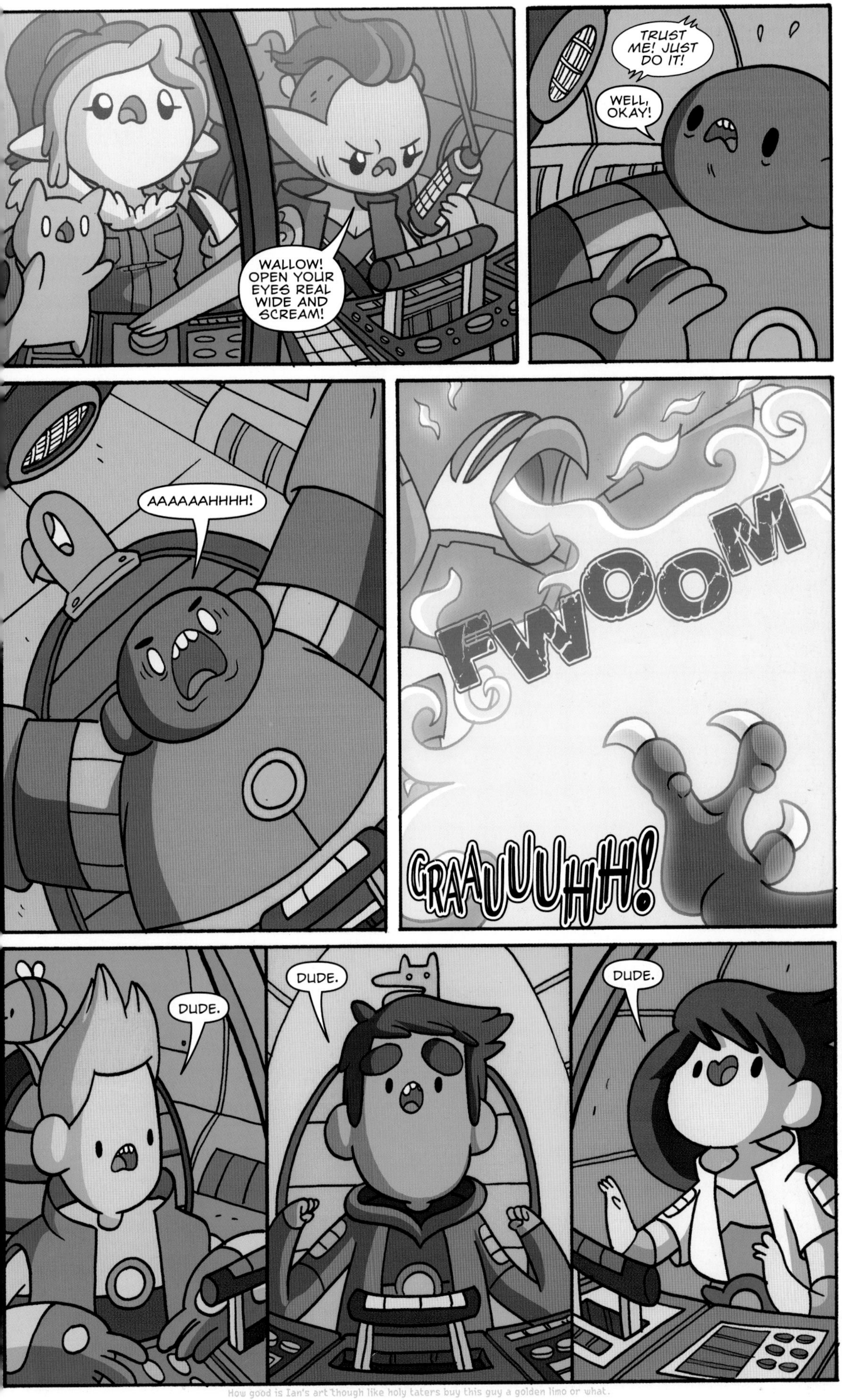
WALLOW! OPEN YOUR EYES REAL WIDE AND SCREAM!
TRUST ME! JUST DO IT!
WELL, OKAY!
AAAAAAHHHH!
FWOOM
GRAAUUUHHH!
DUDE.
DUDE.
DUDE.

How good is Ian's art though like holy taters buy this guy a golden limo or what.

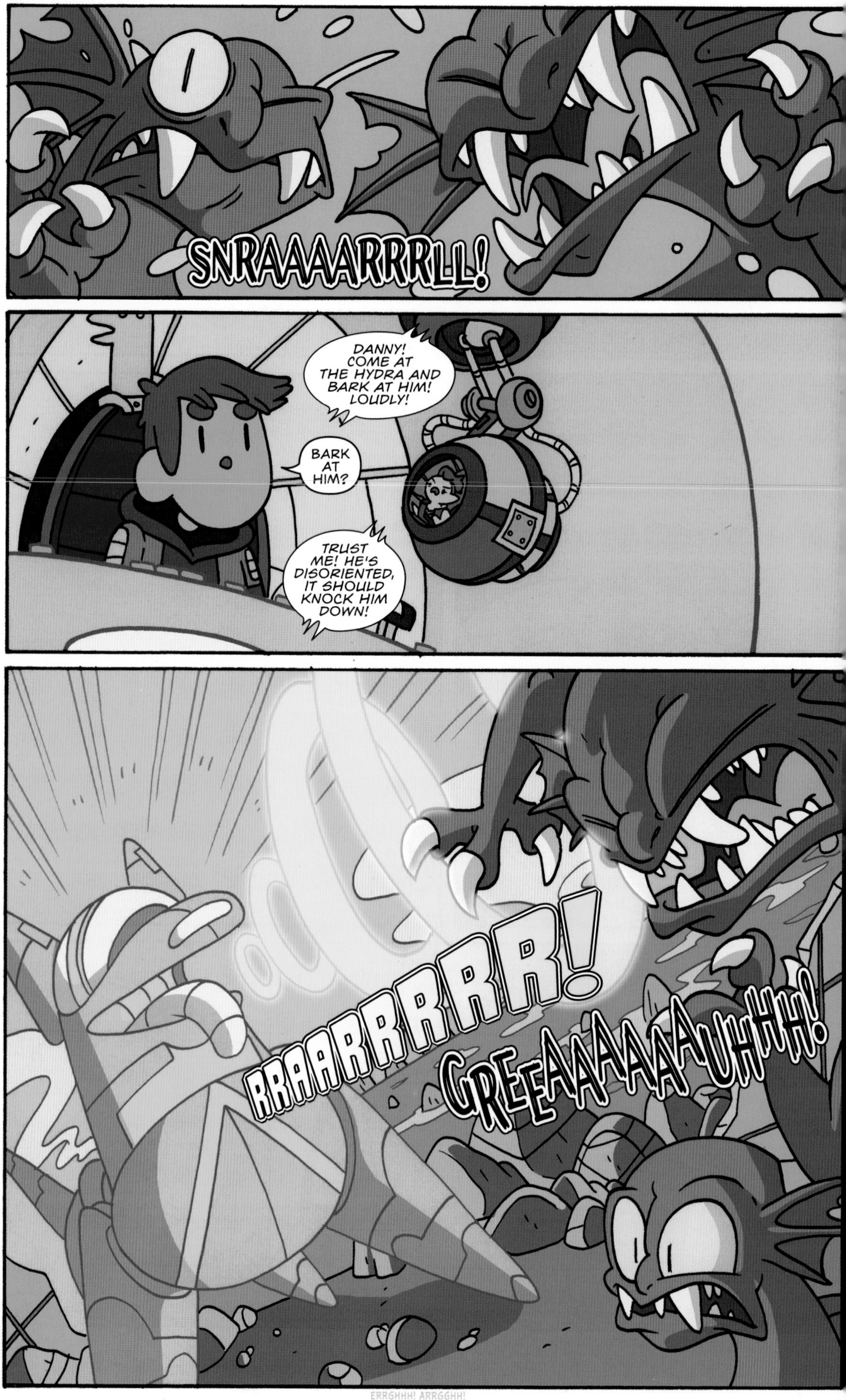
SNRAAAARRRRLL!
DANNY! COME AT THE HYDRA AND BARK AT HIM! LOUDLY!
BARK AT HIM?
TRUST ME! HE'S DISORIENTED, IT SHOULD KNOCK HIM DOWN!
RRAARRRRRR!
GREEAAAAAAUHHH!

ERRGHHH! ARRGGHH!

DUDE!

DUDE!!

DUDE!!!

KRRRACKK

WE DID IT.

YOU TOTALLY DID!

THAT WAS WONDERFUL! EVERYONE'S SHIPS ARE SO NEAT!

CHRIS SHOT AN EXPLOSION FROM HIS BUTT!

YOU GUYS WERE AWESOME! I CAN'T BELIEVE THAT WAS THE FIRST TIME ANYONE FLEW THE STING!

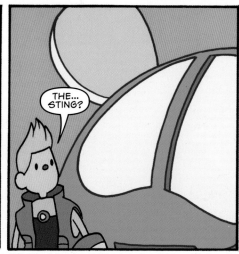

THE... STING?

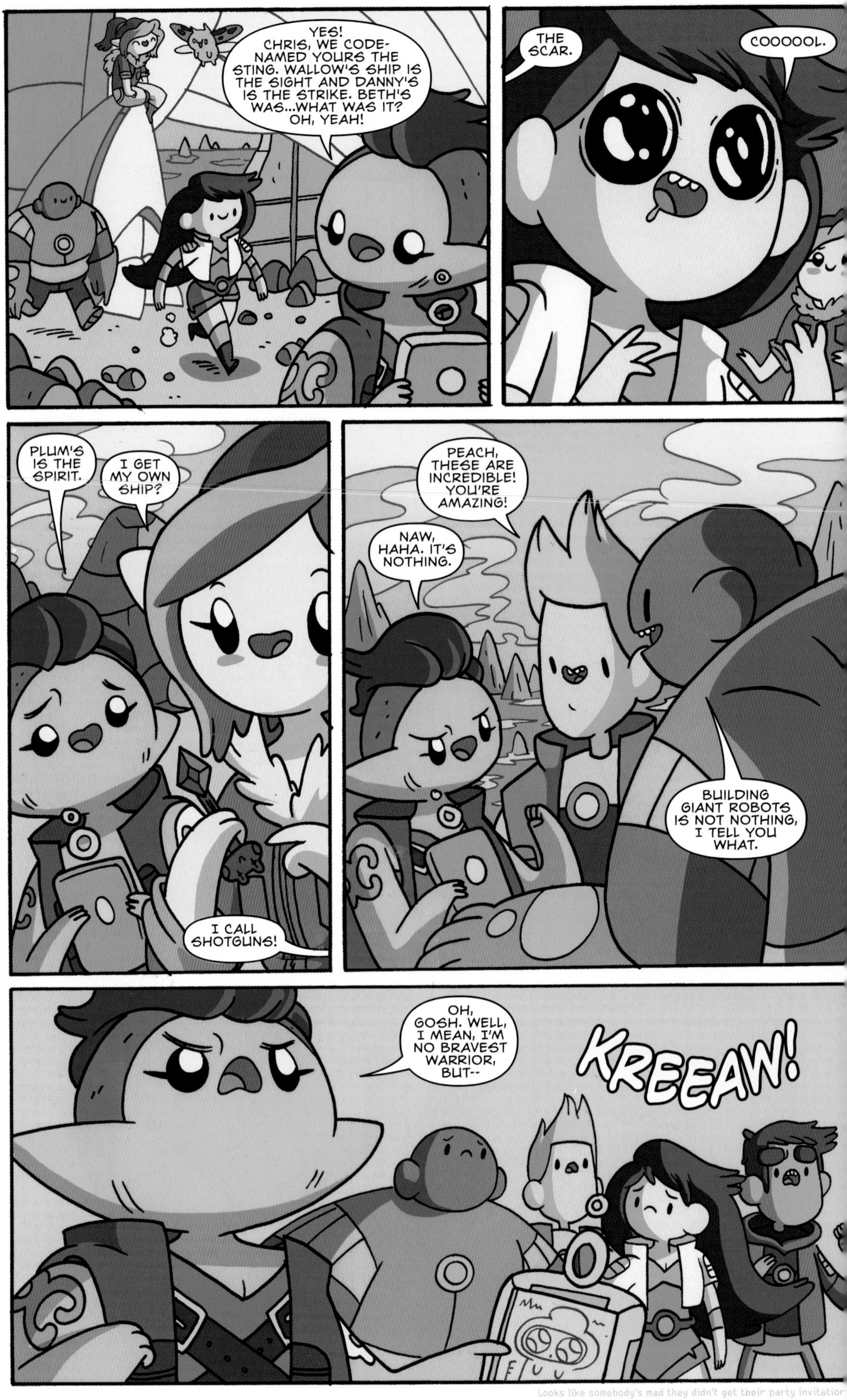
YES! CHRIS, WE CODE-NAMED YOURS THE STING. WALLOW'S SHIP IS THE SIGHT AND DANNY'S IS THE STRIKE. BETH'S WAS...WHAT WAS IT? OH, YEAH!
THE SCAR.
COOOOOL.
PLUM'S IS THE SPIRIT.
I GET MY OWN SHIP?
I CALL SHOTGUNS!
PEACH, THESE ARE INCREDIBLE! YOU'RE AMAZING!
NAW, HAHA. IT'S NOTHING.
BUILDING GIANT ROBOTS IS NOT NOTHING, I TELL YOU WHAT.
OH, GOSH. WELL, I MEAN, I'M NO BRAVEST WARRIOR, BUT--
KREEAW!

Looks like somebody's mad they didn't get their party invitatio

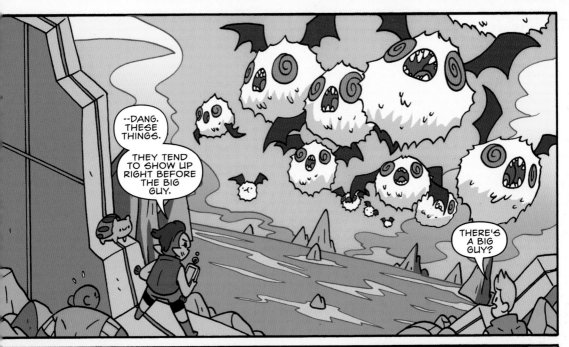

--DANG. THESE THINGS.

THEY TEND TO SHOW UP RIGHT BEFORE THE BIG GUY.

THERE'S A BIG GUY?

THERE'S ALWAYS A BIG GUY.

OF COURSE.

WAIT, HOW BIG?

OKAY, CHANGE OF PLANS. WE'RE SKIPPING RIGHT TO PHASE TWO.

WHICH IS?

Xnij styj: nk dtz ijhtlj ymjxj hnumjwx, dtz fwj rd kfatzwnyj pnsi tk wjfijw.

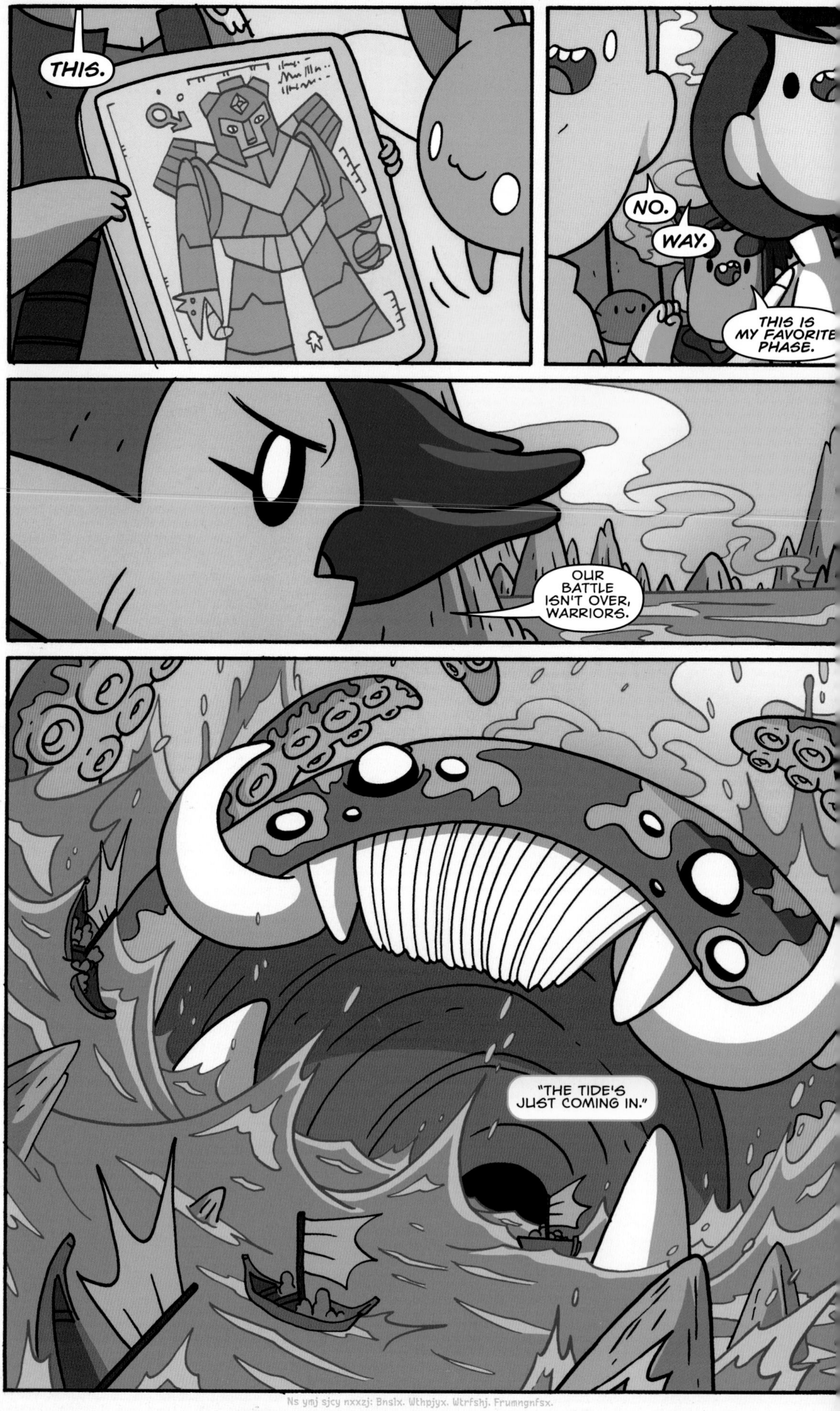
THIS.
NO.
WAY.
THIS IS MY FAVORITE PHASE.
OUR BATTLE ISN'T OVER, WARRIORS.
"THE TIDE'S JUST COMING IN."

Ns ymj sjcy nxxzj: Bnslx. Wthpjyx. Wtrfshj. Frumngnfsx.

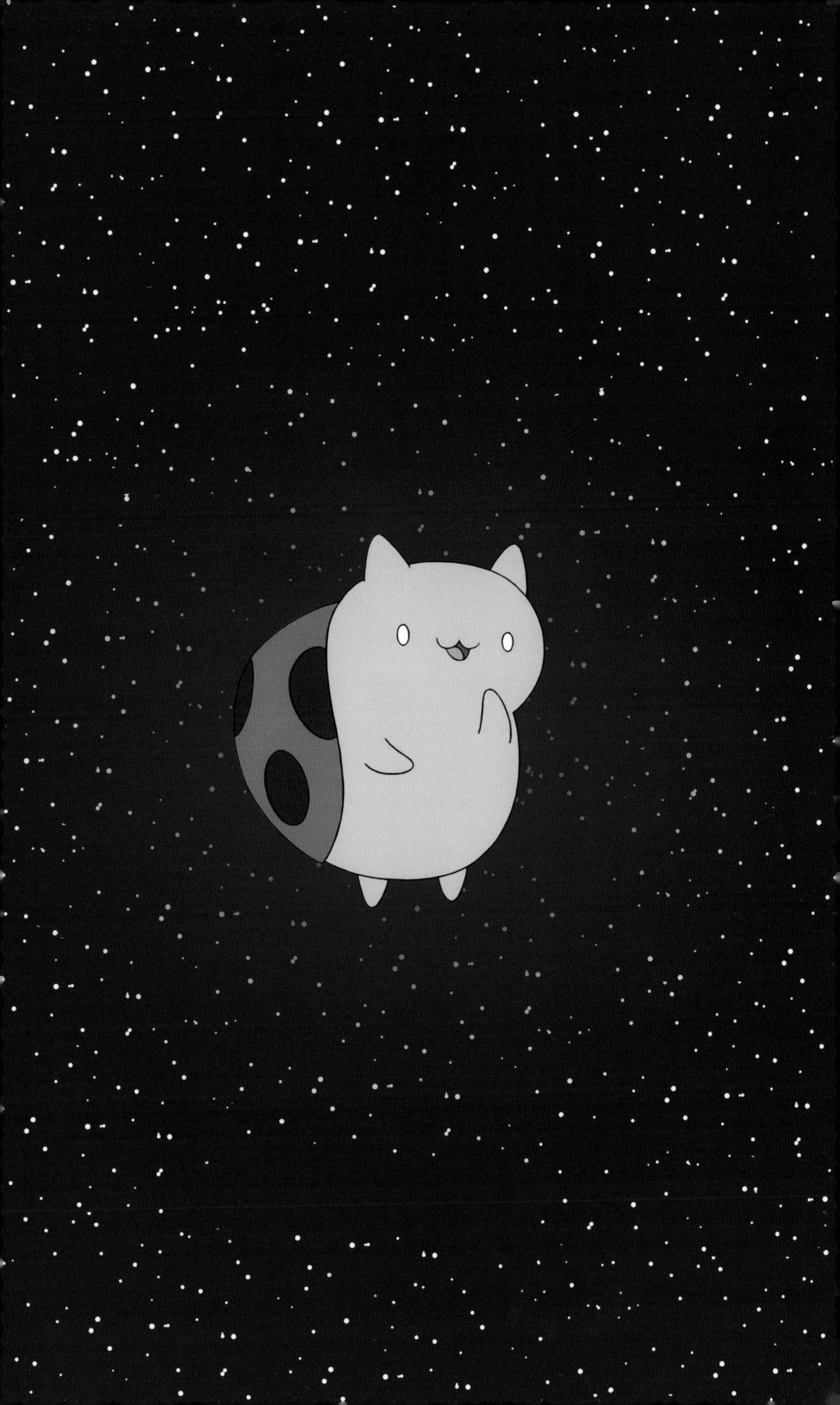

CHAPTER
28

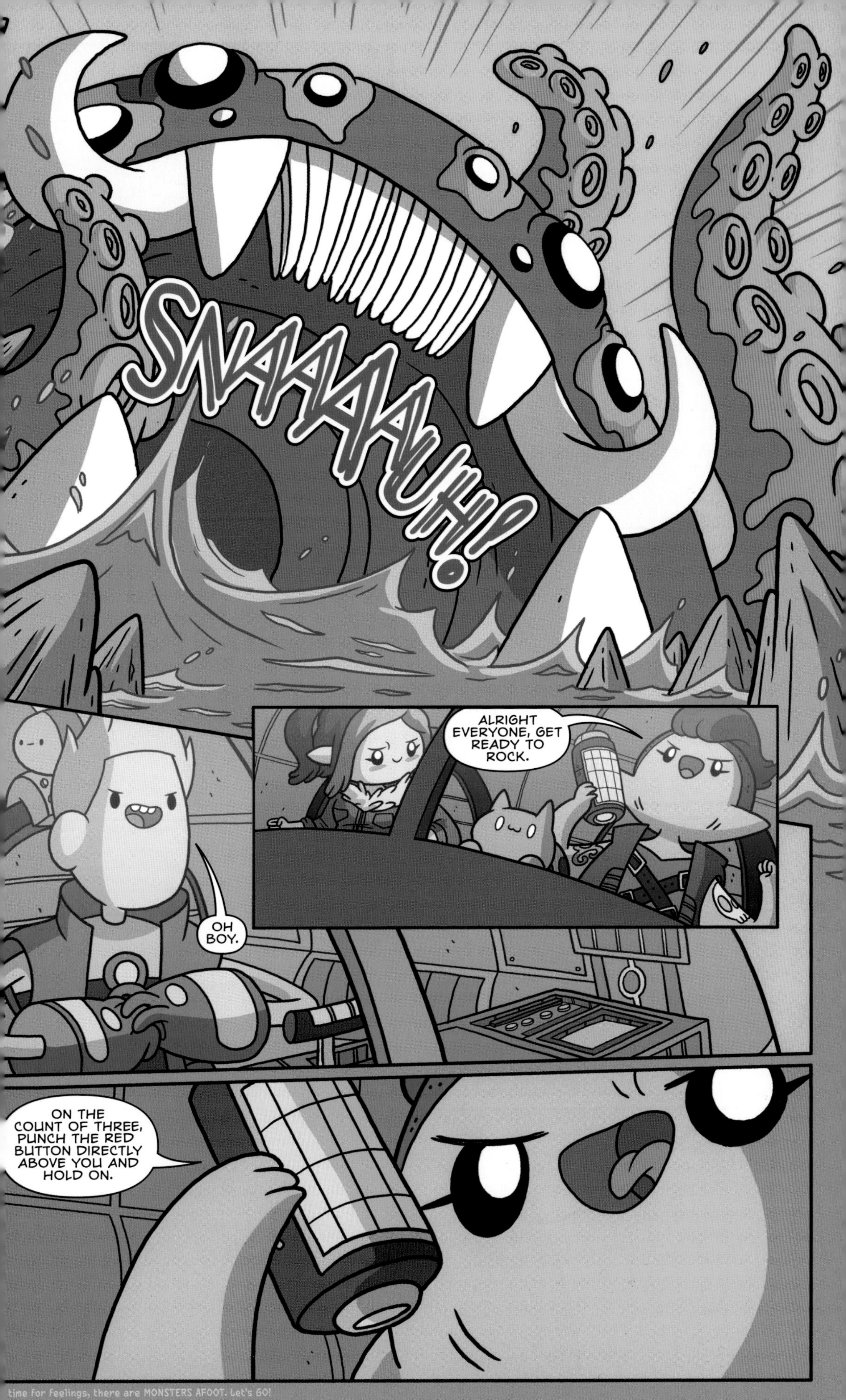
SNAAAAAUH!!
ALRIGHT EVERYONE, GET READY TO ROCK.
OH BOY.
ON THE COUNT OF THREE, PUNCH THE RED BUTTON DIRECTLY ABOVE YOU AND HOLD ON.
time for feelings, there are MONSTERS AFOOT. Let's GO!

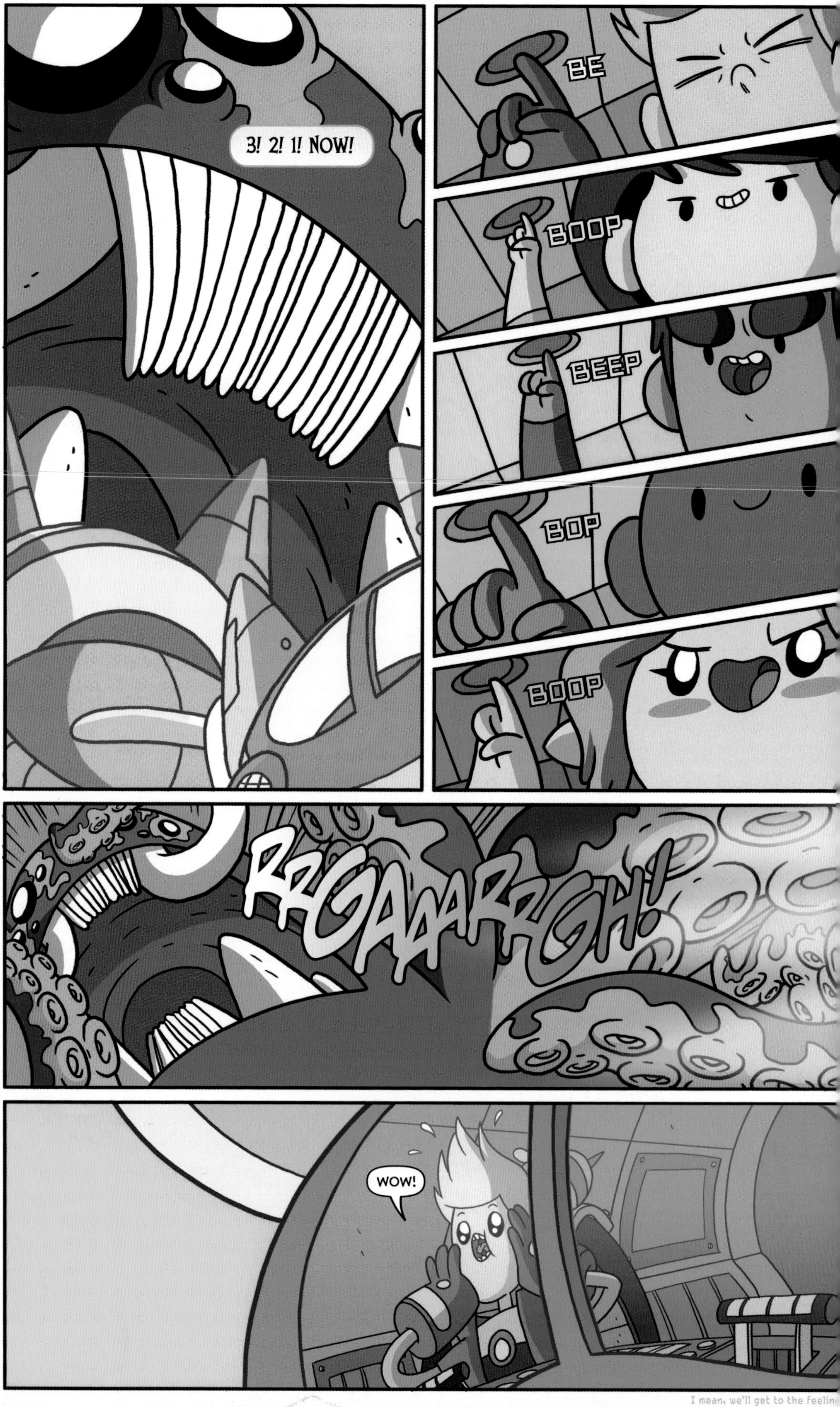
3! 2! 1! NOW!
BE
BOOP
BEEP
BOP
BOOP
RRGAAARRGH!
WOW!

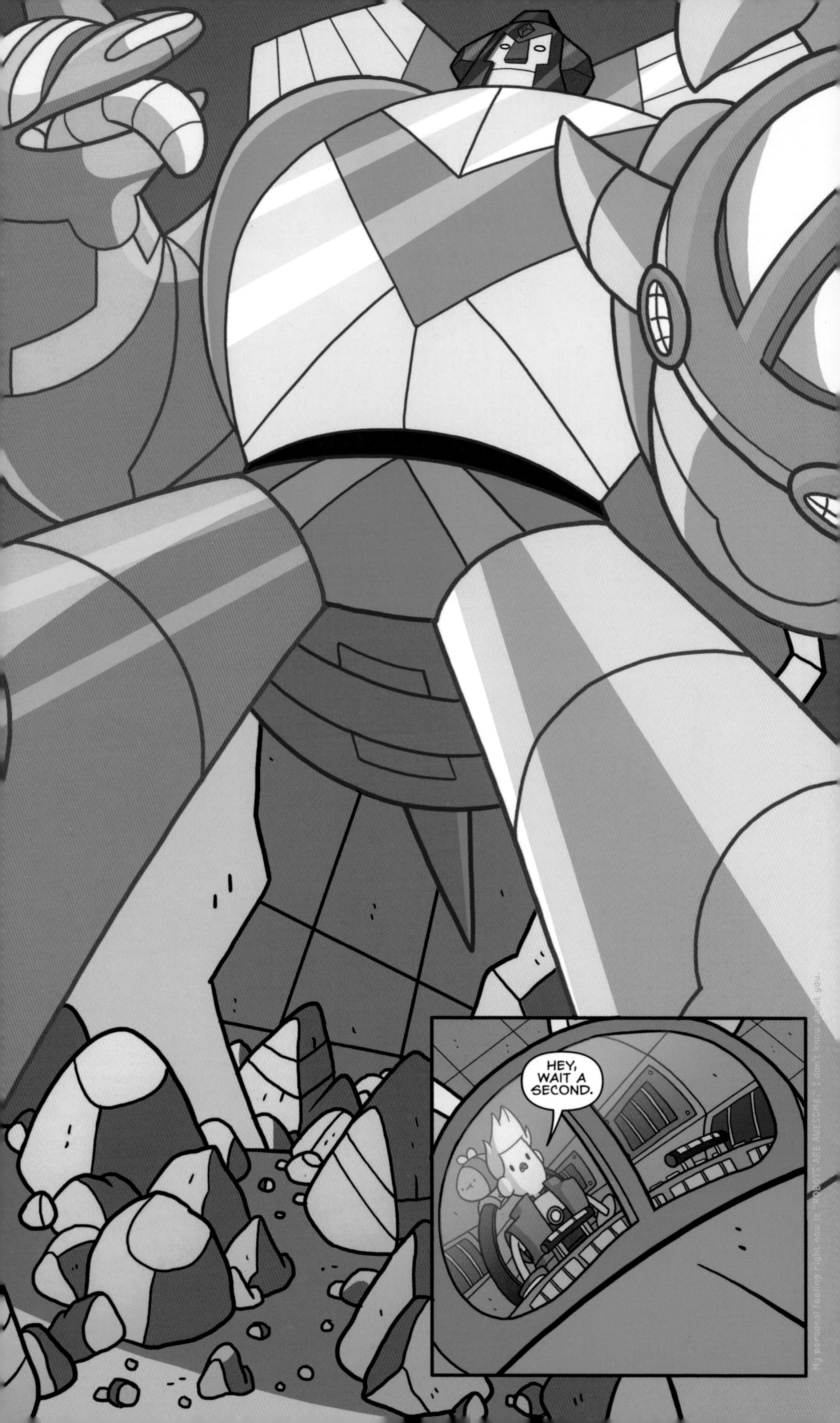
HEY, WAIT A SECOND.
My personal feeling right now is "ROBOTS ARE AWESOME." I don't know about you.

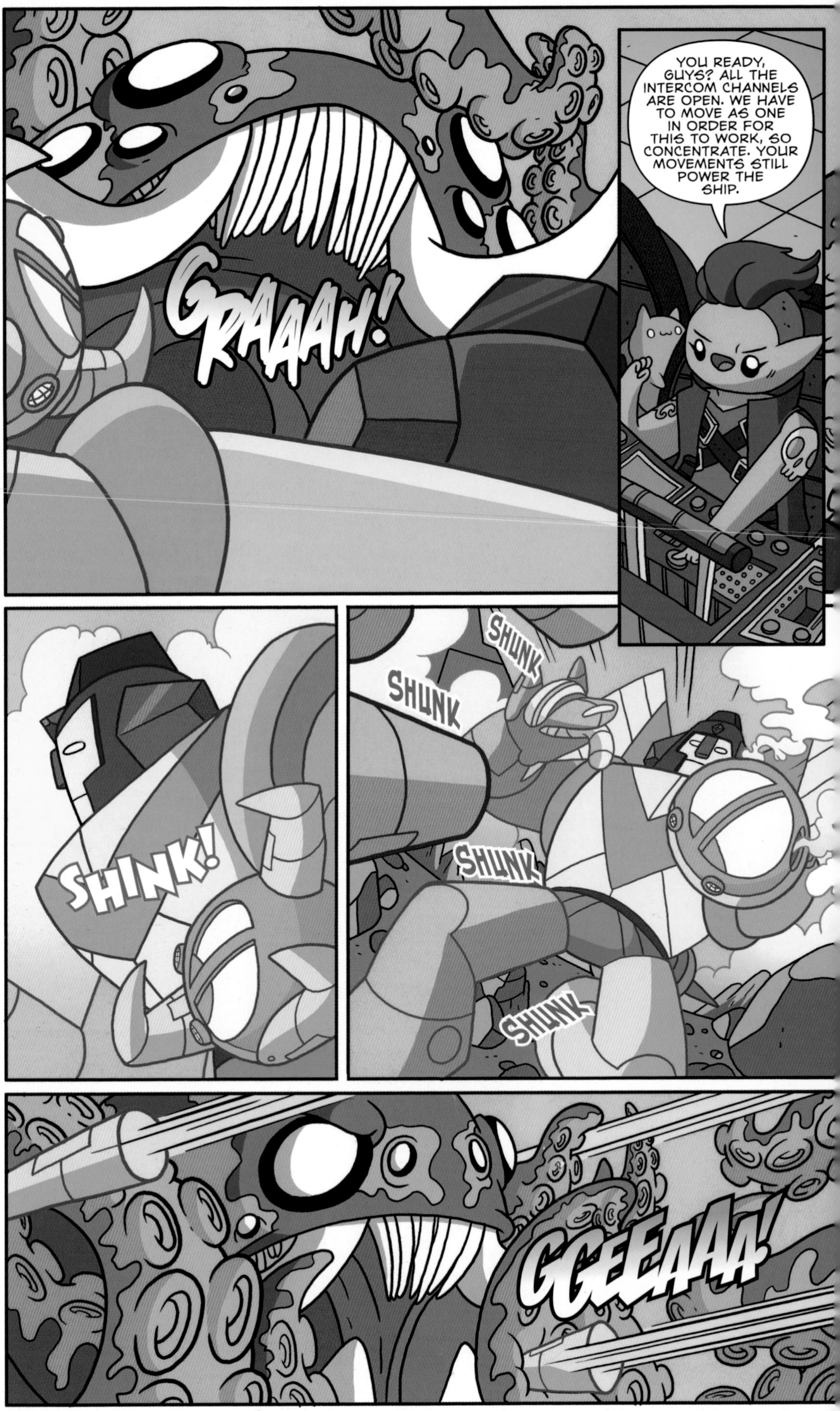
GRAAAH!
YOU READY, GUYS? ALL THE INTERCOM CHANNELS ARE OPEN. WE HAVE TO MOVE AS ONE IN ORDER FOR THIS TO WORK, SO CONCENTRATE. YOUR MOVEMENTS STILL POWER THE SHIP.
SHINK!
SHUNK
SHUNK
SHUNK
SHUNK
GGEEAAA!

This kitten's got claws! Literally! Literally.

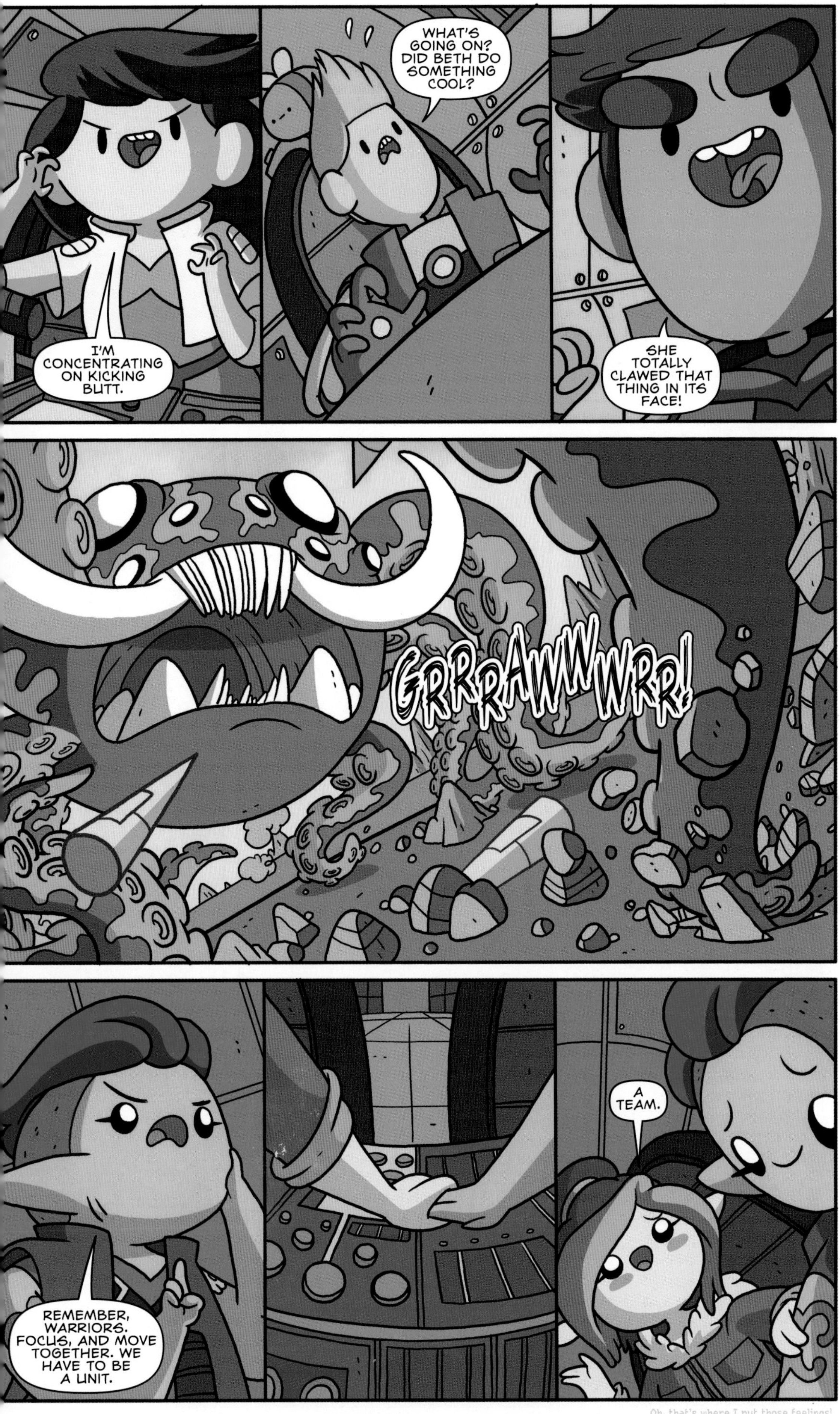
I'M CONCENTRATING ON KICKING BUTT.
WHAT'S GOING ON? DID BETH DO SOMETHING COOL?
SHE TOTALLY CLAWED THAT THING IN ITS FACE!
GRRRAWWWRR!
REMEMBER, WARRIORS. FOCUS, AND MOVE TOGETHER. WE HAVE TO BE A UNIT.
A TEAM.

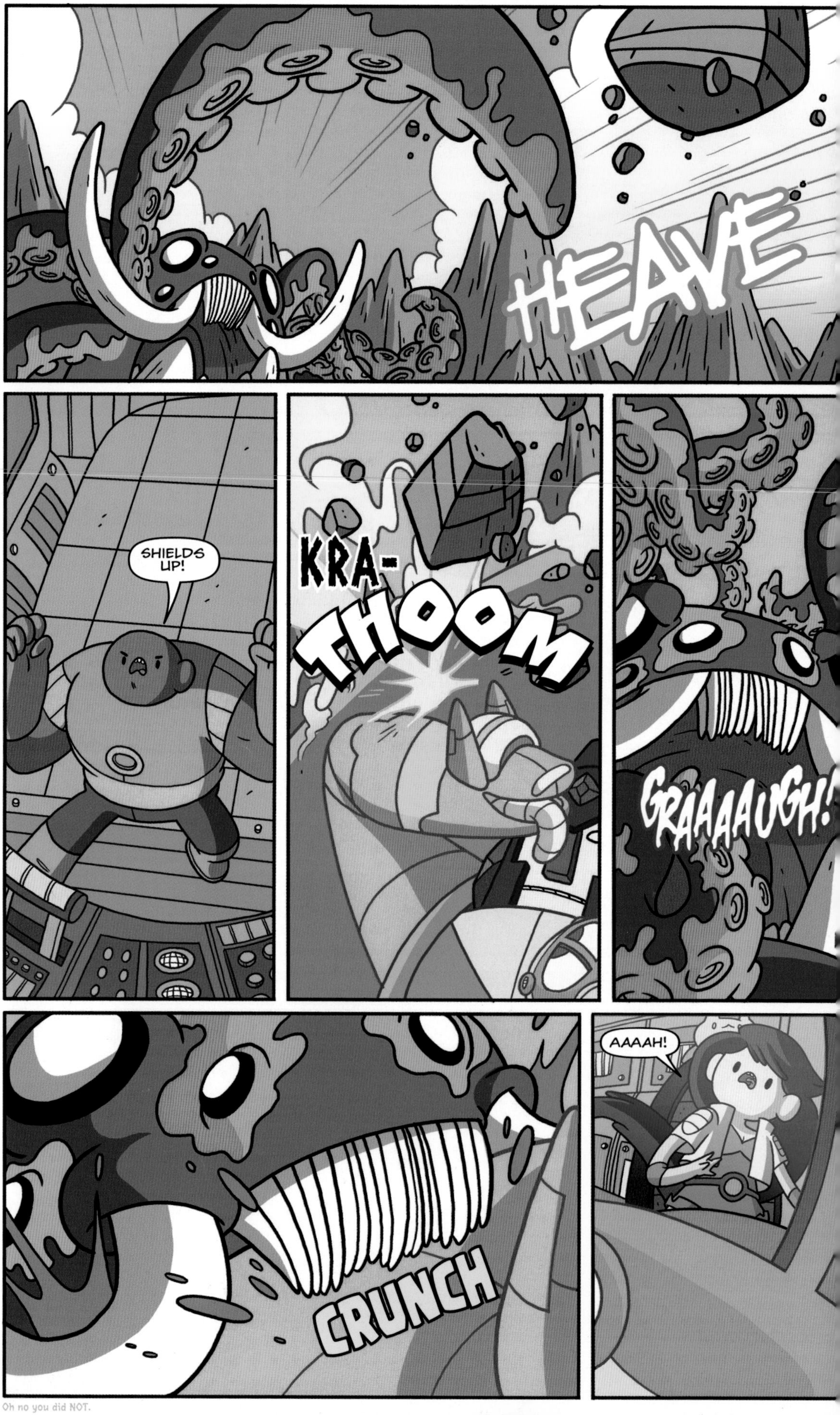
HEAVE
SHIELDS UP!
KRA-
THOOM
GRAAAAUGH!
CRUNCH
AAAAH!

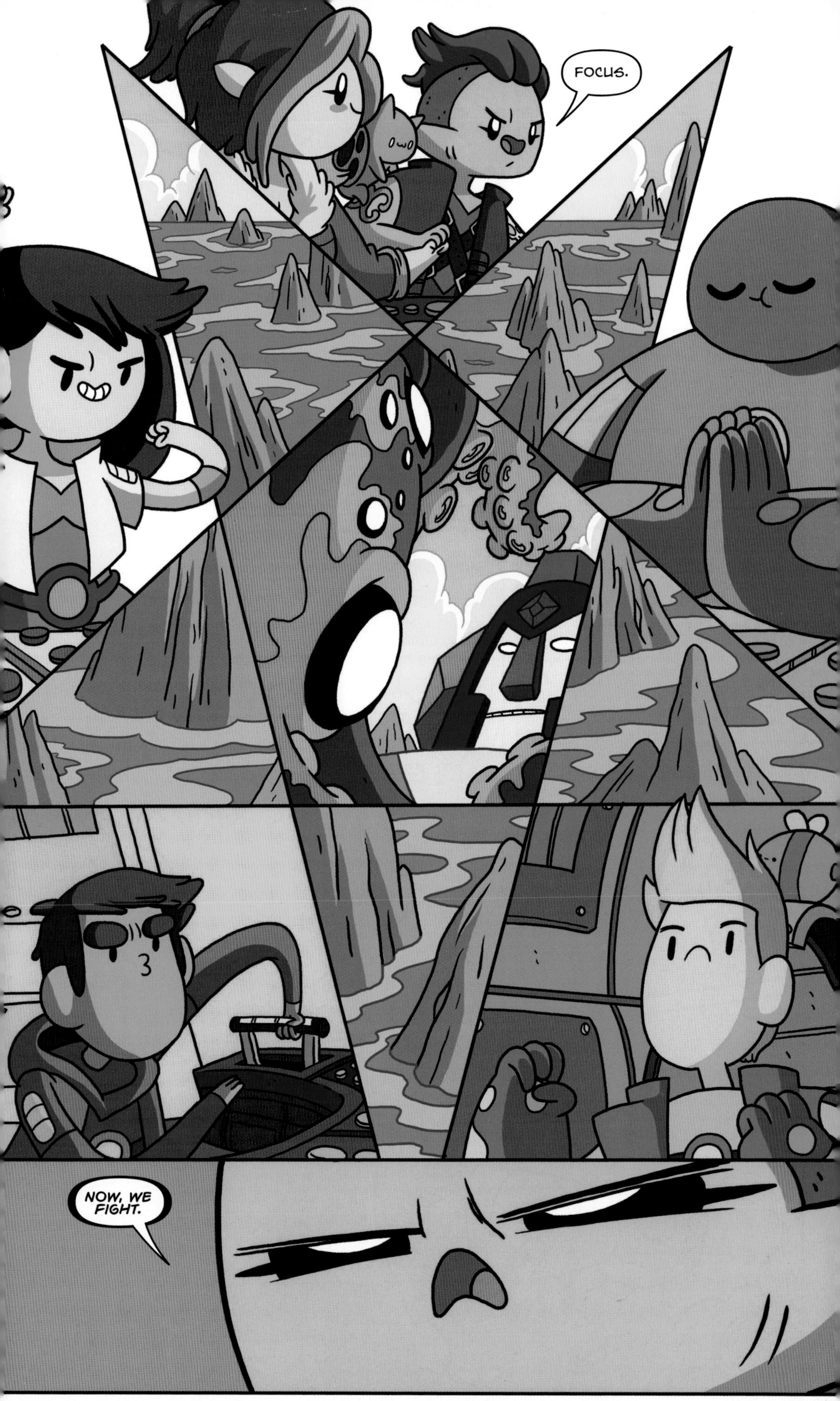
FOCUS.
NOW, WE FIGHT.

I'm pretty sure that by drawing this page, Ian has summoned a demon. Well done, Ian!

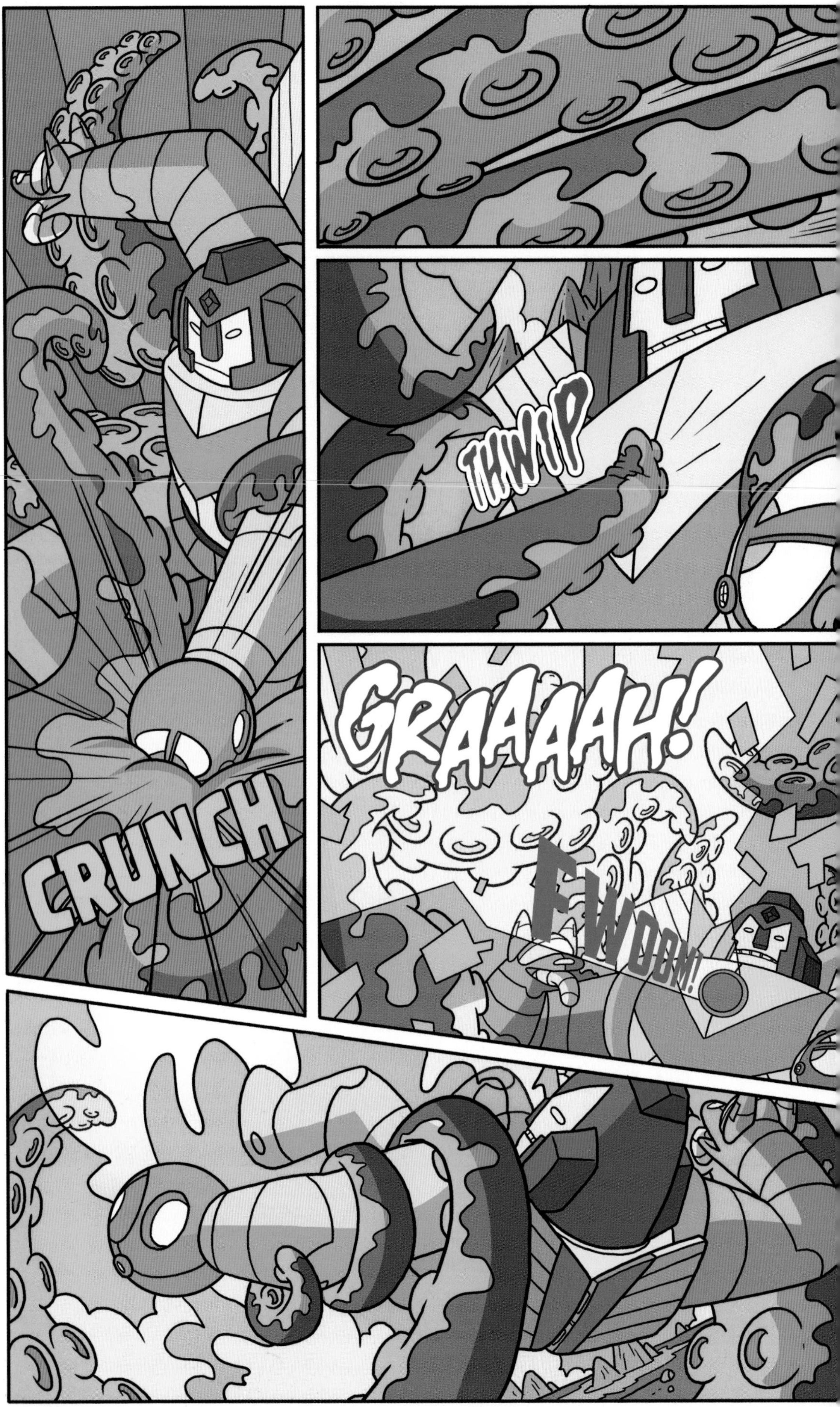
CRUNCH
THWIP
GRAAAAH!
FWOOM!

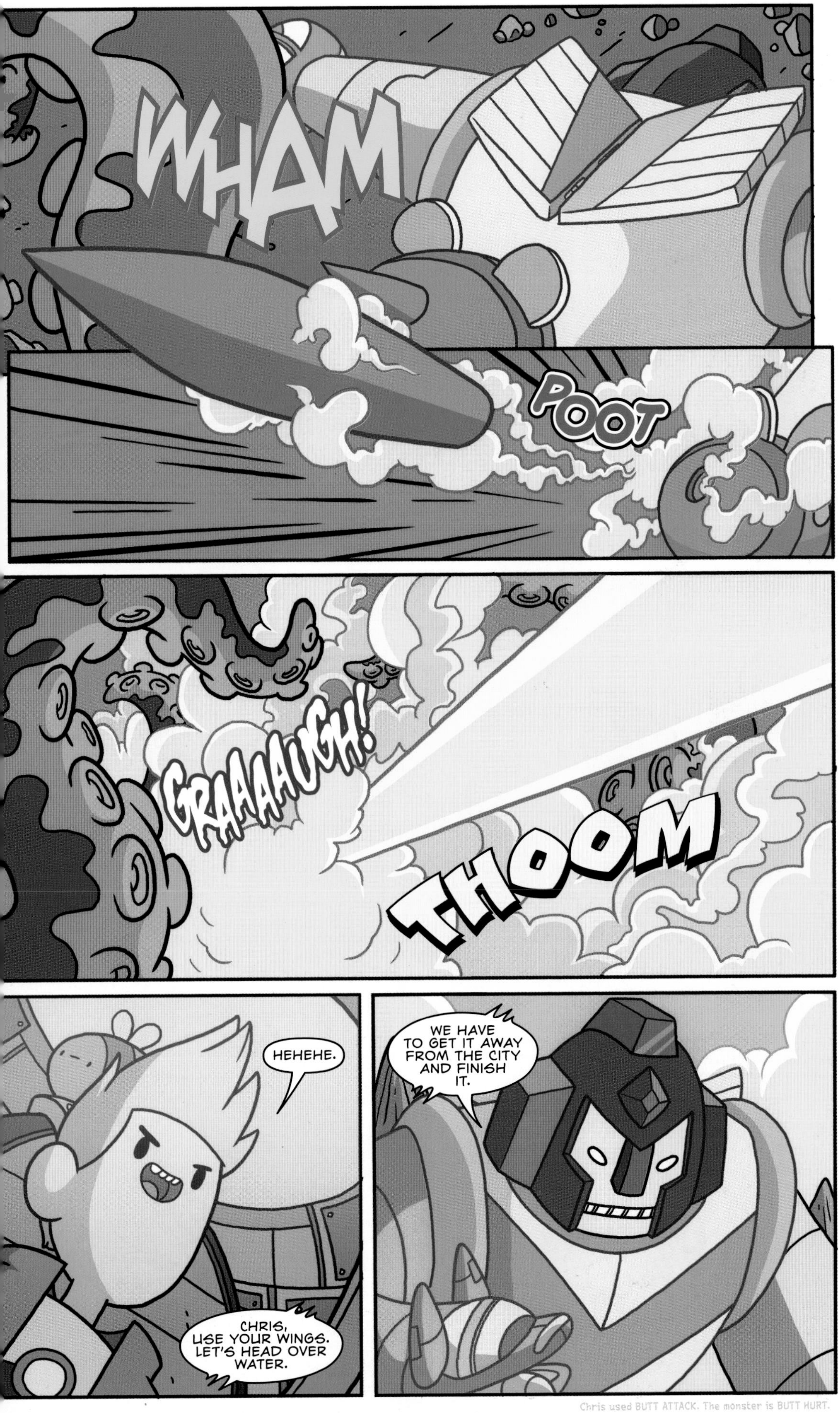
WHAM
POOT
GRAAAAUGH!
THOOM
HEHEHE.
CHRIS, USE YOUR WINGS. LET'S HEAD OVER WATER.
WE HAVE TO GET IT AWAY FROM THE CITY AND FINISH IT.

Chris used BUTT ATTACK. The monster is BUTT HURT.

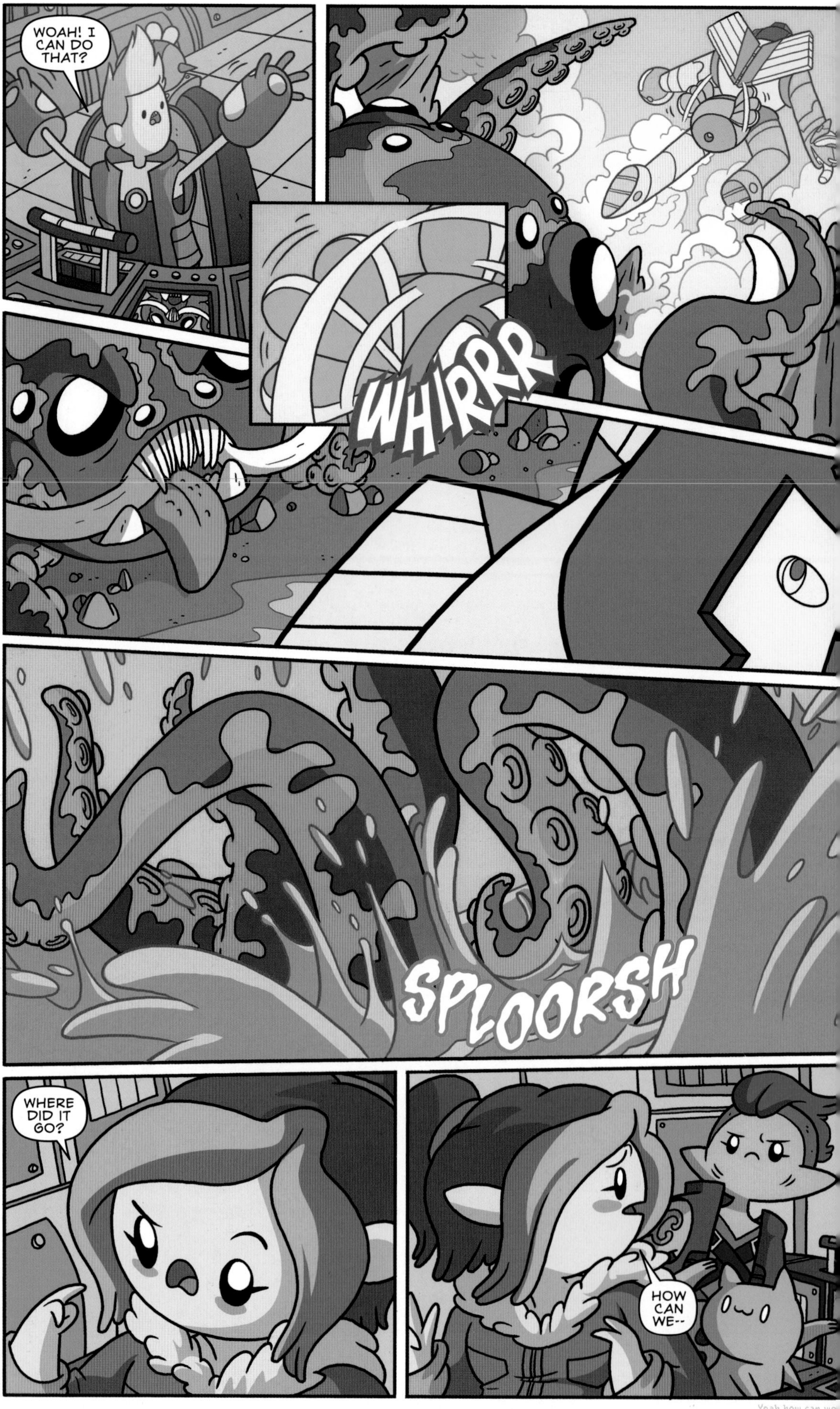
WOAH! I CAN DO THAT?
WHIRRR
SPLOORSH
WHERE DID IT GO?
HOW CAN WE--

Yeah how can we

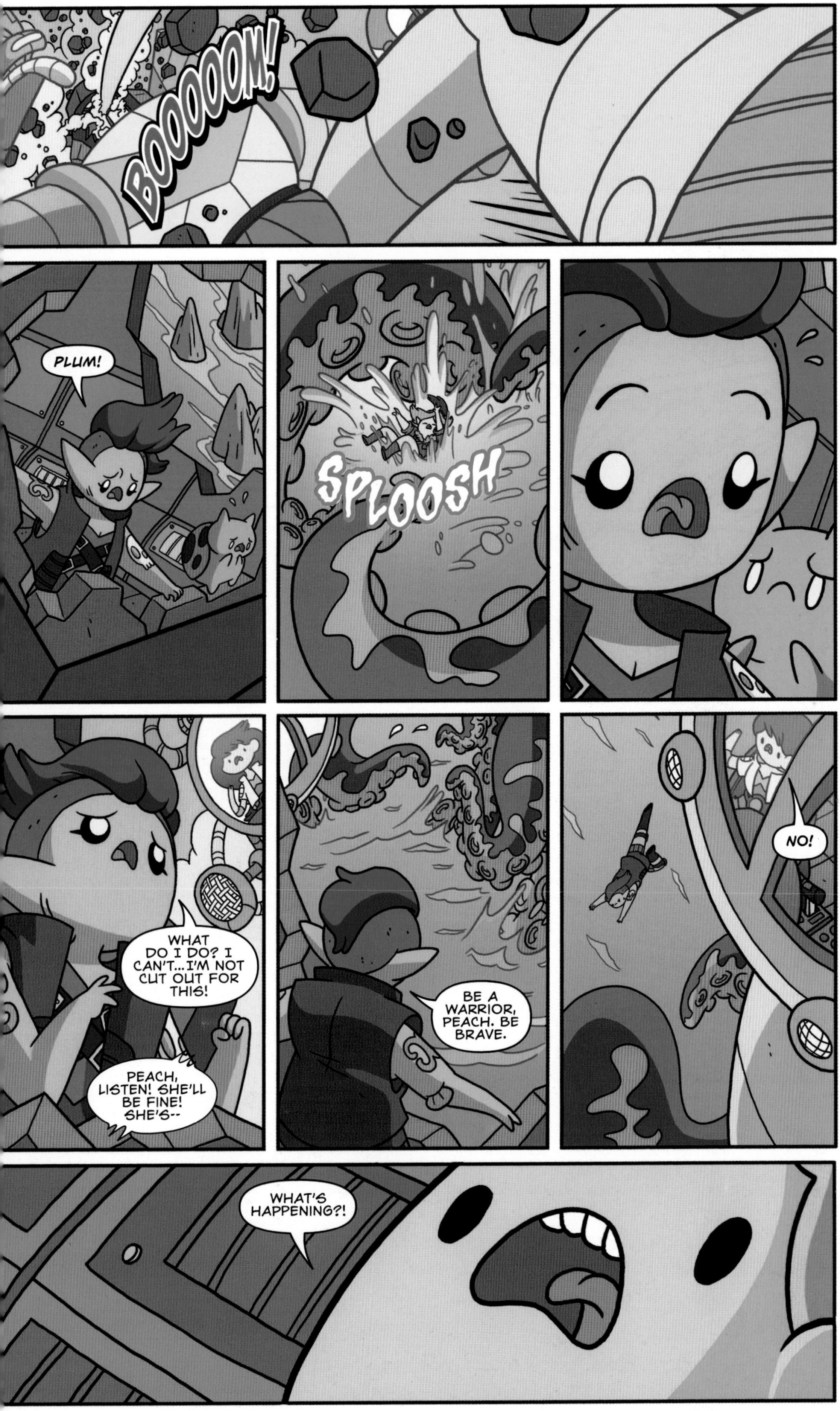
BOOOOOM!
PLUM!
SPLOOSH
WHAT DO I DO? I CAN'T...I'M NOT CUT OUT FOR THIS!
PEACH, LISTEN! SHE'LL BE FINE! SHE'S--
BE A WARRIOR, PEACH. BE BRAVE.
NO!
WHAT'S HAPPENING?!

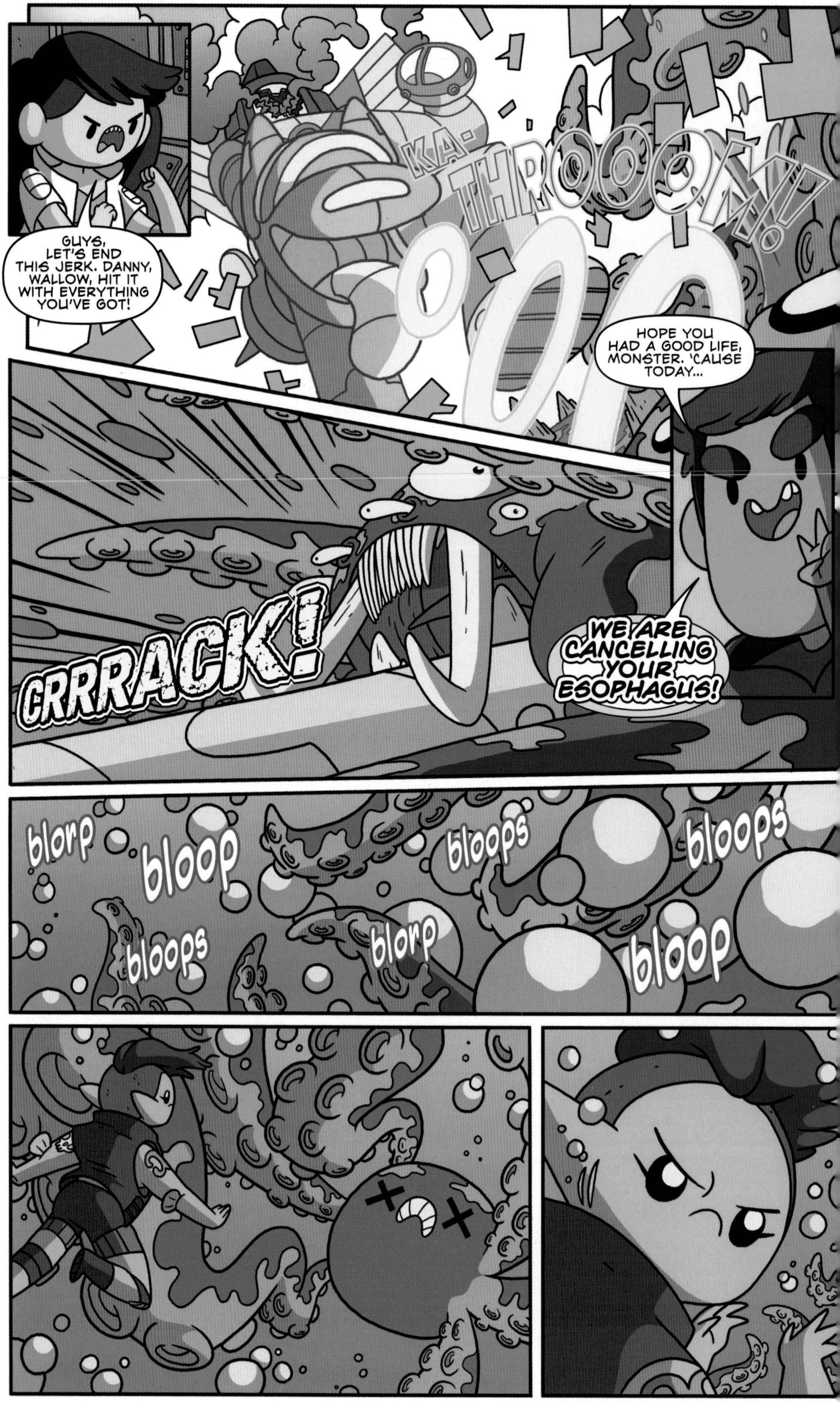
GUYS, LET'S END THIS JERK. DANNY, WALLOW, HIT IT WITH EVERYTHING YOU'VE GOT!
KA-THROOOOM!!
HOPE YOU HAD A GOOD LIFE, MONSTER. 'CAUSE TODAY...
CRRRACK!
WE ARE CANCELLING YOUR ESOPHAGUS!
blorp
bloop
bloops
bloops
bloops
blorp
bloop

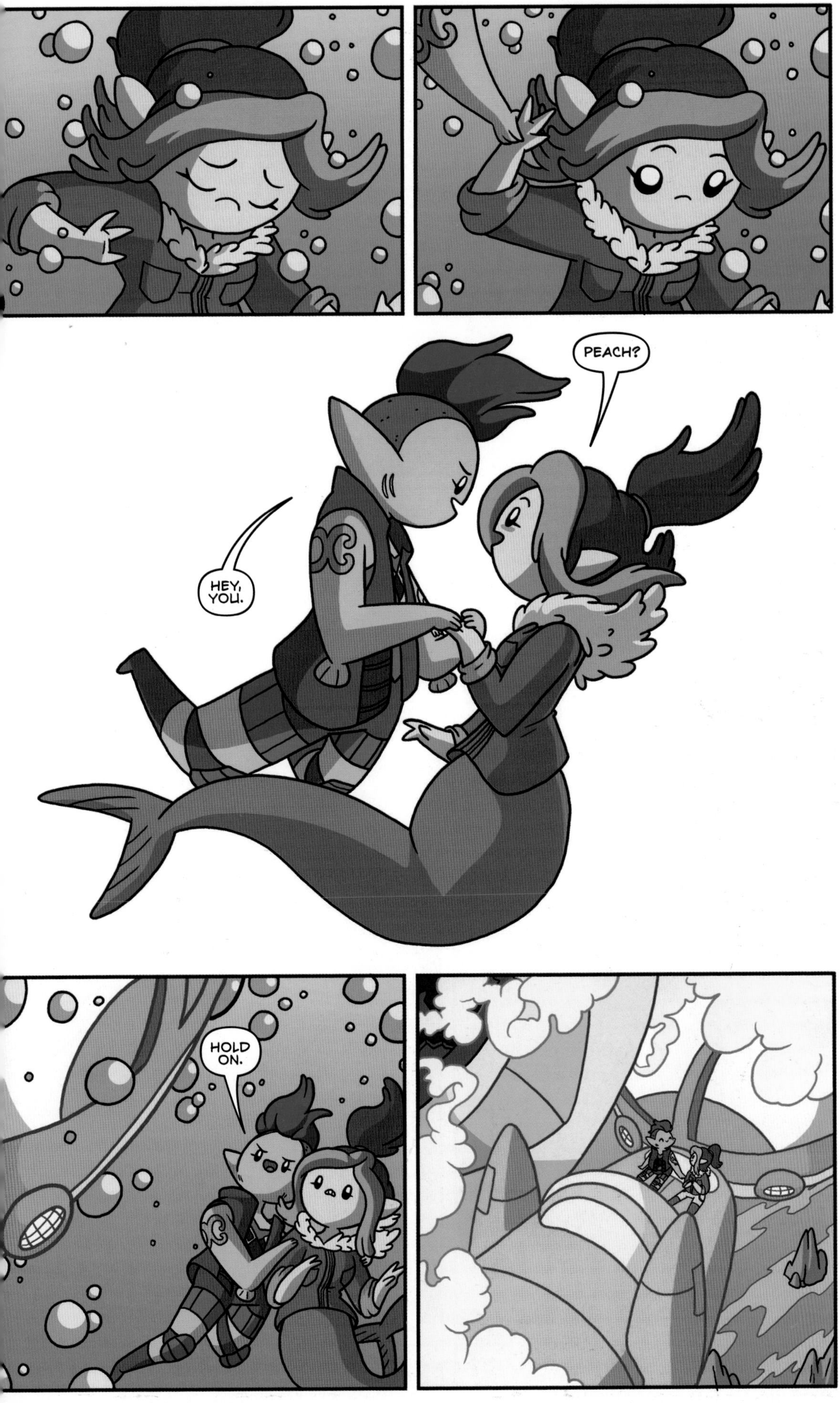
PEACH?
HEY, YOU.
HOLD ON.

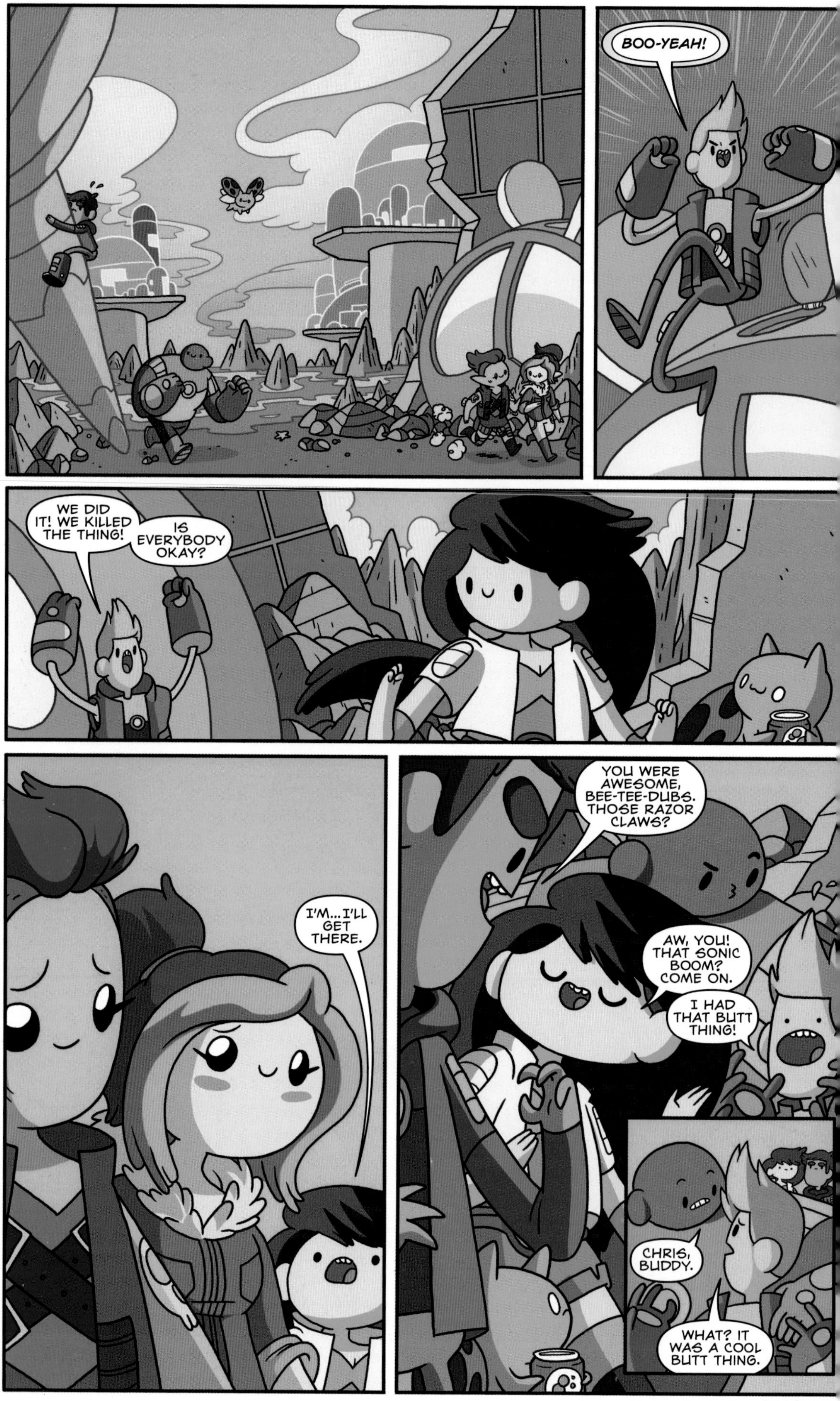

BOO-YEAH!
WE DID IT! WE KILLED THE THING!
IS EVERYBODY OKAY?
I'M...I'LL GET THERE.
YOU WERE AWESOME, BEE-TEE-DUBS. THOSE RAZOR CLAWS?
AW, YOU! THAT SONIC BOOM? COME ON.
I HAD THAT BUTT THING!
CHRIS, BUDDY.
WHAT? IT WAS A COOL BUTT THING.

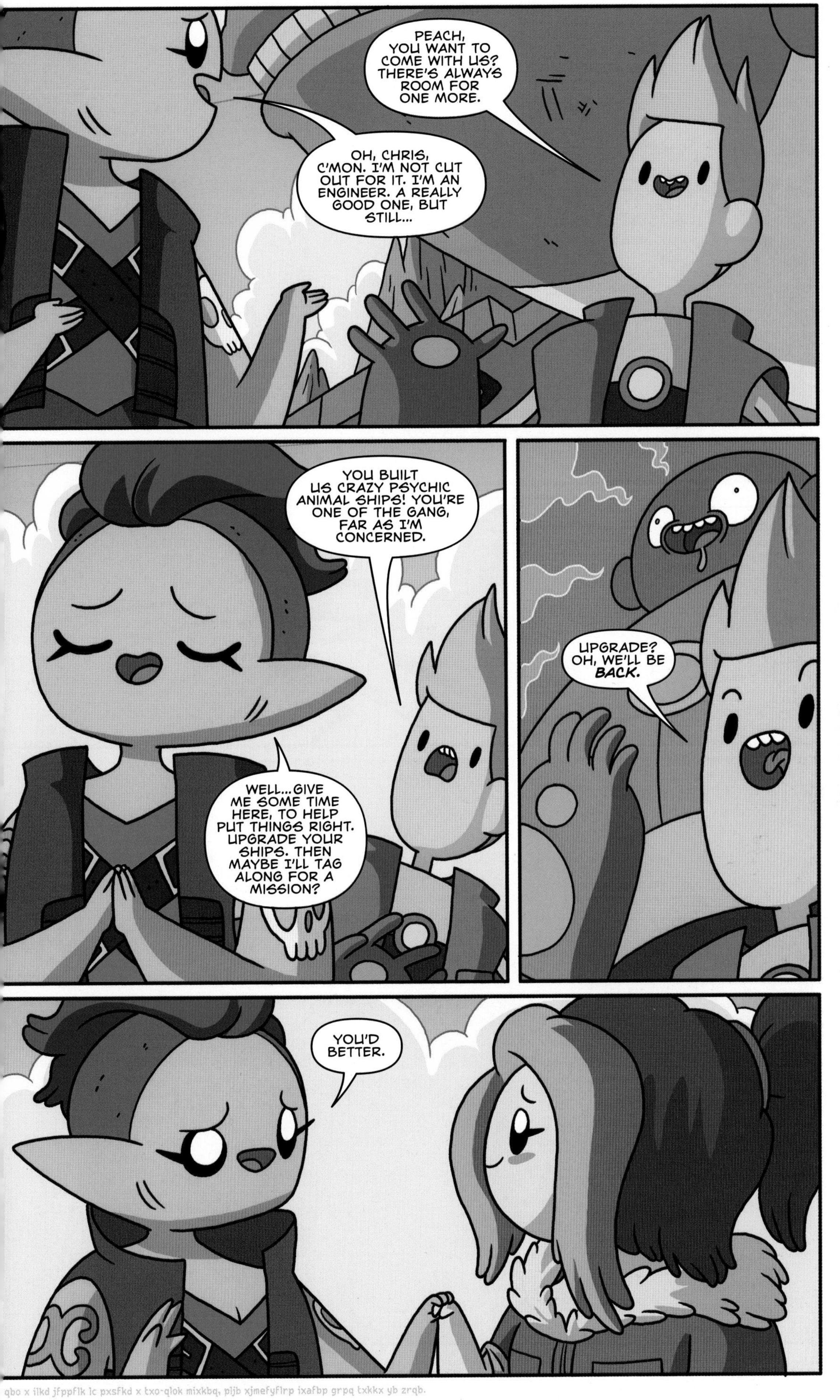
PEACH, YOU WANT TO COME WITH US? THERE'S ALWAYS ROOM FOR ONE MORE.
OH, CHRIS, C'MON. I'M NOT CUT OUT FOR IT. I'M AN ENGINEER. A REALLY GOOD ONE, BUT STILL...
YOU BUILT US CRAZY PSYCHIC ANIMAL SHIPS! YOU'RE ONE OF THE GANG, FAR AS I'M CONCERNED.
WELL...GIVE ME SOME TIME HERE, TO HELP PUT THINGS RIGHT. UPGRADE YOUR SHIPS. THEN MAYBE I'LL TAG ALONG FOR A MISSION?
UPGRADE? OH, WE'LL BE *BACK.*
YOU'D BETTER.

qbo x ilkd jfppflk lc pxsfkd x txo-qlok mixkbq, pljb xjmefyflrp ixafbp grpq txkkx yb zrqb.

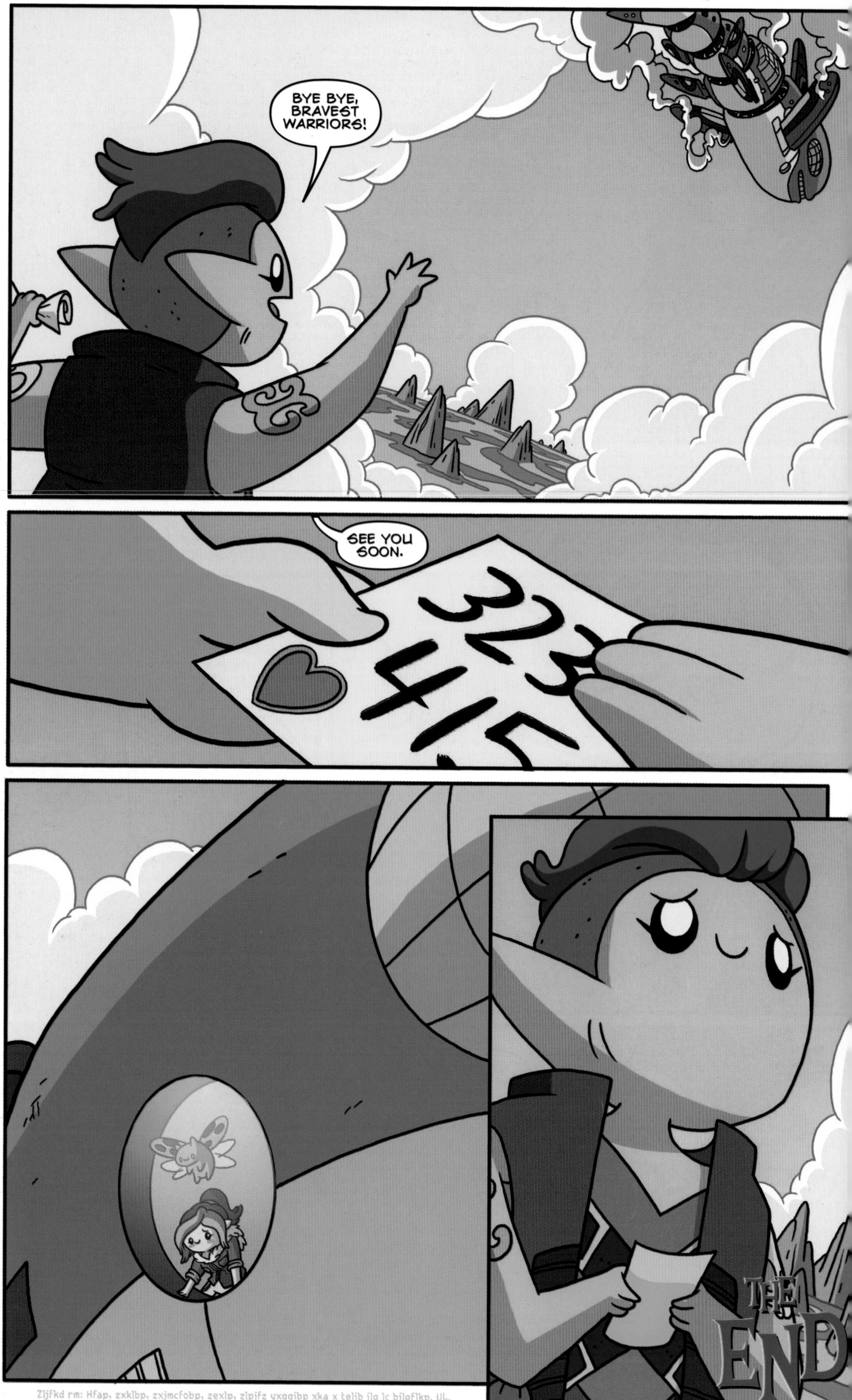

BYE BYE, BRAVEST WARRIORS!
SEE YOU SOON.
323 415
THE END

Zljfkd rm: Hfap, zxklbp, zxjmcfobp, zexlp, zlpjfz yxqqibp xka x telib ilq lc bjlqflkp. UL.

SHORT MISSIONS

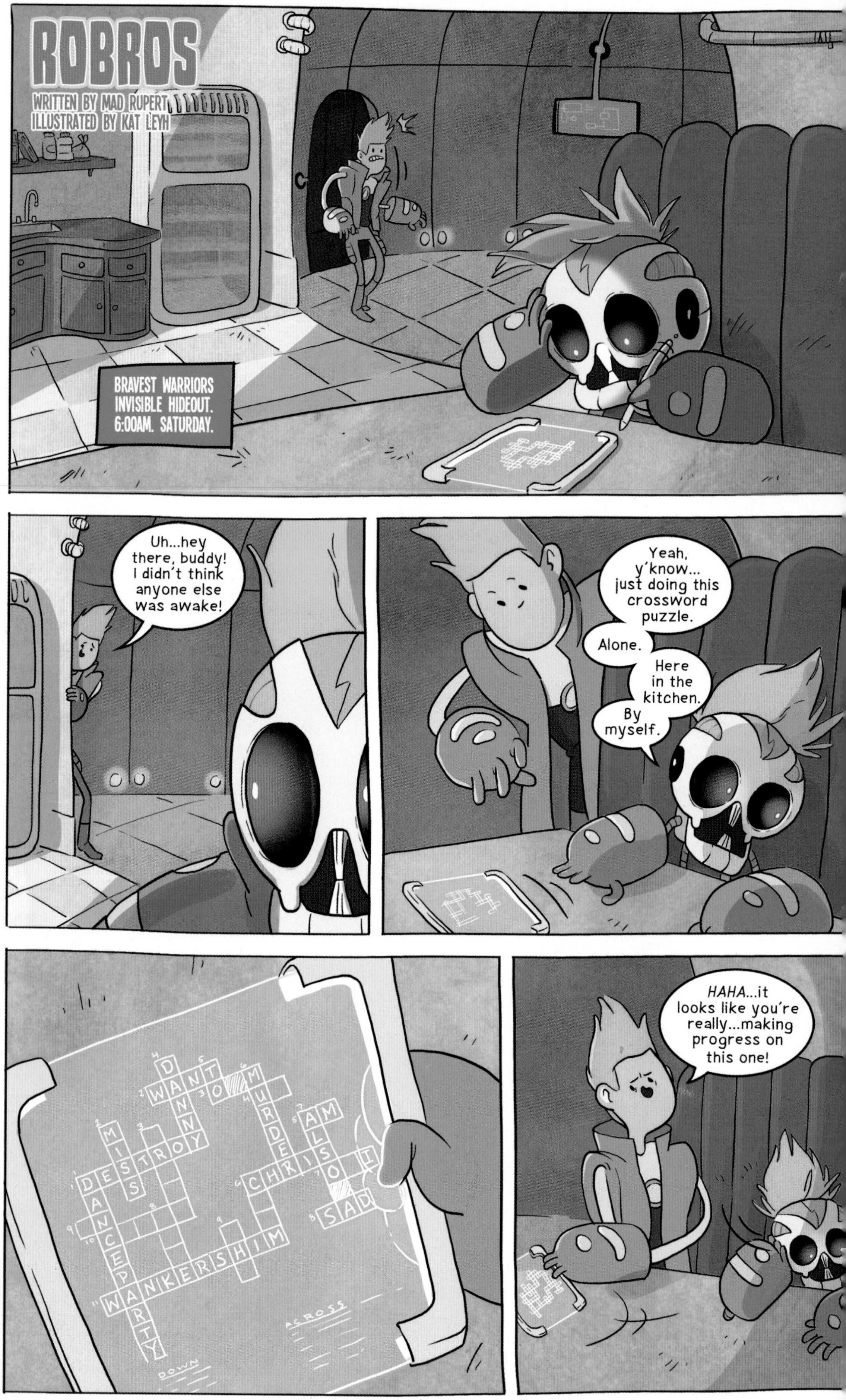

ROBROS
WRITTEN BY MAD RUPERT
ILLUSTRATED BY KAT LEYH
BRAVEST WARRIORS INVISIBLE HIDEOUT. 6:00AM. SATURDAY.
Uh...hey there, buddy! I didn't think anyone else was awake!
Yeah, y'know... just doing this crossword puzzle.
Alone.
Here in the kitchen.
By myself.
WANT
DANNY
MURDER
MISS
DESTROY
AM
ALSO
DESS
CHRIS
SAD
DANCEPARTY
WANKERSHIM
WARTY
ACROSS
DOWN
HAHA...it looks like you're really...making progress on this one!

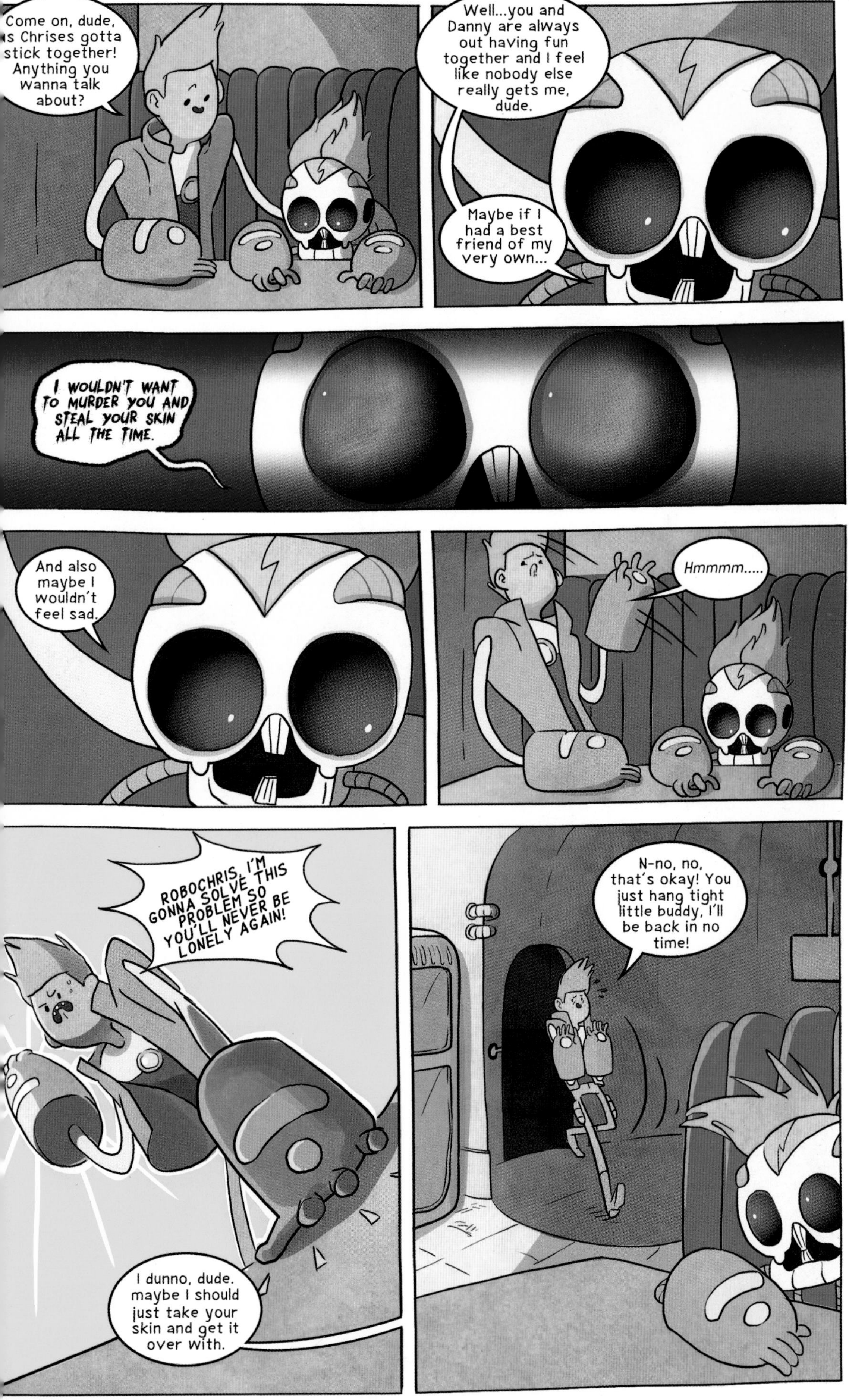

Come on, dude, 's Chrises gotta stick together! Anything you wanna talk about?
Well...you and Danny are always out having fun together and I feel like nobody else really gets me, dude.
Maybe if I had a best friend of my very own...
I WOULDN'T WANT TO MURDER YOU AND STEAL YOUR SKIN ALL THE TIME.
And also maybe I wouldn't feel sad.
Hmmmm.....
ROBOCHRIS, I'M GONNA SOLVE THIS PROBLEM SO YOU'LL NEVER BE LONELY AGAIN!
I dunno, dude. maybe I should just take your skin and get it over with.
N-no, no, that's okay! You just hang tight little buddy, I'll be back in no time!

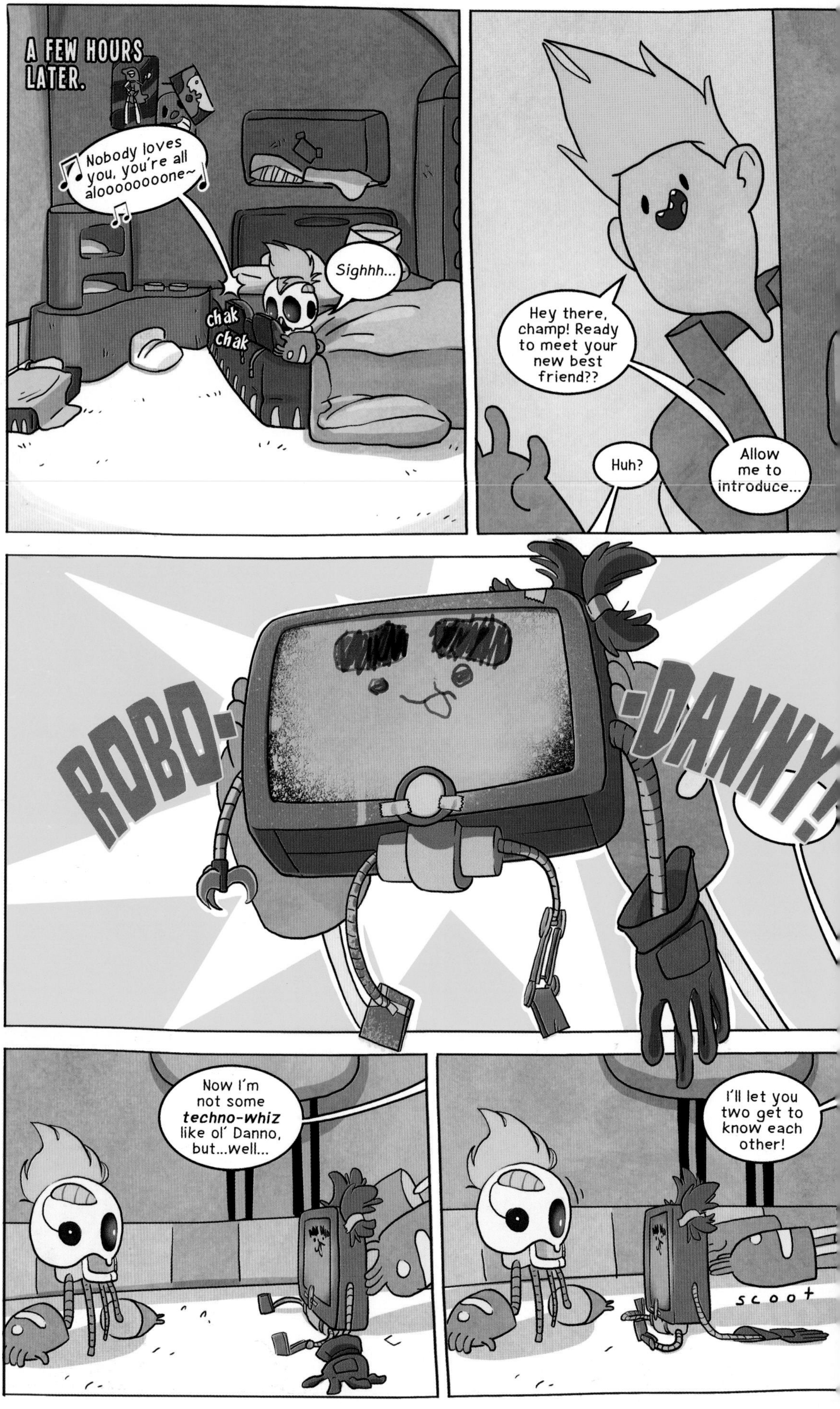

A FEW HOURS LATER.
Nobody loves you, you're all aloooooooone~
Sighhh...
chak
chak
Hey there, champ! Ready to meet your new best friend??
Huh?
Allow me to introduce...
ROBO-
-DANNY!
Now I'm not some ***techno-whiz*** like ol' Danno, but...well...
I'll let you two get to know each other!
scoot

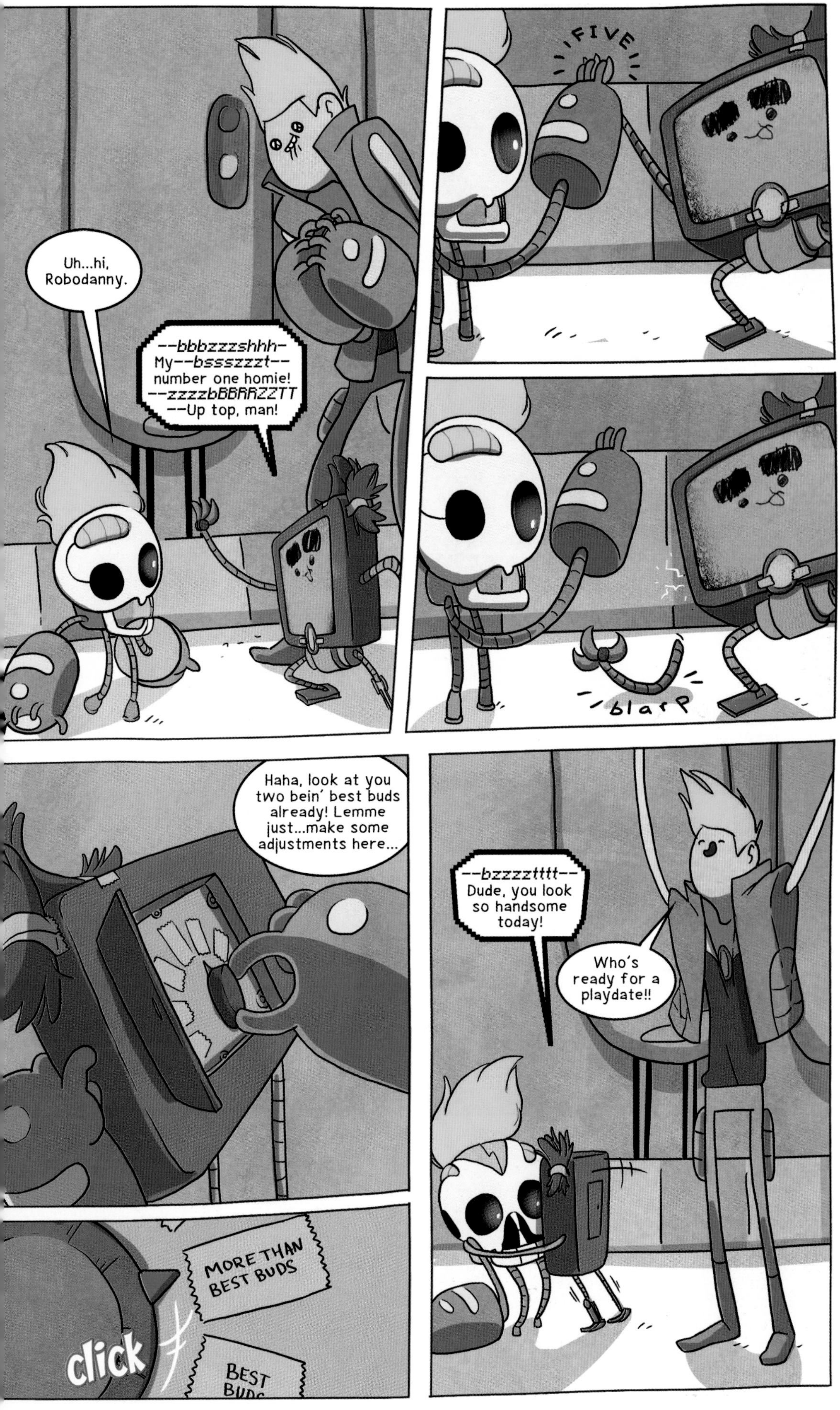
Uh...hi, Robodanny.
--bbbzzzshhh-- My--bssszzzt-- number one homie! --zzzzbBBRRZZTT --Up top, man!
FIVE
blarp
Haha, look at you two bein' best buds already! Lemme just...make some adjustments here...
MORE THAN BEST BUDS
click
BEST BUDS
--bzzzztttt-- Dude, you look so handsome today!
Who's ready for a playdate!!

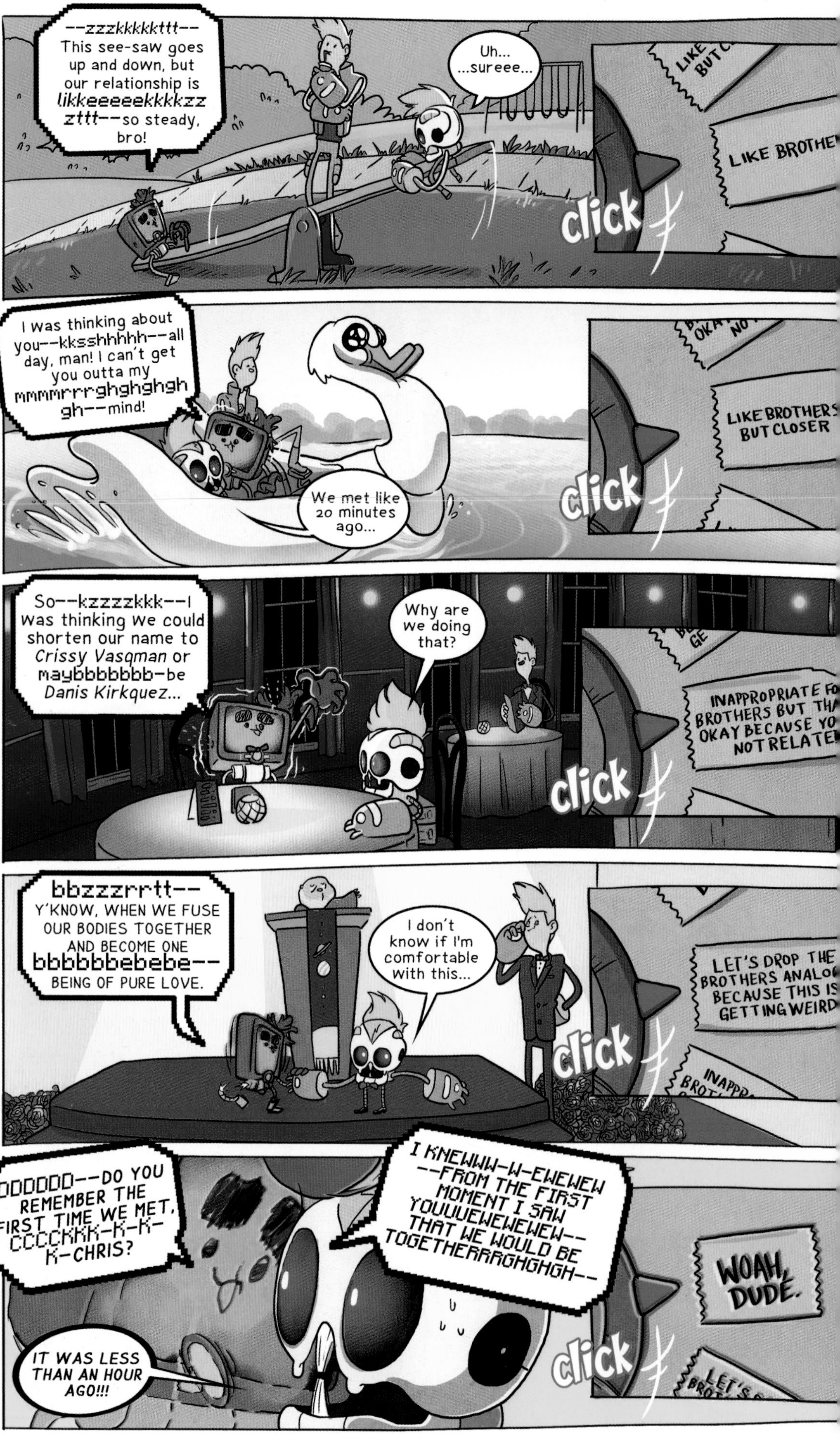
--zzzkkkkkttt-- This see-saw goes up and down, but our relationship is likkeeeeeekkkkzz zttt--so steady, bro!
Uh... ...sureee...
LIKE BROTHE
click
I was thinking about you--kksshhhhh--all day, man! I can't get you outta my mmmmrrrghghghgh gh--mind!
We met like 20 minutes ago...
LIKE BROTHERS BUT CLOSER
click
So--kzzzzkkk--I was thinking we could shorten our name to Crissy Vasqman or maybbbbbbb-be Danis Kirkquez...
Why are we doing that?
INAPPROPRIATE FO BROTHERS BUT THA OKAY BECAUSE YO NOT RELATE
click
bbzzzrrtt-- Y'KNOW, WHEN WE FUSE OUR BODIES TOGETHER AND BECOME ONE bbbbbbebebe-- BEING OF PURE LOVE.
I don't know if I'm comfortable with this...
LET'S DROP THE BROTHERS ANALOG BECAUSE THIS IS GETTING WEIRD
click
DDDDDD--DO YOU REMEMBER THE FIRST TIME WE MET, CCCCKKK-K-K-K-CHRIS?
I KNEWWW-W-EWEWEW --FROM THE FIRST MOMENT I SAW YOUUUEWEWEWEW-- THAT WE WOULD BE TOGETHERRRGHGHGH--
WOAH, DUDE.
IT WAS LESS THAN AN HOUR AGO!!!
click

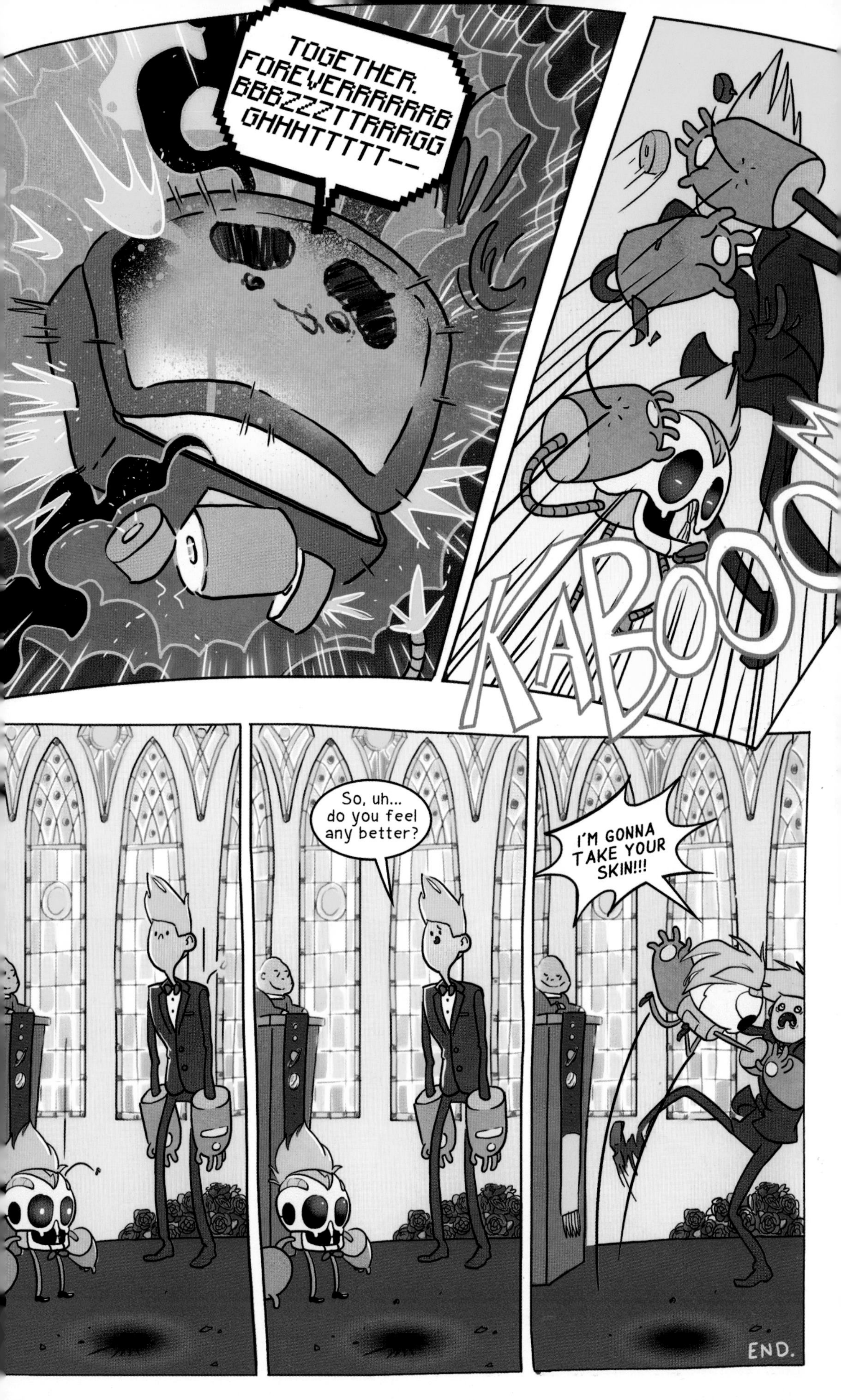
TOGETHER. FOREVERRRRRRB BBBZZZTTRRRGG GHHHTTTTT--
KABOOO
So, uh... do you feel any better?
I'M GONNA TAKE YOUR SKIN!!!
END.

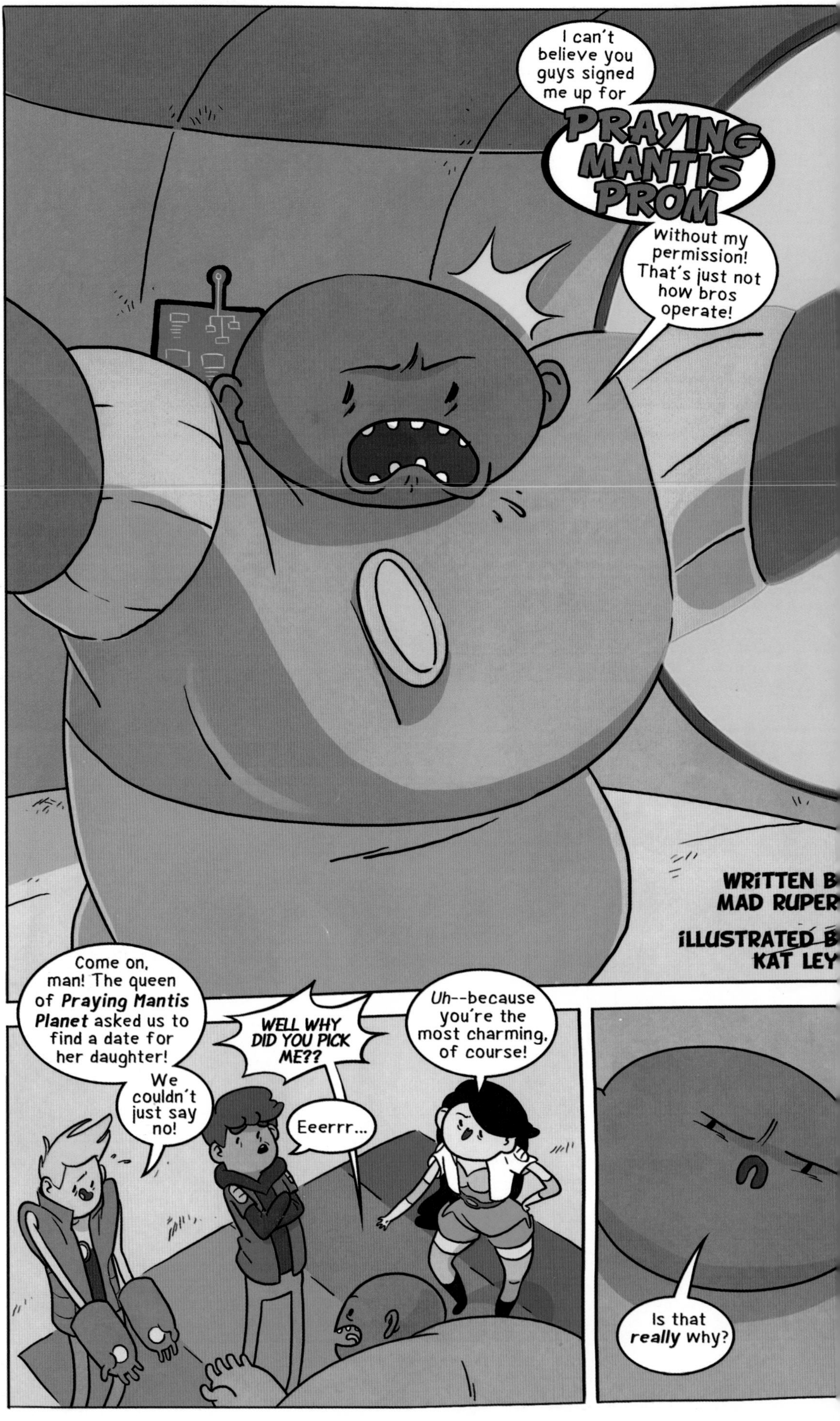

I can't believe you guys signed me up for
PRAYING MANTIS PROM
without my permission! That's just not how bros operate!
WRITTEN B
MAD RUPER
ILLUSTRATED B
KAT LEY
Come on, man! The queen of *Praying Mantis Planet* asked us to find a date for her daughter!
We couldn't just say no!
WELL WHY DID YOU PICK ME??
Eeerrr...
Uh--because you're the most charming, of course!
Is that *really* why?

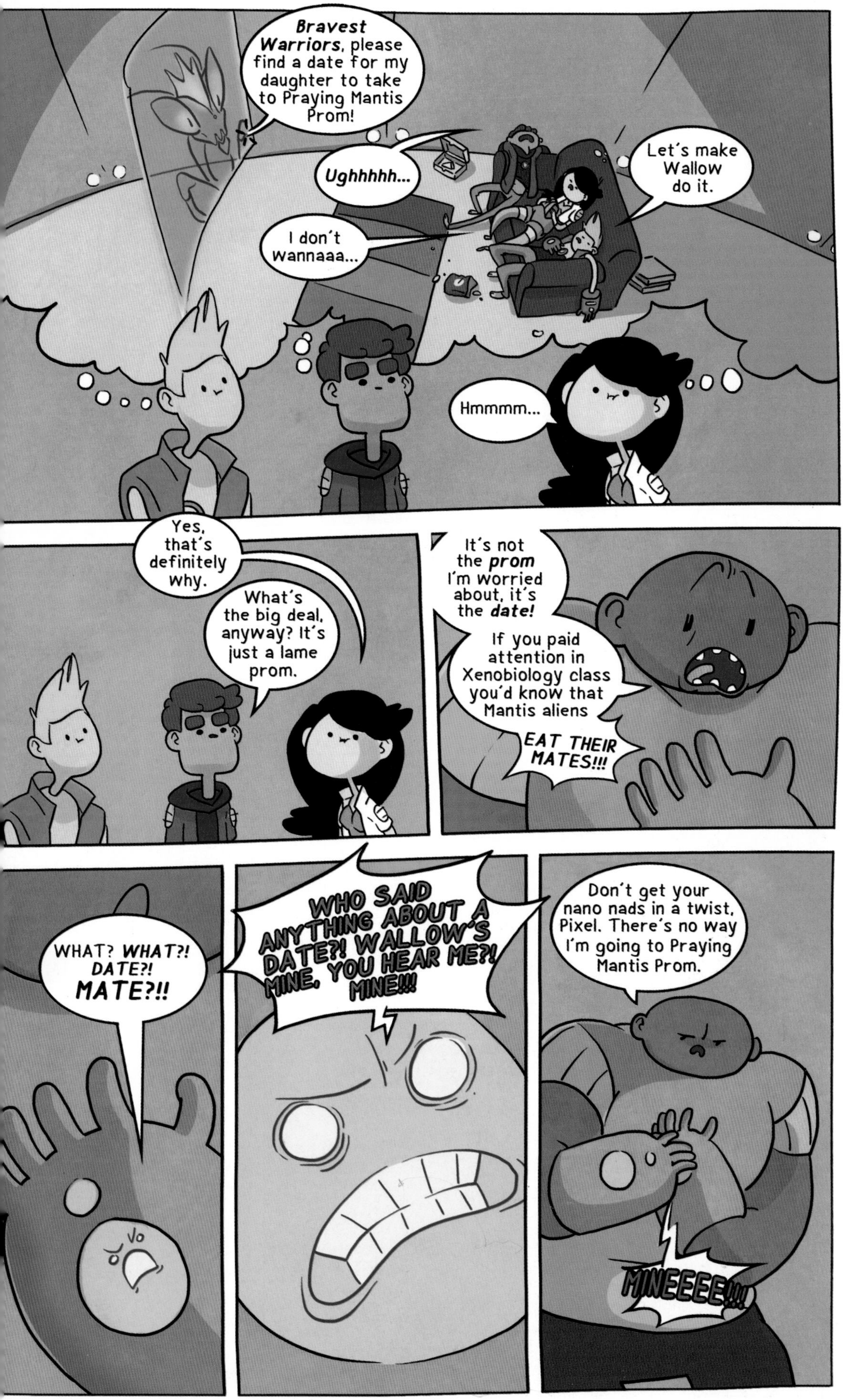
Bravest Warriors, please find a date for my daughter to take to Praying Mantis Prom!
Ughhhhh...
Let's make Wallow do it.
I don't wannaaa...
Hmmmm...
Yes, that's definitely why.
What's the big deal, anyway? It's just a lame prom.
It's not the prom I'm worried about, it's the date!
If you paid attention in Xenobiology class you'd know that Mantis aliens
EAT THEIR MATES!!!
WHAT? WHAT?! DATE?! MATE?!!
WHO SAID ANYTHING ABOUT A DATE?! WALLOW'S MINE, YOU HEAR ME?! MINE, MINE!!!
Don't get your nano nads in a twist, Pixel. There's no way I'm going to Praying Mantis Prom.
MINEEEE!!!

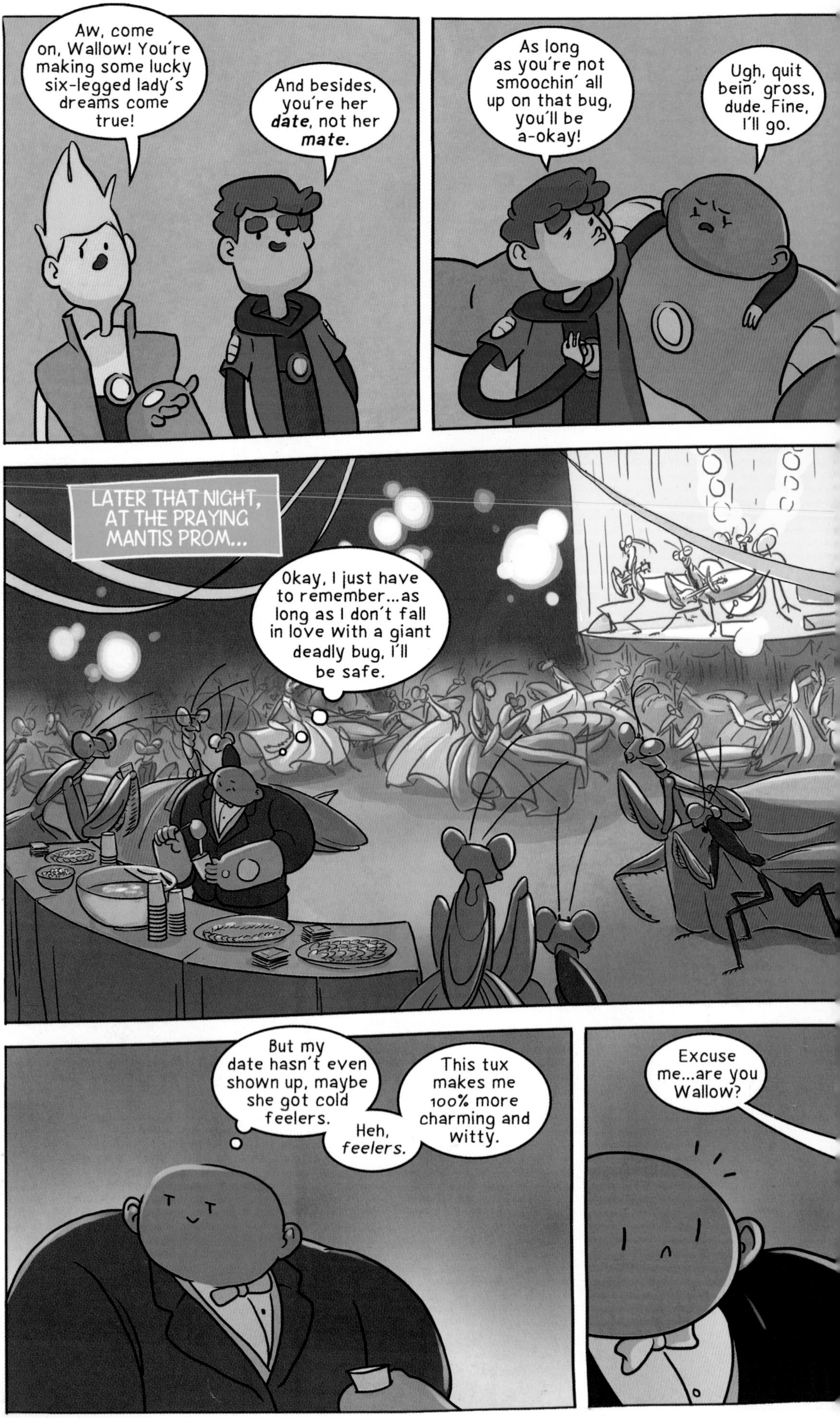
Aw, come on, Wallow! You're making some lucky six-legged lady's dreams come true!
And besides, you're her ***date***, not her ***mate.***
As long as you're not smoochin' all up on that bug, you'll be a-okay!
Ugh, quit bein' gross, dude. Fine, I'll go.
LATER THAT NIGHT, AT THE PRAYING MANTIS PROM...
Okay, I just have to remember...as long as I don't fall in love with a giant deadly bug, I'll be safe.
But my date hasn't even shown up, maybe she got cold feelers.
Heh, *feelers.*
This tux makes me 100% more charming and witty.
Excuse me...are you Wallow?

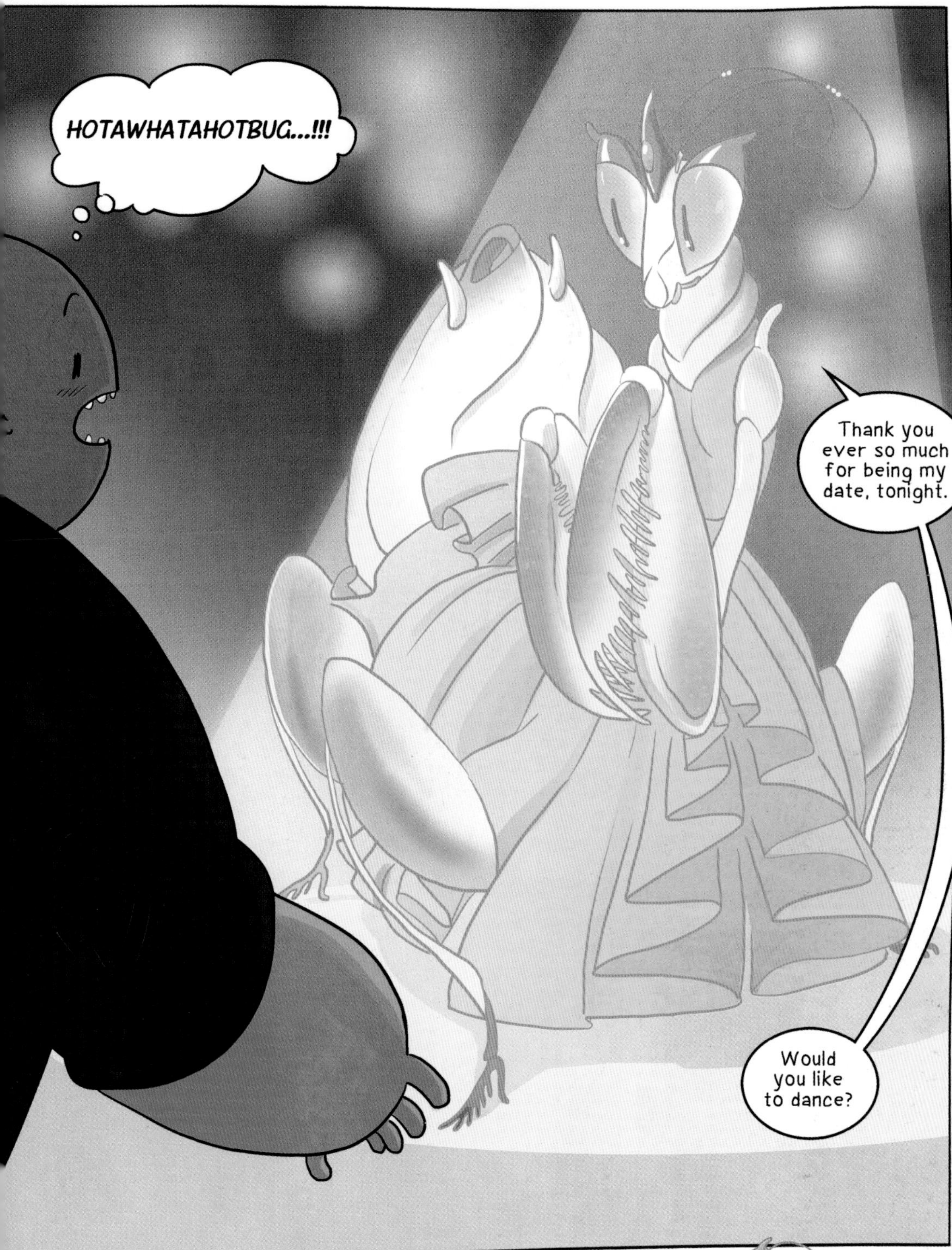
HOTAWHATAHOTBUG...!!!
Thank you ever so much for being my date, tonight.
Would you like to dance?

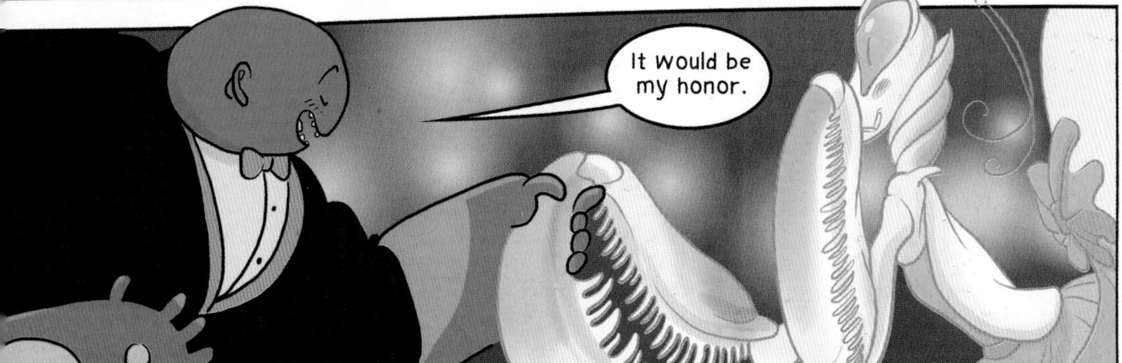
It would be my honor.

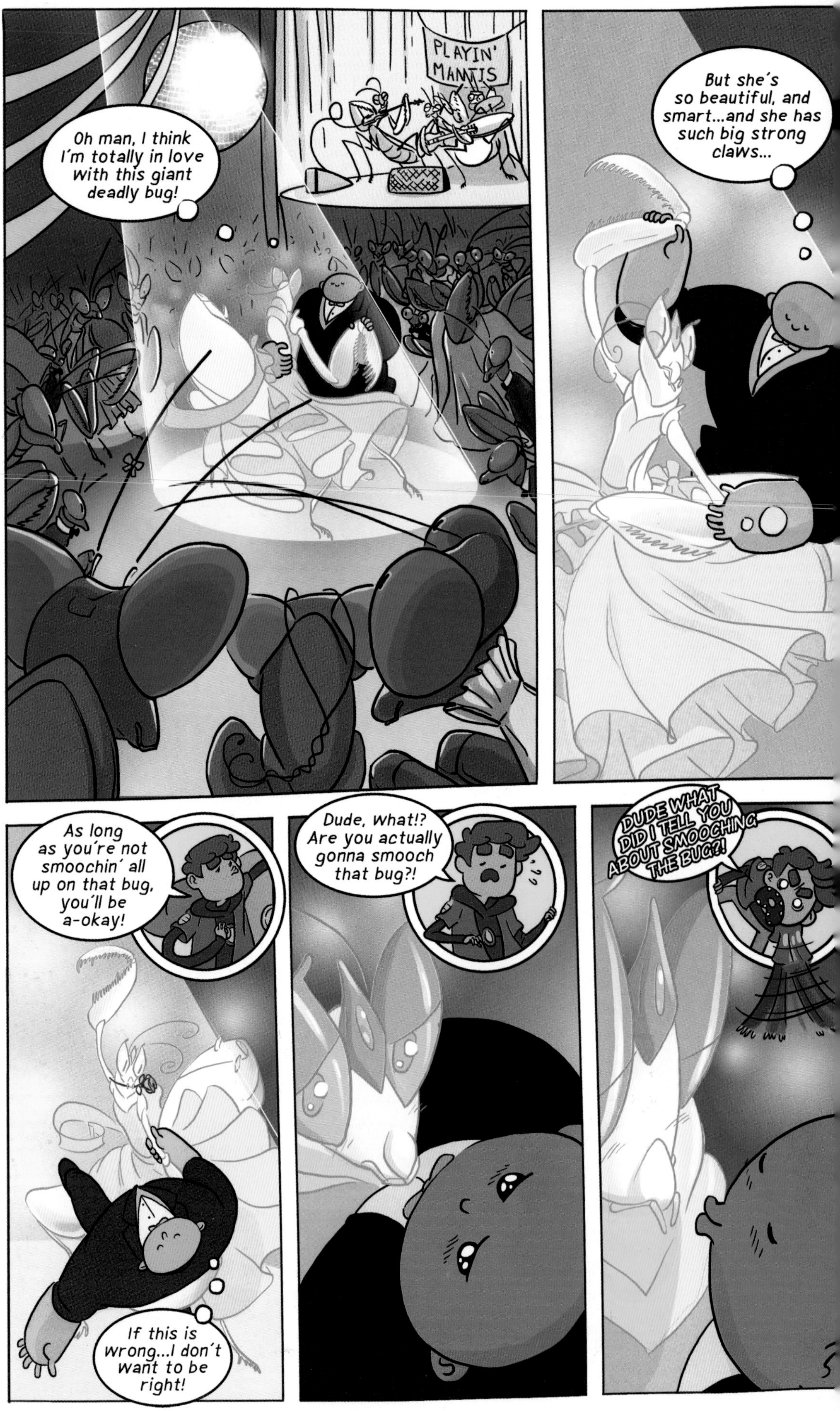
PLAYIN' MANTIS
Oh man, I think I'm totally in love with this giant deadly bug!
But she's so beautiful, and smart...and she has such big strong claws...
As long as you're not smoochin' all up on that bug, you'll be a-okay!
If this is wrong...I don't want to be right!
Dude, what!? Are you actually gonna smooch that bug?!
DUDE WHAT DID I TELL YOU ABOUT SMOOCHING THE BUG?!

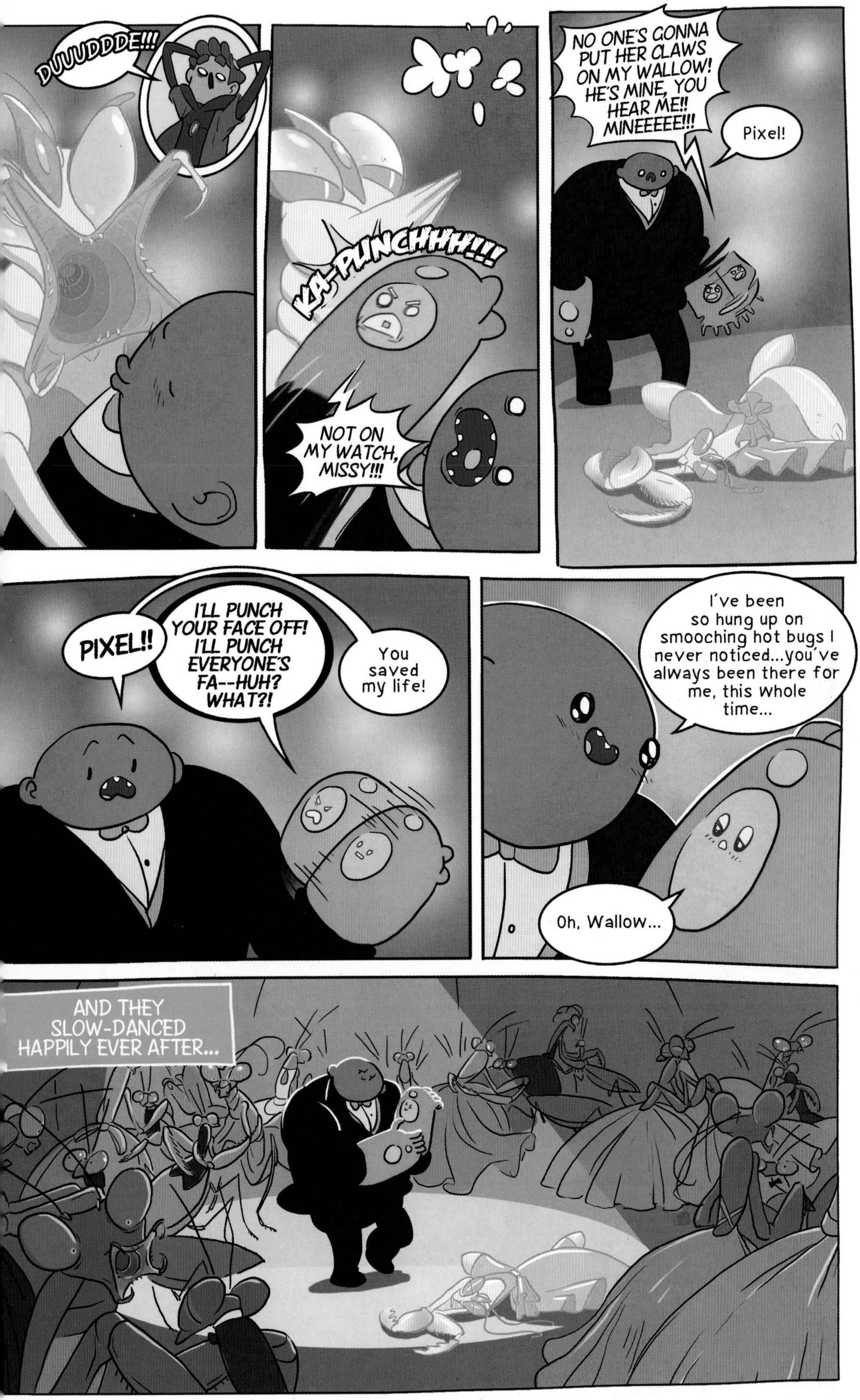
DUUUDDDE!!!
KA-PUNCHHH!!!
NOT ON MY WATCH, MISSY!!!
NO ONE'S GONNA PUT HER CLAWS ON MY WALLOW! HE'S MINE, YOU HEAR ME!! MINEEEEE!!!
Pixel!
PIXEL!!
I'LL PUNCH YOUR FACE OFF! I'LL PUNCH EVERYONE'S FA--HUH? WHAT?!
You saved my life!
I've been so hung up on smooching hot bugs I never noticed...you've always been there for me, this whole time...
Oh, Wallow...
AND THEY SLOW-DANCED HAPPILY EVER AFTER...

END.

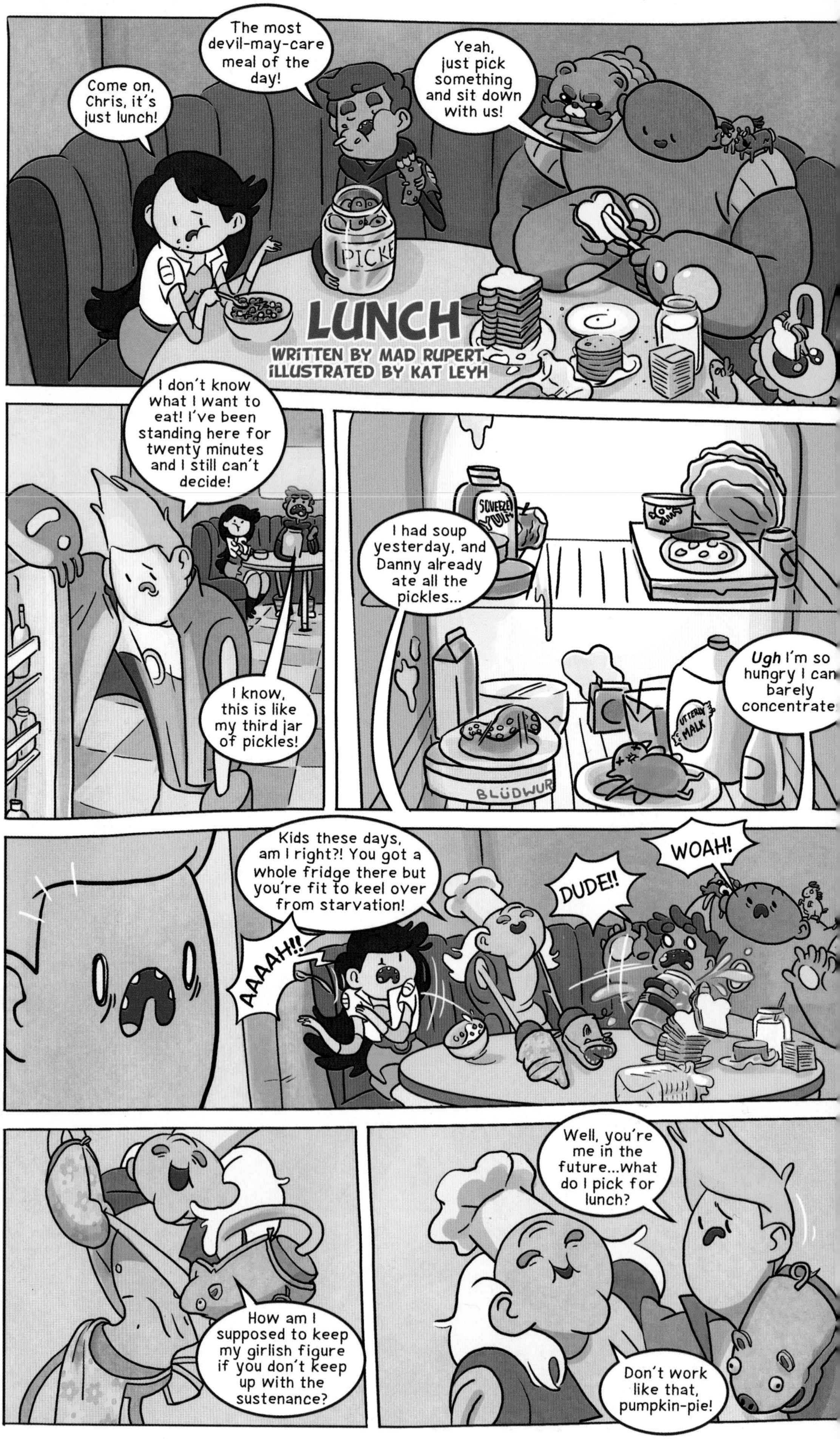
Come on, Chris, it's just lunch!
The most devil-may-care meal of the day!
Yeah, just pick something and sit down with us!
PICKL
LUNCH
WRITTEN BY MAD RUPERT
ILLUSTRATED BY KAT LEYH
I don't know what I want to eat! I've been standing here for twenty minutes and I still can't decide!
I know, this is like my third jar of pickles!
I had soup yesterday, and Danny already ate all the pickles...
SQUEEZE YUM
UTTERLY MALK
BLÜDWUR
Ugh I'm so hungry I can barely concentrate
Kids these days, am I right?! You got a whole fridge there but you're fit to keel over from starvation!
AAAAH!!
DUDE!!
WOAH!
How am I supposed to keep my girlish figure if you don't keep up with the sustenance?
Well, you're me in the future...what do I pick for lunch?
Don't work like that, pumpkin-pie!

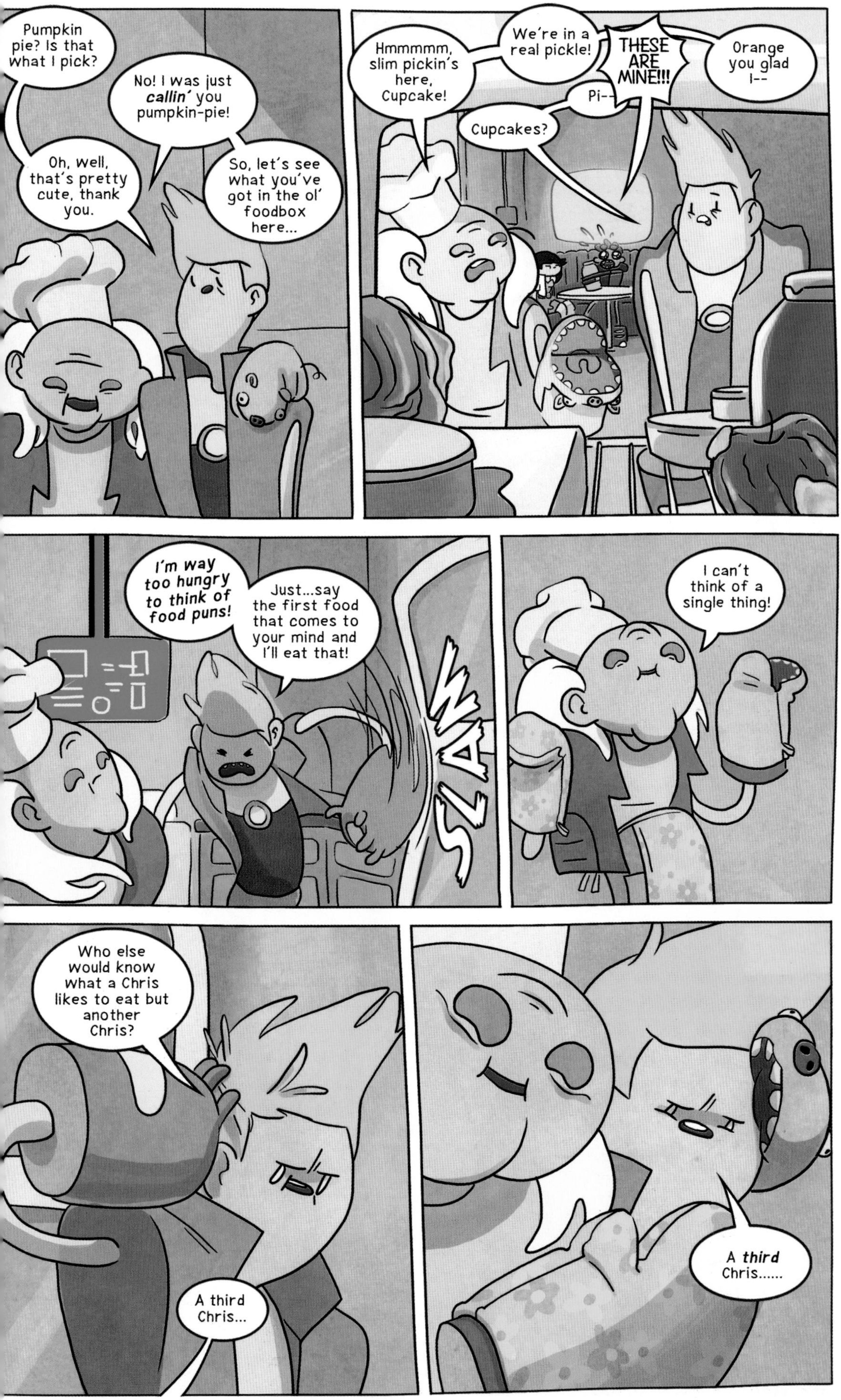

Pumpkin pie? Is that what I pick?
No! I was just *callin'* you pumpkin-pie!
Oh, well, that's pretty cute, thank you.
So, let's see what you've got in the ol' foodbox here...
Hmmmmm, slim pickin's here, Cupcake!
We're in a real pickle!
THESE ARE MINE!!!
Orange you glad I--
Pi--
Cupcakes?
I'm way too hungry to think of food puns!
Just...say the first food that comes to your mind and I'll eat that!
SLAM
I can't think of a single thing!
Who else would know what a Chris likes to eat but another Chris?
A third Chris...
A *third* Chris......

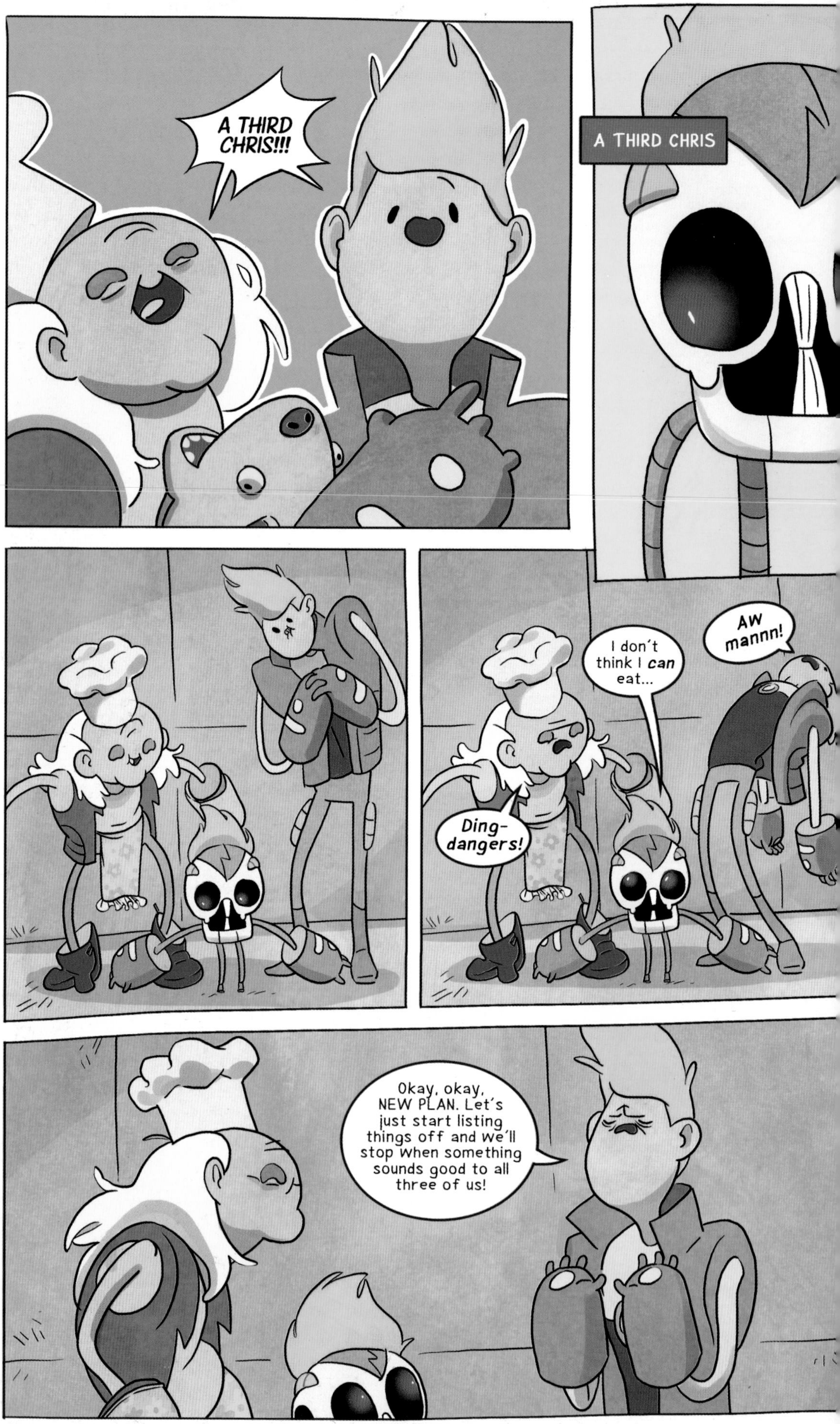
A THIRD CHRIS!!!
A THIRD CHRIS
I don't think I *can* eat...
AW mannn!
Ding-dangers!
Okay, okay, NEW PLAN. Let's just start listing things off and we'll stop when something sounds good to all three of us!

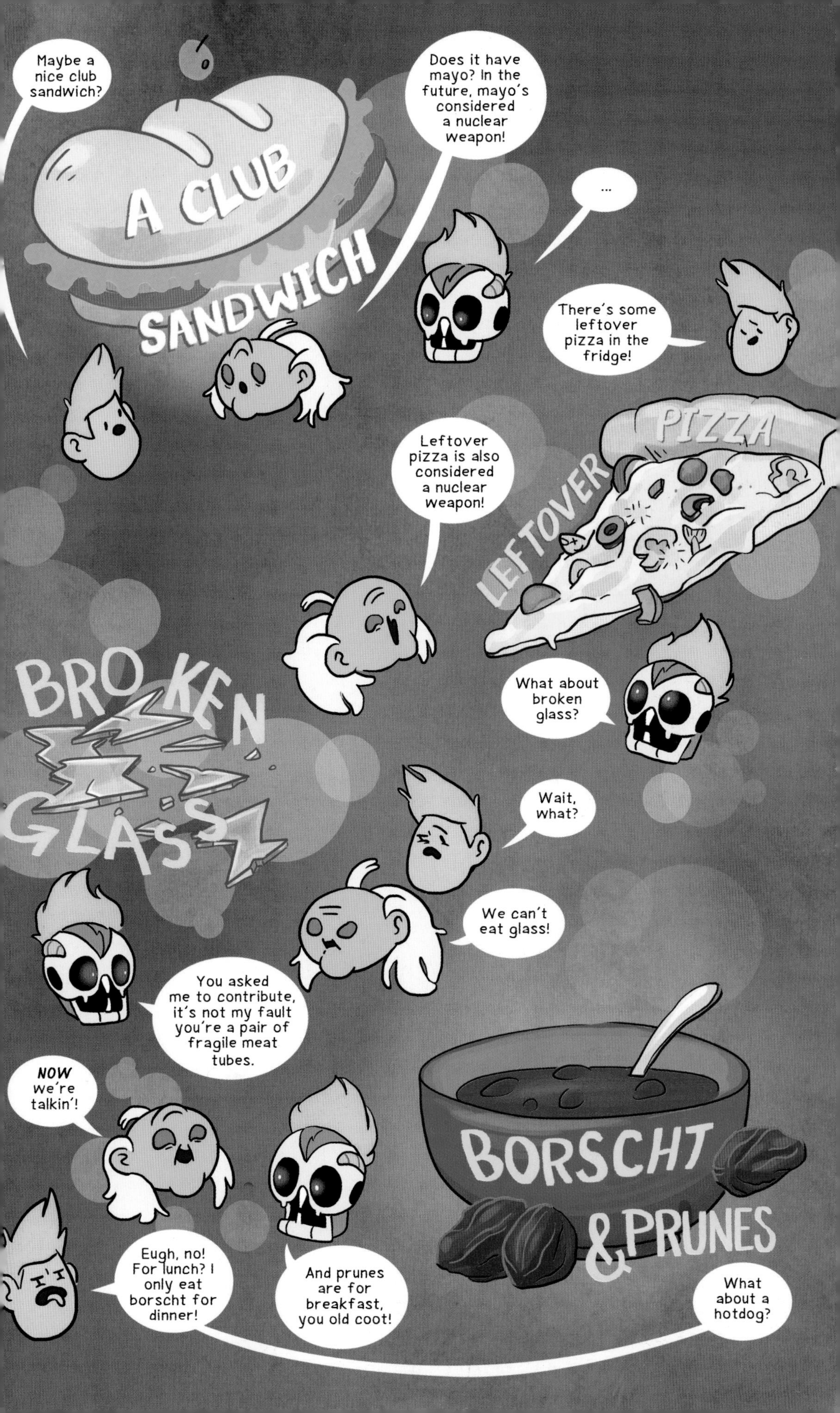
Maybe a nice club sandwich?
A CLUB SANDWICH
Does it have mayo? In the future, mayo's considered a nuclear weapon!
...
There's some leftover pizza in the fridge!
LEFTOVER PIZZA
Leftover pizza is also considered a nuclear weapon!
What about broken glass?
BROKEN GLASS
Wait, what?
We can't eat glass!
You asked me to contribute, it's not my fault you're a pair of fragile meat tubes.
NOW we're talkin'!
BORSCHT & PRUNES
Eugh, no! For lunch? I only eat borscht for dinner!
And prunes are for breakfast, you old coot!
What about a hotdog?

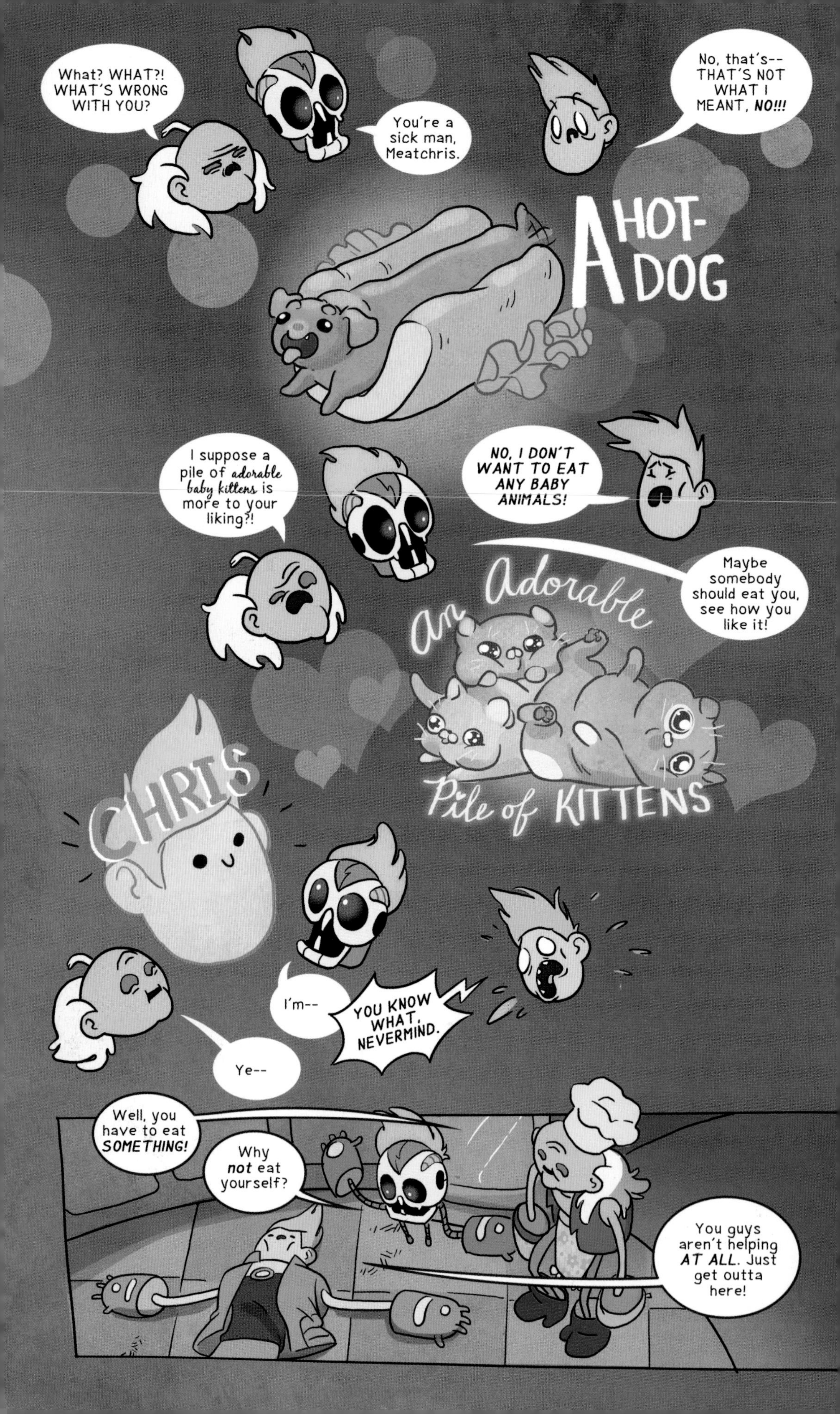

What? WHAT?! WHAT'S WRONG WITH YOU?
You're a sick man, Meatchris.
No, that's-- THAT'S NOT WHAT I MEANT, NO!!!
A HOT-DOG
I suppose a pile of adorable baby kittens is more to your liking?!
NO, I DON'T WANT TO EAT ANY BABY ANIMALS!
Maybe somebody should eat you, see how you like it!
An Adorable Pile of KITTENS
CHRIS
I'm--
Ye--
YOU KNOW WHAT, NEVERMIND.
Well, you have to eat SOMETHING!
Why not eat yourself?
You guys aren't helping AT ALL. Just get outta here!

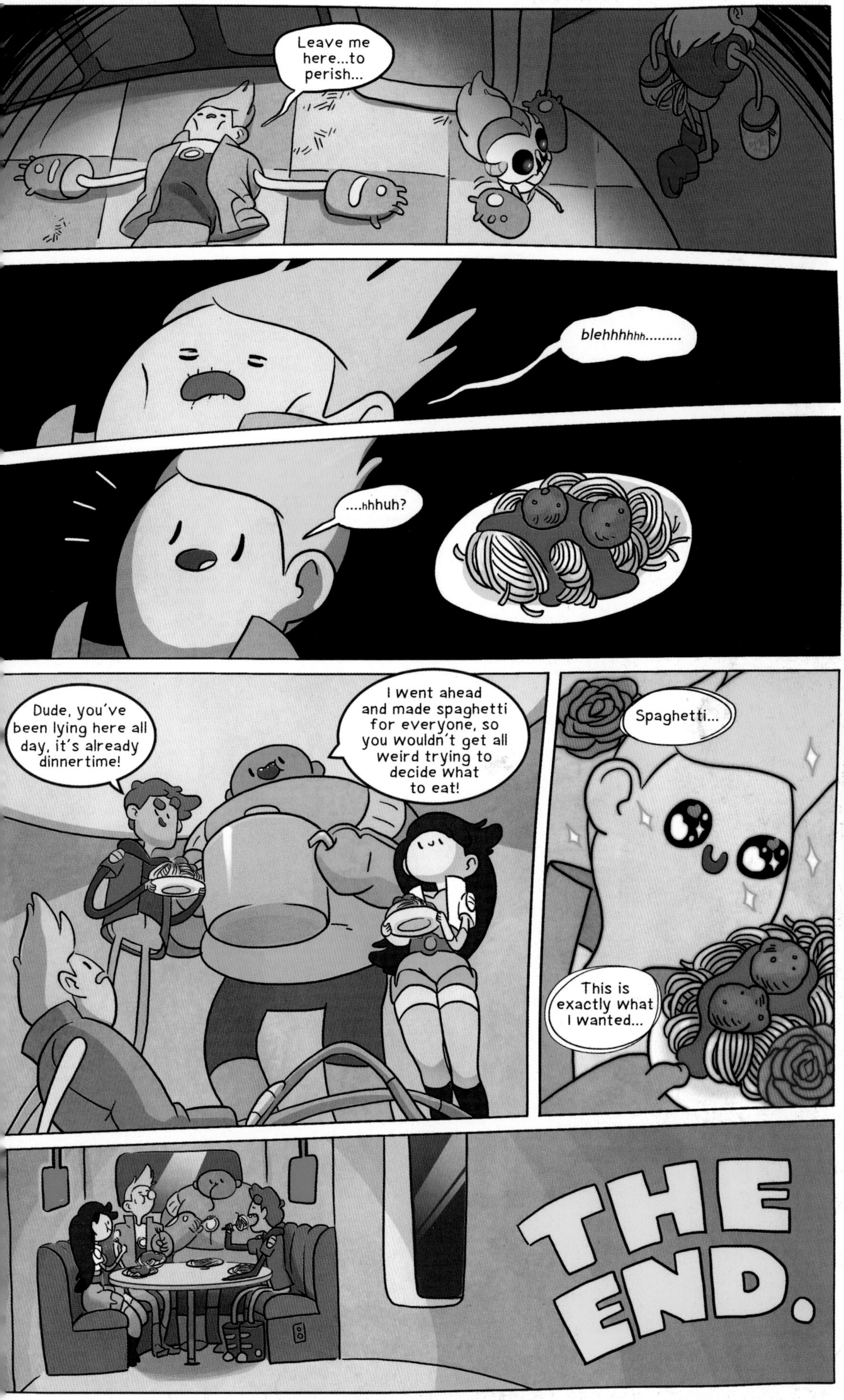
Leave me here...to perish...
blehhhhhh.........
....hhhuh?
Dude, you've been lying here all day, it's already dinnertime!
I went ahead and made spaghetti for everyone, so you wouldn't get all weird trying to decide what to eat!
Spaghetti...
This is exactly what I wanted...
THE END.

COVER 25B
MARIS WICKS

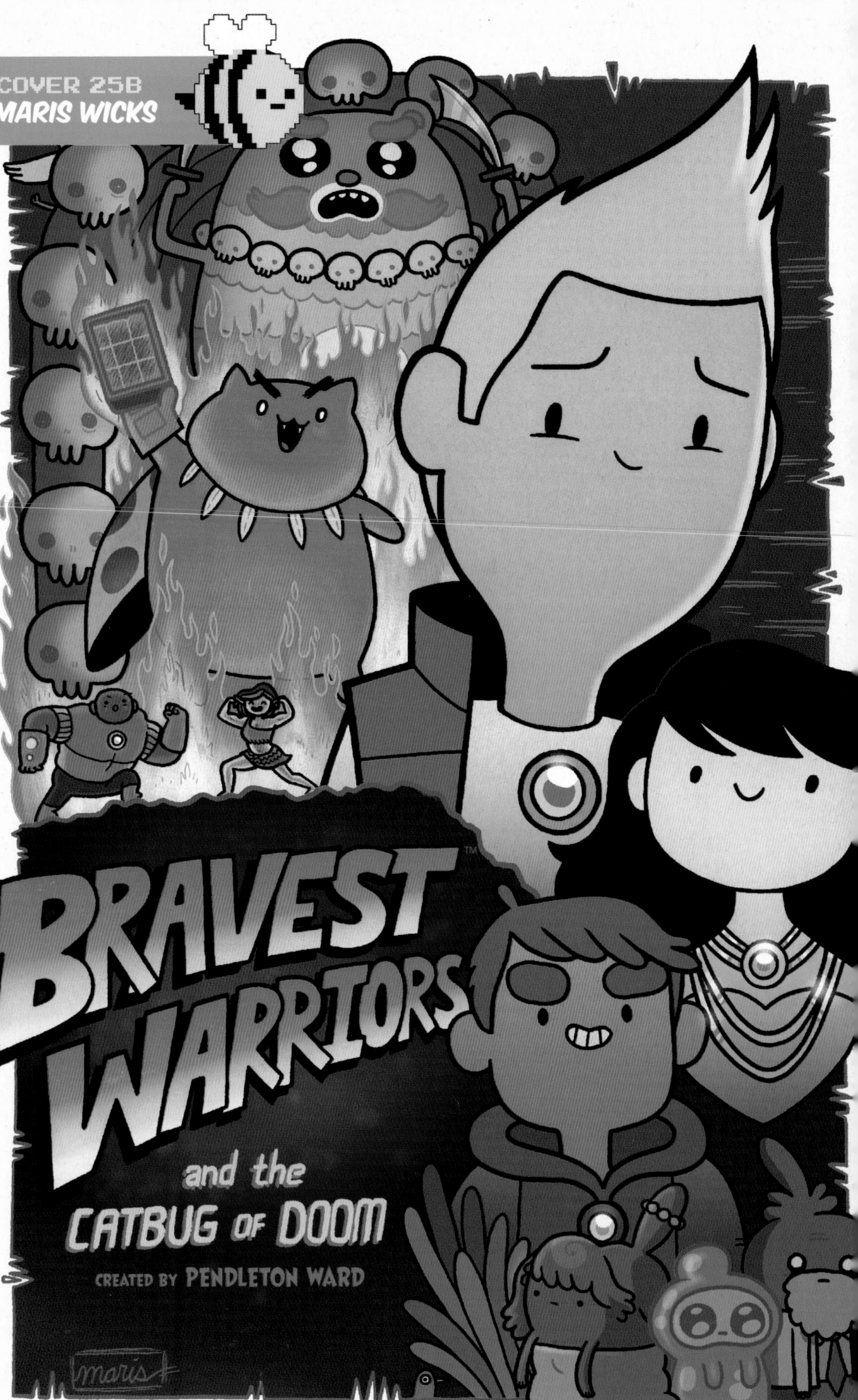
BRAVEST WARRIORS™
and the
CATBUG OF DOOM
CREATED BY PENDLETON WARD
maris

APOLOGIES TO MR. DREW STRUZAN...

THE BRAVEST
ALL OF WARRIORS™

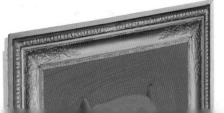

COVER 25 BOOM! STUDIOS EXCLUSIVE
PAULINA GANUCHEAU

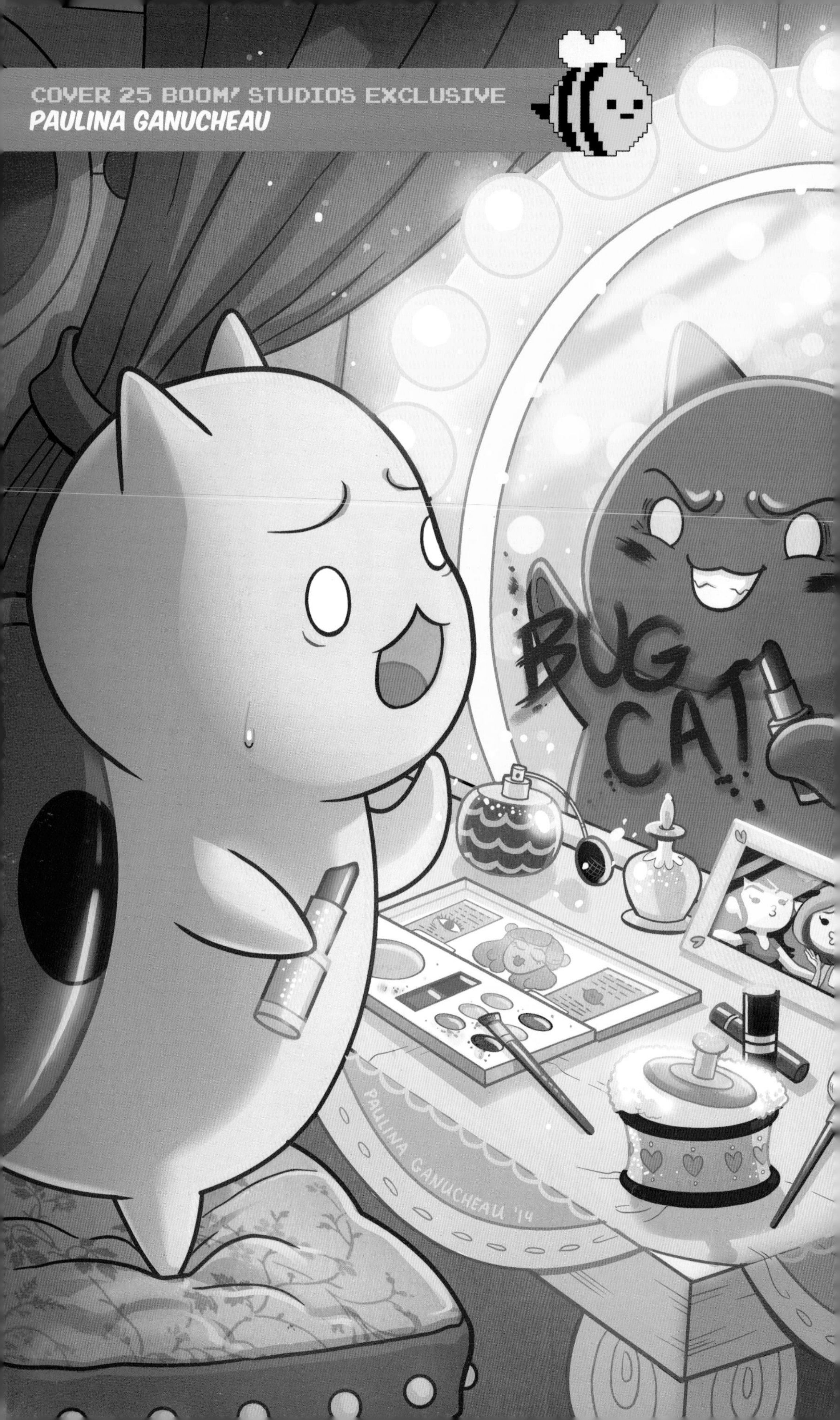
BUG CAT!
PAULINA GANUCHEAU '14

COVER 25 NYCC EXCLUSIVE
KATE LETH

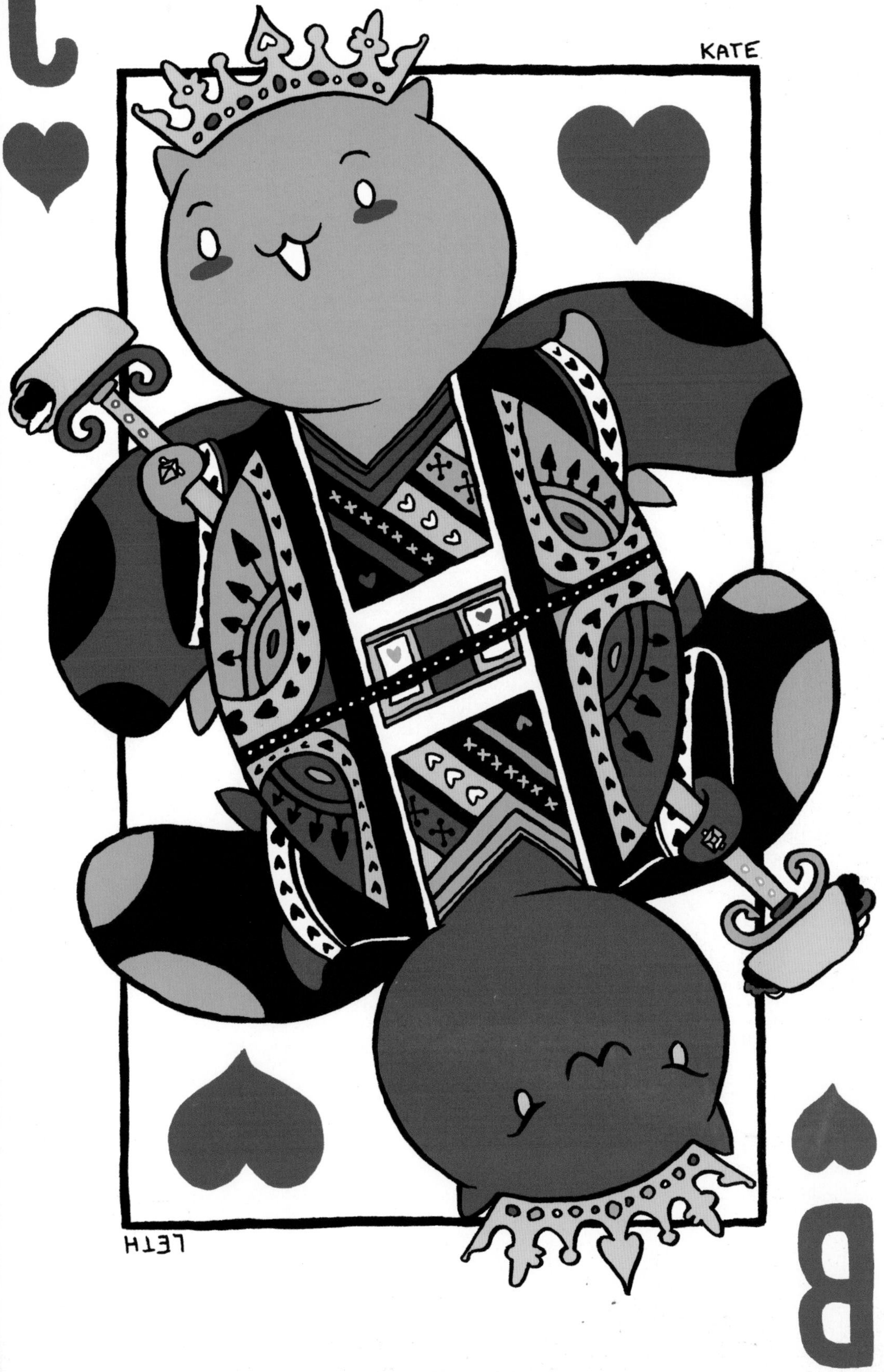
KATE
LETH

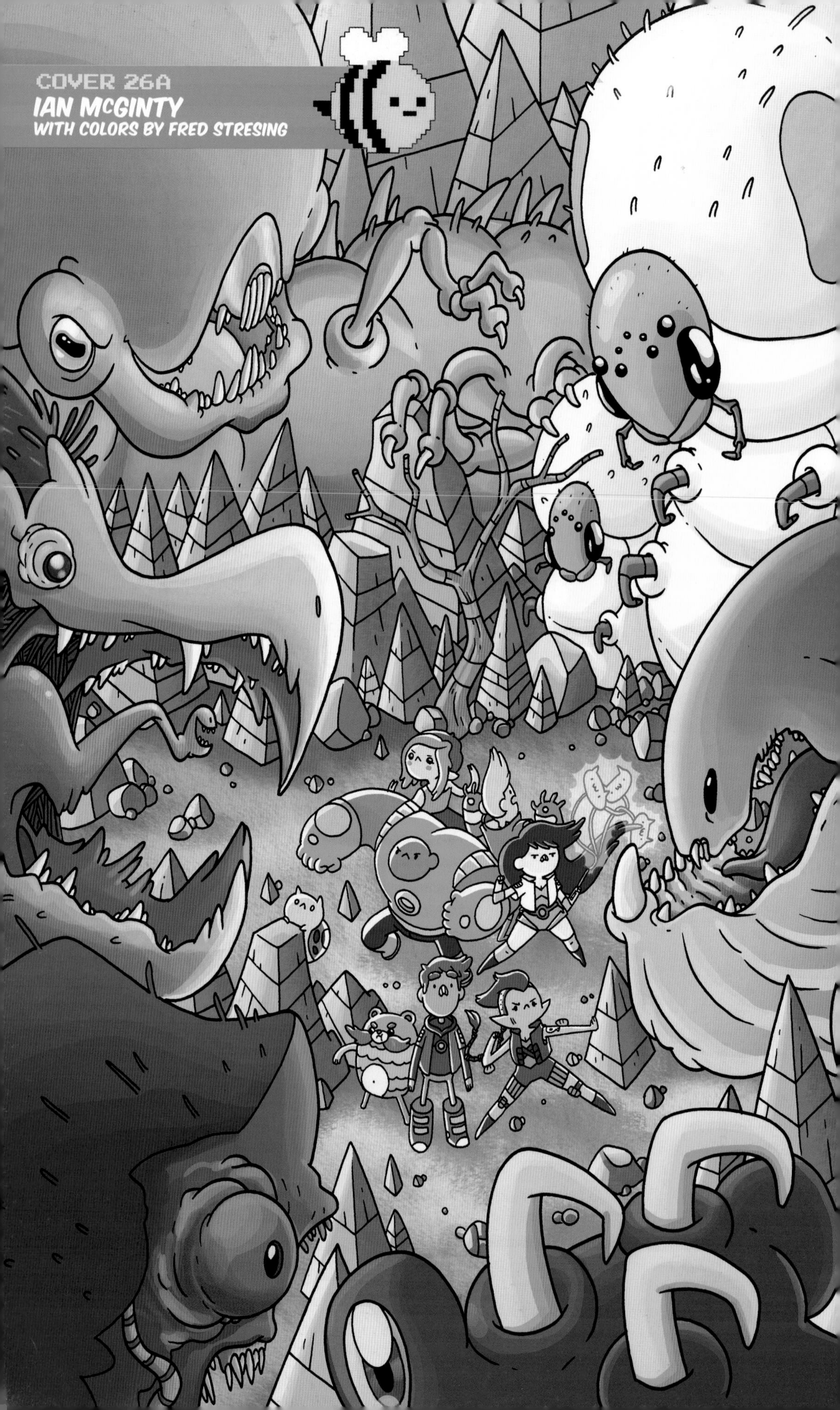
COVER 26A
IAN McGINTY
WITH COLORS BY FRED STRESING

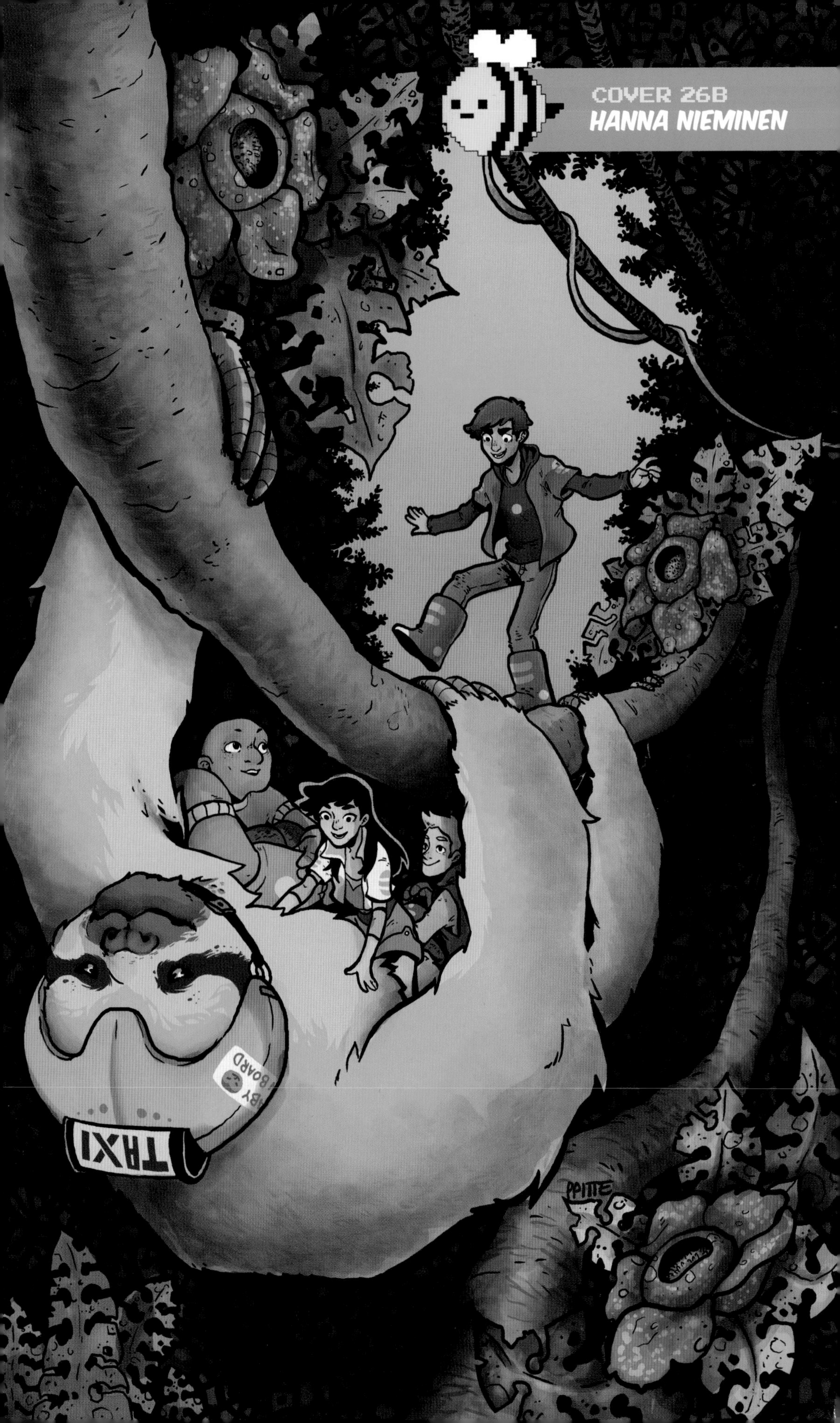
TAXI
COVER 26B
HANNA NIEMINEN

COVER 26C
IRENA FREITAS

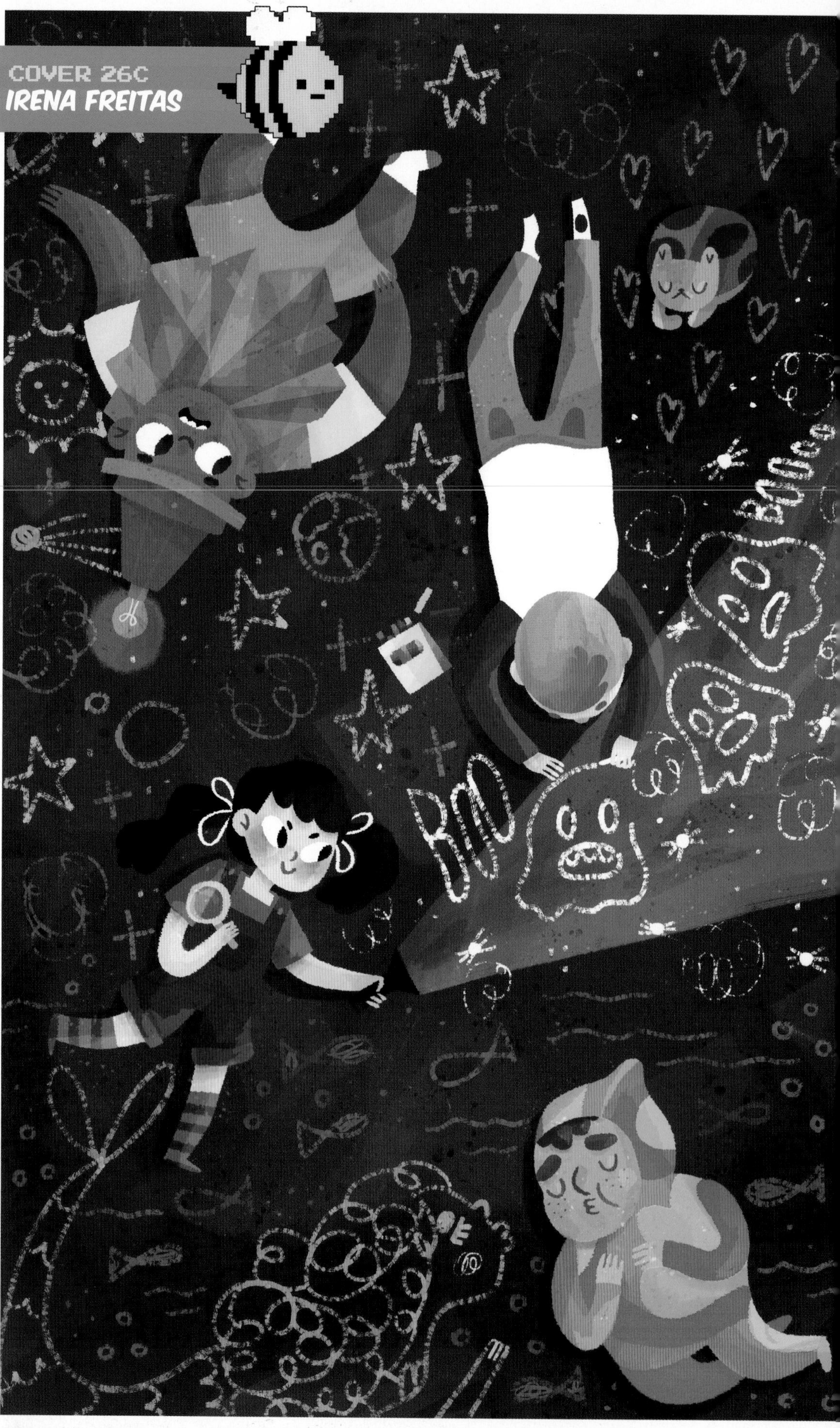
BOO

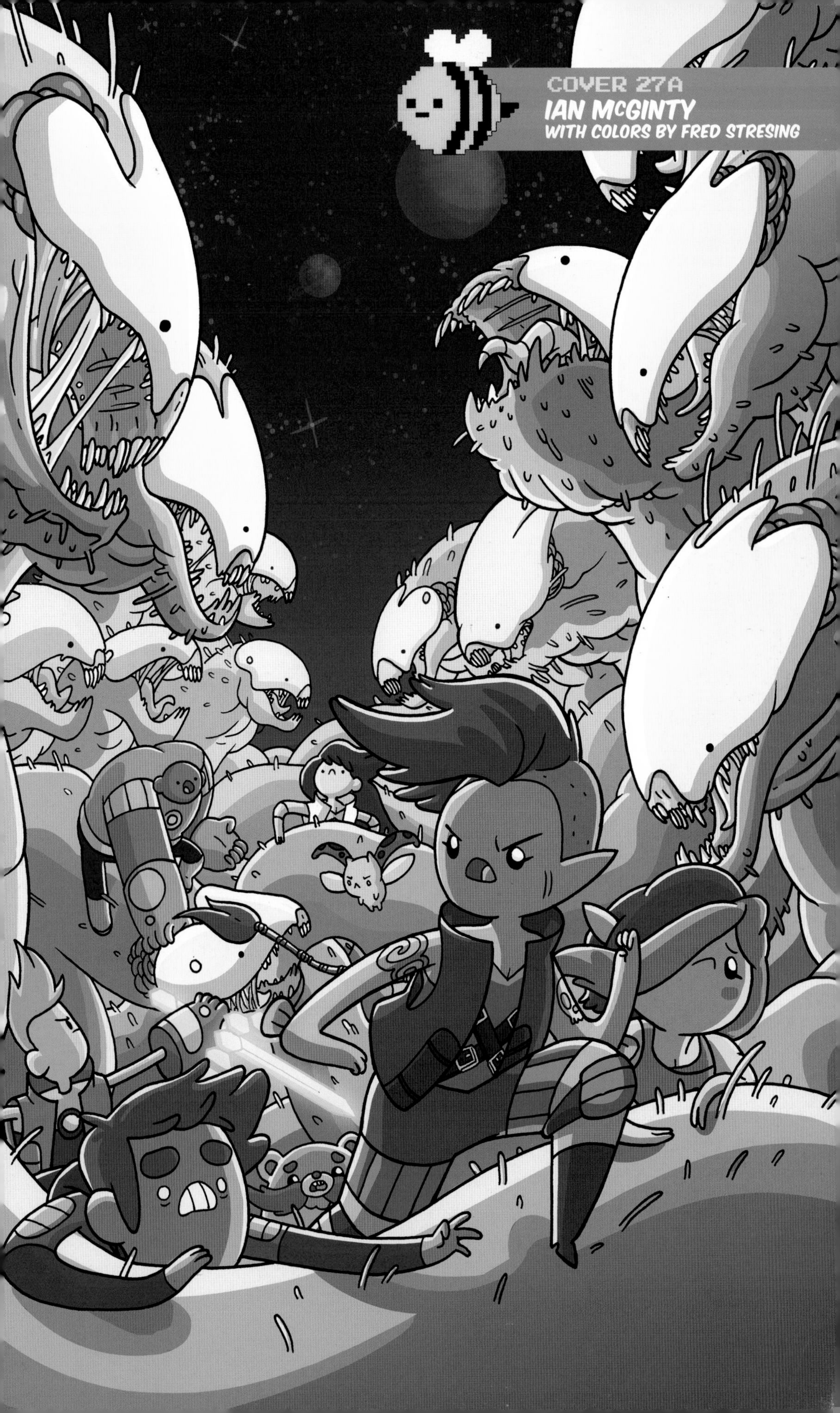
COVER 27A
IAN McGINTY
WITH COLORS BY FRED STRESING

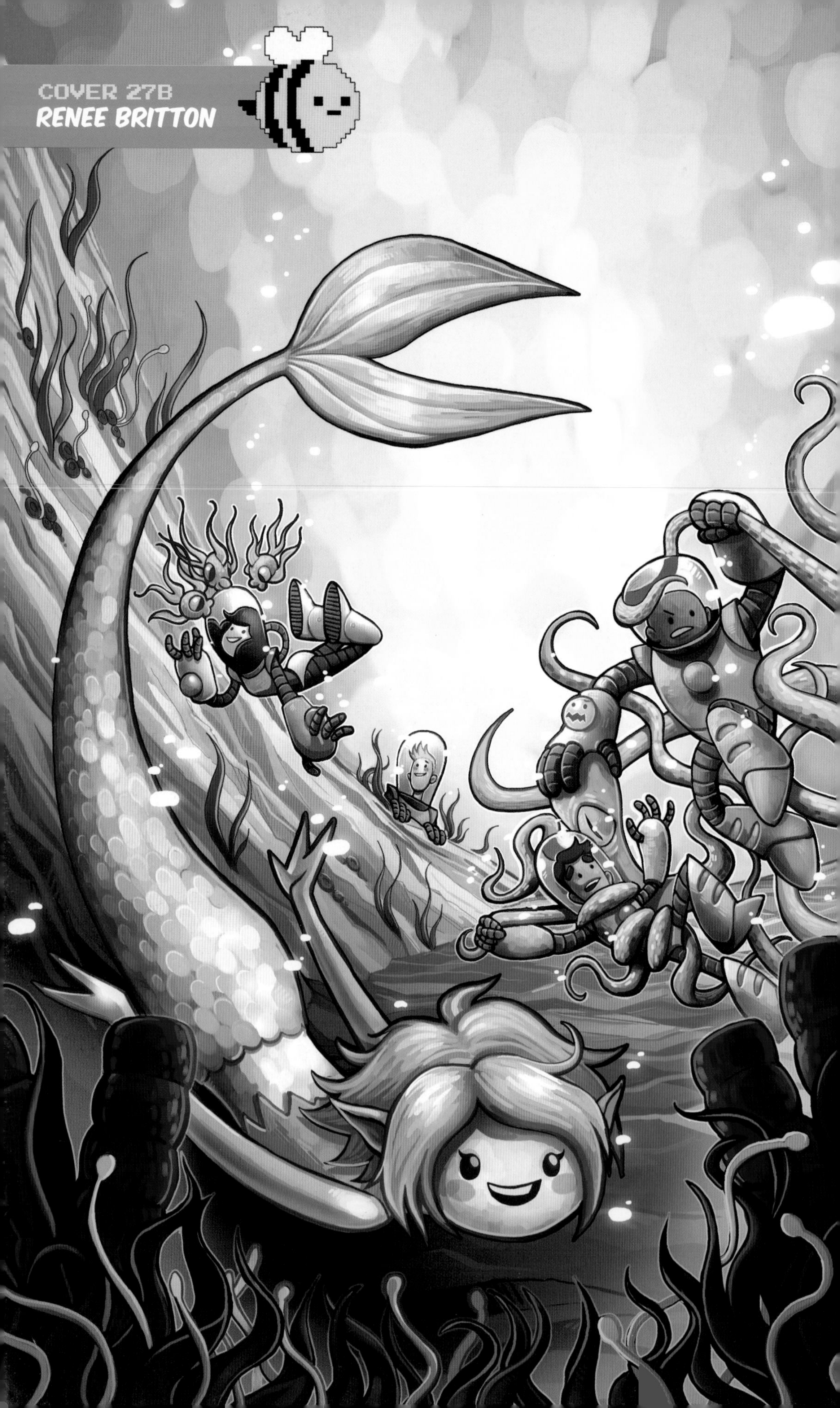

COVER 27B
RENEE BRITTON

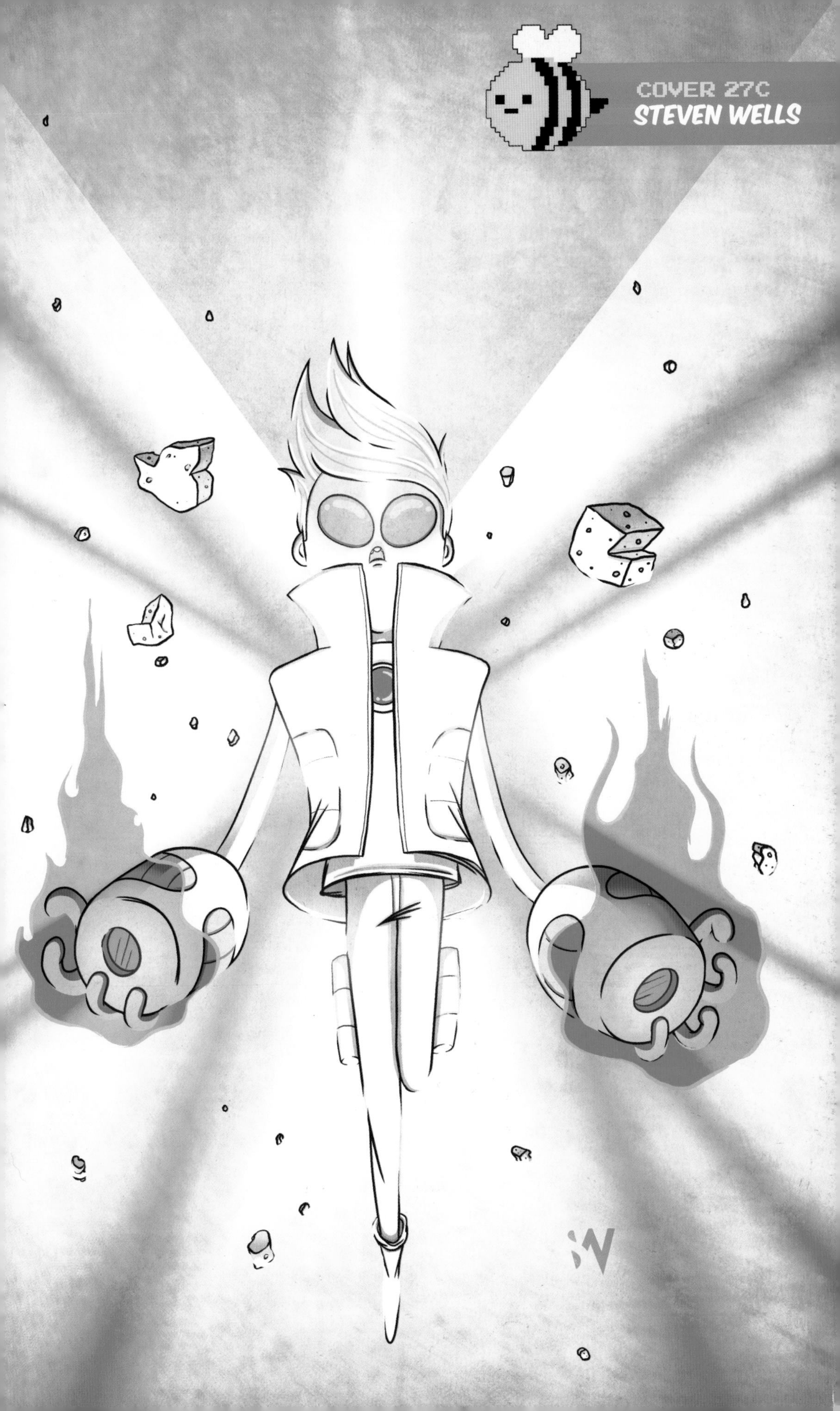
COVER 27C
STEVEN WELLS

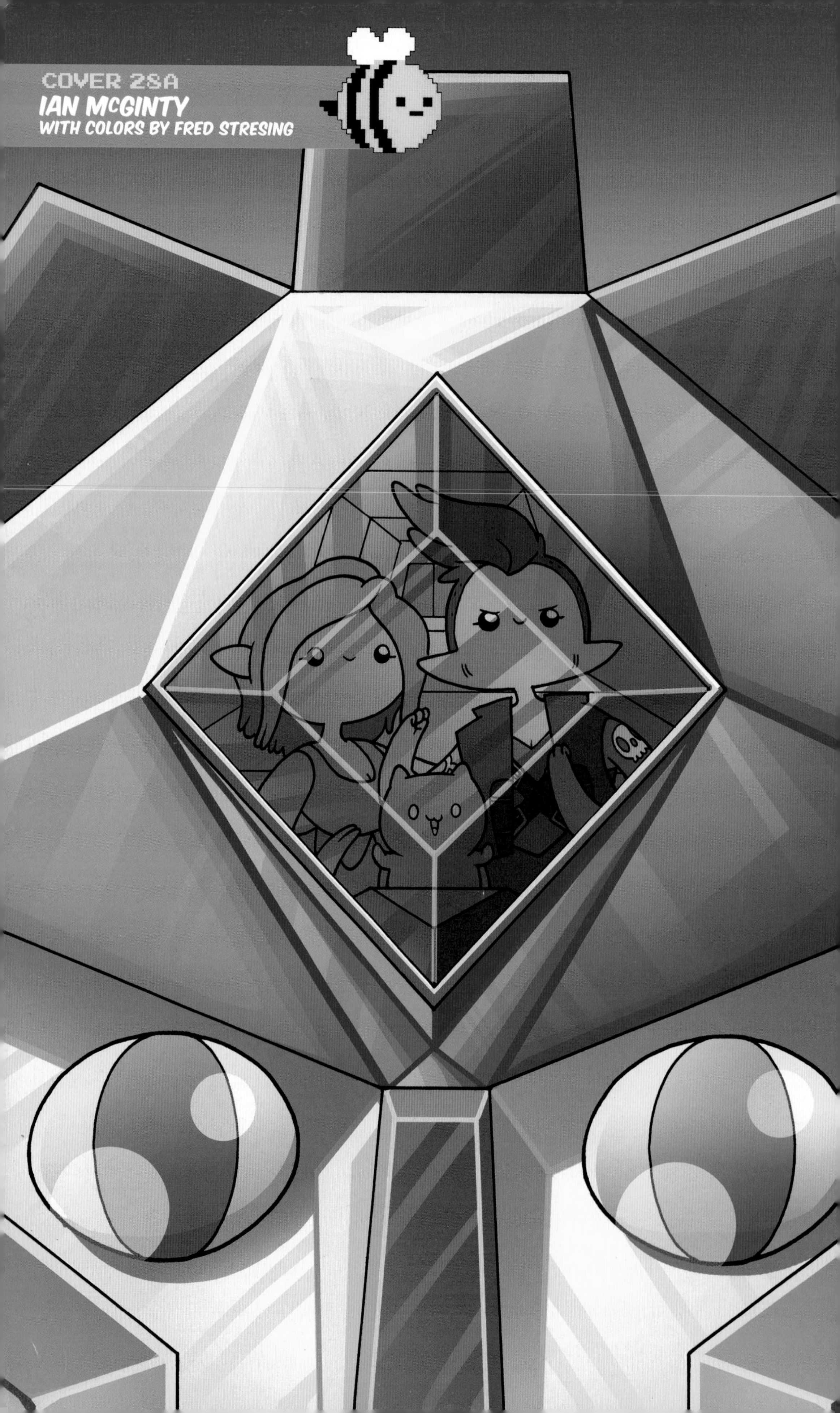
COVER 28A
IAN McGINTY
WITH COLORS BY FRED STRESING

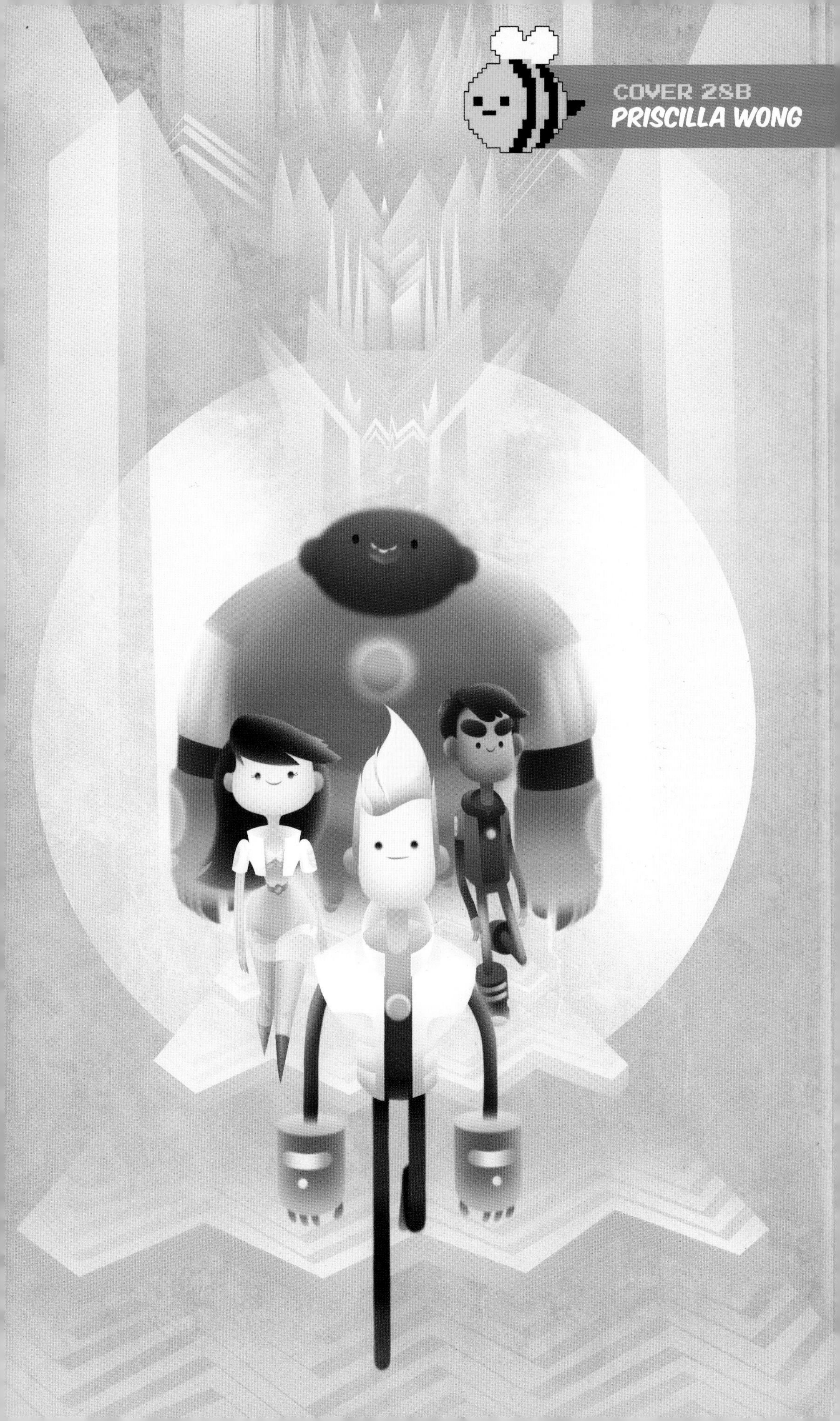
COVER 28B
PRISCILLA WONG

COVER 28C
RACHAEL HUNT

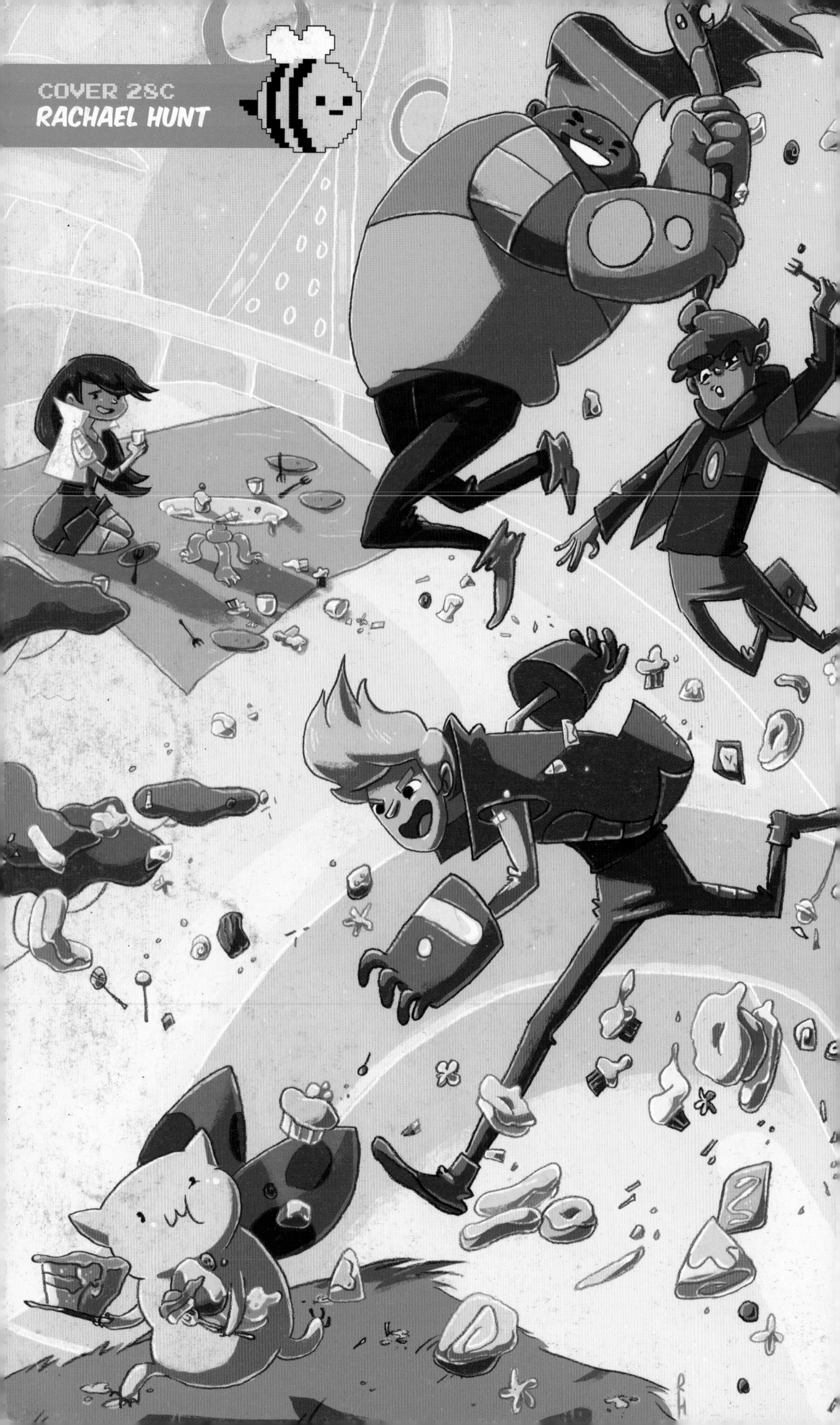